A COLD CASE OF MURDER

A MEG DARCY MYSTERY

BY
JEAN MARCY

New Victoria Publishers

Published by New Victoria Publishers Inc., PO Box 27 Norwich, VT 05055
A Feminist Literary and Cultural Organization founded in 1976.

Cover Design Claudia McKay

Printed and bound in Canada
1 2 3 4   2006 2005 2004 2003

Library of Congress Cataloging-in-Publication Data

Marcy, Jean.
  A cold case of murder : a Meg Darcy mystery / by Jean Marcy.
    p. cm.
  ISBN 1-892281-18-X
  1. Darcy, Meg (Fictitious character)--Fiction. 2. Women private investigators--Missouri--Saint Louis--Fiction. 3. Saint Louis (Mo.)--Fiction. 4. Lesbians--Fiction. I. Title.
PS3563.A6435 C65 2002
813'.54--dc21

                                        2002006880

For Margaret Powell, a straight woman whose bravery and integrity in the face of homophobia challenge us all to be more inclusive.

ACKNOWLEDGEMENTS

This book became a gleam in her eye when Jean found *Lost Caves of St. Louis* by Hubert and Charlotte Rother (St. Louis: Virginia Publishing Co., 1996) at Hayner Library. All the history of St. Louis caves we mention in chapter twenty, Patrick learned from reading this book.

Three groups have helped us by nurturing our work and nourishing our souls:

Alton's Race and Justice Group has offered much support—and gave us the best party for *Mommy Deadest*.

Our Writer's Group (Martha, Jen, Jennifer, and Millicent) have given us critiques which strengthened our work without devastating our tender egos. Martha Miller thrice scoured the book for our most egregious redundancies and clichés. Any that persist are our fault.

Left Bank's Lesbian Reading Group, led by Kris Kleindienst and joined by an ever-changing membership, have been generous and kind to these two writers in their midst, and we relish their wit and insight. As always, Kris in all her guises—intellectual mentor, bookstore owner, community activist, and friend—has promoted our growth and given more support than we can adequately thank her for.

Again we want to thank Tom Stringer, whose knowledge of guns prevents our shooting Meg in the foot.

We are grateful to Claudia, Beth, and Rebecca, who work hard to give our characters the best possible entrance to the larger world. If New Vic didn't exist, neither would Meg and Sarah and Patrick—at least in print.

Not least we'd like to thank you readers who flatter us by attending to the adventures of Darcy, Lindstrom, Healy, and Harvey.

CHAPTER ONE

"I want you to find my daughter's mother."

I blinked. I cleared my throat, just like any bureaucrat. "Well, Ms...Mrs...umm...Mann." She nodded at the second choice. "Mrs. Mann, we don't normally handle domestic cases here at Miller Security. Divorces, custody..." I turned my palms up in an apologetic gesture.

"I understand, Ms. Darcy. But I need someone I can trust. My husband cannot find out what I'm doing." Unlike most people, she managed to lower her voice as her tension grew.

"I can recommend several reliable firms. The agency next door is—"

"Uncle Truman says I can trust Walter Miller with anything." Her eyes were gray, their black pupils widened. She was the antithesis of my usual client. The guys who sit across my desk most often own lumber yards or small construction firms. They want cheap and perfect solutions to real security problems.

Diane Mann put her hands flat on the edge of my desk—soft, pampered hands with a wide wedding band. "And I saw your name in the papers and on TV this summer. I know you don't scare easily."

Actually I scare quite easily. I know from experience the damage violence does to ordinary lives. Along with Lindstrom, my almost-girlfriend, and Patrick, my best friend, I was still recovering from the mayhem in that much-publicized case.

But there were days when I missed the adrenaline-pumping danger and regretted the dull routine that left me bored stiff now that my buddies were engaged in their own lives and projects.

"Those cases weren't ones we chose. They aren't our normal line of work. I really think—"

She interrupted again. "I don't want to lose my daughter. My husband will do anything to keep her. He's a very dangerous man."

She had just the right balance—the startling words, the persuasively reasonable tone. Then she threw the net over me. "Your uncle promised me you'd look into it."

I looked at her again. She seemed to me like a Junior Leaguer who'd come into the city for a day's shopping. Her blue wool skirt suit was tidy and smart, classic rather than stylish. Her hair was perfect in spite of the sleet outside. I put her age at forty. Her makeup was subtle. The gray eyes framed with liner, mascara and god-knows-what-else still looked shrewd to me.

I felt a wave of annoyance. Colleen had told me when I'd seen the unfamiliar name on today's appointment book that the client's uncle was Truman Partridge, the man who had saved my Uncle Walter's life in a nasty little Korean War fight. I'd never been sure if the fight was US Army-approved or one that took place in one of the dozens of little bars Walter had explored while a grunt. Walter, of course, made sure he was out of the office when Truman's niece made her appearance to call in this old debt. Walter hated family cases. He swore we'd never take them. Except, of course, when he owed his life. In that case, my time could be spared. My uncle, her uncle, all the crisscrossing, binding loyalties.

I didn't stifle my sigh. "Is there a beginning to this? Maybe you can start there."

I suppose she'd rehearsed it several times before she came. She was thirty-eight and married to a man twenty-two years her senior. Eight years ago they'd adopted a baby. Jessica was delightful, their only and much-cherished child. But cracks and fissures had appeared in the marriage. Diane Mann wanted out, but she also wanted to make sure she could take her daughter with her.

I looked up from the notes I was scribbling on a legal pad. "You think your husband will try to get custody of Jessica?"

"I know it. Doug's a completely determined man, and he dotes on Jessica."

"You know joint custody is becoming more common; it might be best for—"

"He'll never allow it."

"He may not have a choice. I'm not sure what the law—"

"He's a retired police officer and very powerful, well-connected." She was growing impatient at my inability to appreciate what she was up against.

I cast my eyes down my page of notes. "Why do you want to find your daughter's biological mother?"

"Because there's something wrong about the adoption. Doug knew about it. He lied to me."

Lies in a marital context didn't seem the earth shaking stuff that wins or loses custody cases. I waited.

"Doug told me Jessica was the illegitimate daughter of his wild niece Marianne. He made me promise not to talk about it—the family would be scandalized and Marianne's heart was broken. When we got the baby, I was so thrilled I didn't ask questions. Doug handled everything about the adoption. I never signed papers or went to court." She sent me a questioning look: was I following?

I nodded.

"But last year Marianne came back to St. Louis—she'd been living in Ohio. She was dying and we took her in. After all, I owed her so much. She and I became close as I cared for her. Just before she died, I couldn't abide the silence any longer. I thanked her for giving us Jessica." Here Diane Mann paused and waited until I raised my head from my notes. "Marianne said she'd never had a baby."

"Did you confront your husband with Marianne's denial?"

She nodded emphatically. "He told me to stay out of it. It was none of my business." Her voice said she still felt that outrage. "None of my business *who* Jessica's mother was!" She heard herself, reined in. "Not that it matters in some ways—she's a perfect little girl. But it matters that Doug would lie to me about it."

"Could Doug have been the father? Was there someone he might have had the child with before you were married?"

She shook her head. "No. I'm sure the baby isn't his. We were married for ten years when Jessica came."

"How about an affair after you married him?"

"No. Whatever his faults, he's never been a womanizer."

I wasn't convinced she'd have known if Doug had cheated on her, but for now I filed the thought away.

"Did he offer you any explanation after you confronted him?"

"He said her mother had died."

"In childbirth?"

"Shortly after in an accident."

"What about the baby's father?"

"A bad guy, he said. With no interest in the child."

"What else?"

"Nothing. He'd found the baby through work."

"Who handled the adoption?"

"Willard Gardner. He was the attorney for Heitner Associates.

7

Doug has worked for them for years—moonlighting before he retired and full-time now."

Heitner. Where had I heard that name? Before I asked, she went on to explain—Heitner Associates used to be Heitner Brewery. A faint click of recognition for me. Way before Anheuser-Busch became a triumphant behemoth, St. Louis had had as many family-owned breweries as my cat Harvey has wiles. Diane Mann added that the adoption process had been started very soon after Jessica's birth—under a month. Jessica was born eight years ago, December 13. Diane told me again how the baby had brightened her life.

I was sorry to spoil the moment. "Mrs. Mann, I'm not clear on what you hope to gain. Let's say you're right—that there was something fishy about the adoption and Willard Gardner, presumably an attorney in good standing, either went along with it or was fooled—"

She bristled. I continued, keeping my voice non-judgmental. "Just suppose all that happened as you suggest. Won't undermining the legitimacy of the adoption jeopardize your own custody of Jessica?"

She shook her head; a natural flush deepened the blush she had applied to her cheeks. "It would never come to that, don't you see? If I have something to block Doug, to embarrass him—something to hold over his head—"

I sighed. No wonder Walter avoided divorce cases. They were minor civil wars, fought outside the Geneva conventions. Reputations were shredded; kids burned in the heat of the battle. Those who counseled sanity became the enemy.

Even so, something about her fierceness attracted me. She was trying to use her wits to outfox this man she saw as ruthlessly determined. Was he?

"Did he threaten you?" I asked.

She looked at me, taking my measure. "Not what you think, not with hitting."

"Has he ever hurt you? Physically?"

Her face changed. "Oh no—not really. Years ago he slapped me a couple of times, but nothing—" She stopped. I was unsure what nothing meant in a world where face slaps were in bounds.

"A big guy?"

"Yes, but really—"

It was my turn to interrupt. "Ever strike Jessica?"

"Never!" I wasn't sure if the outrage was on behalf of her husband, her daughter, or herself.

"Then what?"

"Just that forbidding glare he has—don't cross me." Her eyes pled with me to glide over this, to make it easier on her.

I scanned my notes. She wasn't yet ready to go below the surface of his abuse, but I had enough.

"You'll take it?" she asked.

I hesitated. A wife-beating cop is not so very rare, but a chance to even the score is. I knew I'd like to be the girl to do it.

She renewed the emotional pitch. "I need your help. To keep my daughter, I have to find out where Jessica's mother is."

"Who Jessica's mother is," I corrected her, signaling my capitulation.

Diane Mann had handed me a wad of twenties instead of a check. Her husband would see the checkbook. I gave the cash to Colleen, started a file and made careful notes of all Diane had told me, including her dictum never to call her. She would call me, regularly.

At four-thirty Colleen stuck her head in my door and said she was closing shop early; she was on the way to the bank and then heading home because the sleet wasn't letting up. I considered the matter and decided to follow her example.

Miller Security shares an asphalt parking lot behind the building with the agency next door. I ducked my chin into the collar of my parka, squinting my eyes against the slanting assault of ice. I was too lost in thoughts of Diane Mann's problem to understand his first words.

"Meg, don't go yet." Patrick caught me as I was opening the Plymouth's door. Some detective I am. I hadn't seen his MG on the other side of our neighbor's van. Why was he here?

"I need to borrow your office for a few minutes," he said, as though he'd heard my question.

Patrick occasionally fancies the detective's life in spite of his close contact with me for the last four years. Scenarios of Patrick's impersonating a PI swam through my head. But I didn't want to argue while my lashes were growing icicles. I held the back door for him, then, inside, resumed my interrogation. "What do you need the office for?"

"E-mail. Our phones are out at home." We had separate apartments in a four-flat on Arsenal.

"Our phones? Mine, too?"

"Yep. I tried yours, too. Dead."

"Why?" As soon as it was out of my mouth, I realized the folly.

Patrick's grasp of things mechanical and technological is even weaker than my own. His specialties are books, local history, and gay gossip.

"I don't know. They're just dead. No dial tones. No anything. It's probably the ice."

"Have you called the phone company?"

"Not yet. I need to e-mail Joseph. He said he'd wait up for me."

I glanced at my watch. It was nearly eleven P.M. in Oxford, England. I unwillingly carried the six-hour time differential in my head because of Patrick's habit of mentioning the time in England twice daily. His pining for Joseph was really getting me down. I motioned him into my office.

"Thanks, Meg. You've saved my life."

"I'm going to call the phone company from Colleen's desk. You can use my computer."

I wandered through the building to the reception area. It took me a few seconds to find the phone company's number, then some patience to get through the automated trouble-reporting program. I made two calls, one for Patrick's number and one for my own.

I yanked open one of Colleen's drawers. Our receptionist/assistant keeps her desk entirely too neat. All the paper clips nestled in their round hole. I knew from experience that every pen in Colleen's desk would work perfectly. I grabbed a small yellow pad and started a to-do list for the Mann case. I looked up Heitner Associates for Willard Gardner's phone number and jotted it on my list.

I heard Patrick shut down my computer.

"Did they say they'd come fix our phones?" he asked.

"I only got to register my complaint with a machine. It assured me a technician would be out to check it."

"I told Joseph to e-mail me here."

"What's wrong with the bookstore?" Providing postal service for the lovelorn Patrick struck me as a thankless and time-consuming job.

"You know those guys, Meg. Sandra would read it, and Bobby would probably post it on the bulletin board."

"Maybe they'll fix our phones tomorrow. It has to be the ice if both our phones are out. Did you check downstairs?"

"Nobody home when I left. Maybe the Duc family will be back by the time we get there. You going out with Sarah tonight?"

"I doubt it. She's hot on the trail of another cold case. Some old kidnapping that ended in a child's death."

I sighed. Sarah Lindstrom was perfectly happy to be too busy to have dinner with me. When she had been transferred to dealing with cold cases while she recovered from injuries received during our previous case in July, she'd feared being squeezed out of the St. Louis Police Department. However, even decade-old cases couldn't contain her geyser of ambition. She was setting a new land-speed record by clearing in four months seven cases that had been dead and buried. Bill McClellan had done a whole column on her success last week. If the department thought Sarah Lindstrom would crawl politely back into the closet and while away her career being grateful not to be fired, they were wrong. Although Lindstrom had been outed against her will, she had never hung her head and wasn't going to start now. All talk about quitting the force and becoming a PI had dried up with her very first cold case, a six-year-old murder of an elderly man. And gone, too, was even the hint she had shown of needing me. I was back to my former status as a part-time thing. A mere distraction.

"Meg. Surely it isn't that bad." Patrick was commiserating, so my disappointment must have bubbled up to my facial expression. "How long has it been since she called?"

"Well, she called yesterday, but it has been a week since we've done more than a quick meal and a kiss."

"A whole week?" His incredulity was insincere.

"Yeah, I know—since August for you. But Joseph's in Oxford. He can't do any better."

"Let's go home and console ourselves. You buy the beer, and I'll call for the pizza."

Just as we were headed for the back, Walter lumbered in. His unruly hair, once vibrantly red and now fading to white, was full of ice beads. Mikie, his small poodle, trotted three steps ahead of him.

"Hi, Walter," Patrick said.

"Hi, Patrick." Walter turned to me. "Truman's niece come to see you today?"

I was still miffed that he had dumped Diane Mann on me, but I wouldn't give him the pleasure of seeing my reservations about the case. "She sure did. Diane Mann. Looks to be an interesting one."

Walter's eyebrows arched, but he decided not to press his luck. "Good, good. Don't forget the Galleria tomorrow." Walter had landed the security contract at yuppie heaven somehow, and the profits from that would keep us in donuts for a while if we could get a semi-reliable work force to do mall security.

"We start interviewing at ten, right?" I asked, to reassure him I remembered.

Walter nodded.

"I think I'll call Colleen and see if she can come in at eight so we can get a jump on this Mann case," I said.

"Good, good. See you later." Walter nodded again and turned his size thirteens toward his office. Mikie scampered after him.

"Ready?" Patrick asked, stretching his long arms above his head.

"Give me a second. I'd better give Lindstrom a buzz."

Patrick sent a smug look. Despite my resolve, I still buckled first.

"Since our phones are down," I offered lamely.

One reason Lindstrom was racking up such an amazing solve rate was that she tended to work eighteen-hour days. Not surprisingly, she was still at her desk.

"Lindstrom here," she said, the familiar brusque voice clear.

"Darcy here," I said. I told myself such mild mockery was really affectionate teasing.

"Ah, you!" As always, I wasn't quite sure about the spin on *her* words.

"Yeah, me. Patrick just dropped by. Our phones are out. So I thought if you called—"

"Thanks. Give me a call when you're reconnected." Friendly. Practical.

"We were just going home to order pizza. Want to join us?"

"Ah, well, I'd love to. But I'm just about to leave the office to interview a witness in the Grierson case."

"The old kidnapping?"

"That's it." A pause. "Eat a slice for me," she said in a cordial but signing off tone.

"From your lips to my hips," I said. I didn't want her to know I was disappointed, that I was more interested in her company than in pepperoni and beer.

Patrick had followed me into my office and was listening without pretense. Lindstrom and I said goodbye.

"The good detective is busy?" he asked.

I nodded. "Probably only hours away from cracking another one."

"You aren't happy?"

"Of course, I'm happy. Who isn't against crime?"

"Hmm." He kept his blue eyes fixed on my face.

"Don't hmm me. Being a one-woman force for justice is time-consuming."

CHAPTER TWO

St. Louis is a Southern city in many ways, but our climate will not cooperate with our desire to be warm and lackadaisical. We've learned the hard way to invest in salt and City Works Department overtime. And so, as I drove southwest on Gravois Tuesday morning, the street was clear and dry.

Inside Miller, Colleen had already brewed the coffee and plopped a white bag of something on the small kitchen table when I let myself into the squat red brick building a few minutes early. Colleen is bright and often bored with the phone answering and simple bookkeeping that Walter originally hired her for. So I try to use her considerable intelligence as our link to the Web, and for occasional all-purpose lying and conniving, she's pretty handy, too.

Sometimes I wished Colleen liked me more, but I try not to whimper. Her loyalty to Walter is unwavering. I opened my office and turned on my computer, then went searching for her. I found her at her desk with the yellow pages open to hospitals. She looked up with knitted brows. "Here's what I've got so far, can you think of any others? Alexian Brothers, Barnes, Deaconess, DePaul, Incarnate Word, Jewish, Lutheran, Missouri Baptist, St.John's Mercy, St. Louis University Hospital, and St. Mary's."

"Hospitals? Incarnate Word's closed and—"

"I know that, but it was operating when the baby was born. What's her name again?"

"Jessica Mann now, but we don't know what name her biological mother gave her."

"Okay, do you want me to start scratching around on the Internet and see what I can find?"

"Yeah. Diane Mann said a corporate attorney, Gardner, handled the adoption, but I think we'd be better off approaching him already knowing some things. I suspect his sympathies will be with Doug Mann and not Diane. Maybe you should go to the *Post* and get all the announced births for that month, and while you're there, you can search for the mothers' names in obituaries. Just in case Mann was telling the truth when he told Diane that the baby's mother was dead less than a week after the birth."

"Not everyone publishes a birth announcement. If the mother was planning to give the baby up for adoption, I don't imagine she'd want it in the *Post*."

"Diane doesn't know anything about the circumstances of the birth. Maybe we'll hit it lucky. I can search the Internet and make calls to hospitals between interviews today," I said.

"If the birth mother wasn't planning on adoption, she might have had the baby baptized or christened."

"Oh no, there must be a million churches, not counting synagogues, mosques, and temples."

"Probably not a million, Meg. Do you think the baby's mother was murdered?" Colleen asked.

"He said an accident. But I guess she might have been. Maybe it was something that some buddy of his on the force responded to."

"And maybe he just stole the baby from some poor woman who got arrested." I was amazed at Colleen's scorn for our city's finest. Nothing I knew about her background or family would result in quite that much cynicism about the police.

"What's in the bakery sack in the kitchen?" I asked.

"Custard-filled donuts. You have to save two for Walter. He needs them if you're going to be interviewing for security guards all day."

"How many do we have coming in?"

"Three every hour. A total of twenty-four guys today."

"Hey, that's too many. We need a lunch break at least."

"You have a break from twelve-thirty to one, but you can't quit till six-thirty."

"God, Colleen. Are you trying to kill us?"

"Walter says you have to have two classes of twenty hired and ready for training by Friday. You interview again on Thursday."

I decided not to ask what the training schedule looked like. That misery could wait until after the donuts.

The first applicant didn't look promising. His dishwater blond hair was clean, but it looked like it had been cut by his younger brother. He was unattractively thin and gangly, almost adolescent. To make all the physical impressions worse, he didn't offer his hand or meet my eyes.

"Jerry?" I extended my hand, but from a distance so he would have to come to me.

It took him a millisecond, but he got it. "Un-huh. Yes, ma'am. I'm Jerry Cross."

Well, there was a mother or a grandmother on the job somewhere. Even when asking for a job, the average twenty-year-old doesn't ma'am me.

"Come on back, Jerry. Walter will be here in a few minutes, but we need to get started."

I pulled Jerry's resumé from the file. "You worked with Burns for a couple of months? Why did you leave?"

"The water pump busted on my car. My brother said he'd help me fix it, but it took him three days to find the right pump at the junkyard. I had to quit."

Uh oh. Another young man with the "I have no control over my ability to get to work" fallacy. Ten points off.

"I really liked it, though. That's why I called right away when I saw you guys' ad."

Something perverse in me took over. I wasn't Jerry's mother, or even yet his employer—but I had to nag.

"The Burns office. That's just a block from the Jefferson Avenue bus route, isn't it?"

Jerry looked blank. When he realized what I meant, he frowned. "Yeah, but I was workin' way out in Ballwin. You can't get there on the bus. Not at night, anyway."

I conceded the point with a nod.

"What didn't you like about your job at Burns?" If he told me his boss was a prick, I'd point him out the door. Just then Walter lumbered in, Mikie dancing behind him.

"Sorry I'm late, Meg. Howard called just as I was leavin' the house. You ready for another cup?" He poured coffee into his plain white mug—well, white on the outside, anyway. He held the pot over my cup. I nodded.

"Walter, this is Jerry." I handed him Jerry's resumé, and Walter sat down and started reading. Mikie sniffed around a bit, including at Jerry's ankles, and, finding nothing noteworthy, trotted off to see if Colleen was in yet.

I did all the preliminary reading of resumés and most of the reference checking. Walter tended to make hiring decisions based solely on his prejudices and staring into the eyes of the applicants. Flinchers need not call back. Walter dropped the resumé on the table and gave Jerry a skeptical look. Jerry blushed. I was at least gratified that he hadn't thought to stand and offer his hand to Walter either.

But the interview seemed to turn a corner; Jerry's answers grew more confident. By the time Walter was walking Jerry back out, I jotted a couple of notes on the resumé and started the "maybe" pile.

We had two no-shows and a day crammed with the oddments of humanity that think they want to be security guards. It is always a quirky variety, maddeningly so when we had to have twenty of them hired and ready to train in less than forty-eight hours. Mostly, Walter and I agreed about their potential as employees, if not always their relative worth as members of the new world community.

By three-thirty I desperately wanted to take a nap. By four-thirty we had seventeen possibles. The last one was a slender woman named Andy with a bushel-basket of naturally curly red hair. She was smart as well as pretty, and I had Walter pinned to the mat seconds after she was gone. Walter doesn't think attractive women make good team members. I try not to draw personal conclusions.

When Andy left, I walked down the hallway from Walter's office to the reception area. Colleen was just back at her computer from her mission to the library, her nose and cheeks red with cold. She was typing intently. For the first time in memory her coat was draped over a client's chair instead of hung on the coat tree in the corner.

Before I could develop a quip on this state of affairs, Colleen spoke. "Meg, will you get me a cup of tea?"

I waited a beat while I swallowed my surprise. Colleen never asked for favors in this category. "Sure," I said. "Earl Gray, right?"

"The stronger the better." She was peering at her steno pad, though her fingers hadn't stopped their quick march across the keyboard.

When I returned, I announced my deduction. "You've got some leads."

She nodded, took a cautious sip of the tea. She tilted her head toward the printer, just delivering the last sheet. I picked up the four pages. I'm sure Colleen was doing filing when she was in the womb—her organizational gene was that strong. Each page was set up in identical format, and she'd left spaces for us to pencil in new information.

"Do you want separate folders for those?" she asked.

I shook my head. "Nah. I'll just keep them in the case file for now."

She shrugged but made no comment. I wasn't going to spoil her mood—neither cold rain nor chapped cheeks nor sloppy filing was going to bring her down.

I pulled the other client's chair around behind the desk and to her side so that we could look together. None of the pages held more than a few lines of type, but I knew how much work had gone into the gathering.

Eight years ago in St. Louis four women had given birth, then died shortly afterward—within the same three-week period.

The first, Tawnese Johnson, had been twenty-three, and together her name and North Side address suggested her race. Colleen and I exchanged a look.

I spoke first. "Diane Mann didn't say Jessica was a white baby." I hadn't asked to see a picture of the child. More surprisingly, Diane hadn't offered to show one.

Colleen shrugged.

Before the library had kicked her out at closing time, she had managed to make a copy of the *Post's* story on Tawnese Johnson's death. The young mother had rated only a three-column-inch story buried in the Metro section. She'd been killed by a boyfriend and left behind three kids. Three column inches. For the next three mothers we didn't have the details, merely the day of death.

Janice Holmes had died ten days after giving birth. Diane Mann had said Jessica was a week old when they'd gotten her. I suspected it wouldn't be easy to distinguish a ten-day-old from a seven-day-old baby. Janice had lived in Florissant and been survived by a husband, Kenneth, and two kids. No racial assumptions leapt out from that set of data. Janice had been twenty-seven.

I was surprised to find myself growing gloomy. My maternal instincts are pretty limited, but even the bare facts of the deaths of two young mothers tugged at my soft spots.

I expected Colleen, a confirmed and conventional het with her own steady boyfriend and advanced plans for their rose-covered cottage, to be similarly touched. But her eyes were glittering—and not, I felt sure, from cold or tears. She was as obsessed in pursuit of a lead as Detective Sarah Lindstrom or PI Meg Darcy.

"Look at this one," she said, pointing to Teresa Rushing, a mere seventeen when she'd died; her death had occurred an exact week following the birth of her child.

Rushing had been survived by her mother and a brother. Neither of us recognized Rushing's street address.

"Seventeen," I said.

Colleen nodded. "But look at those dates."

"Could be coincidence."

She gave me a look, the sort I haven't seen since quitting therapy.

I tried a ploy that had never worked then either—I changed the subject. "But something else is fishy. Her obituary didn't list a daughter as a survivor."

Colleen took the Rushing page and made a note. "I'll check it out."

The last page named Jenetta Wilcox. She was forty-two and the mother of four kids. Her husband was Frank, and they lived in University City. Her baby had been born three weeks before her death.

"This is great work, Colleen."

And it was. Searching through weeks of microfiched birth and death announcements wasn't exciting stuff—except that for Colleen it had been.

"I'll go back tomorrow and look for more specific stories on their deaths—just in case there was any other news coverage," she said, the thrill of the chase creeping into her voice. Then she looked at me. "I mean, if that's okay with you and Walter."

She knows she's indispensable to the running of the office.

I hesitated. I'd promised Walter I'd see the two applicants who hadn't fit into today's schedule. He planned to be out of the office till noon. Colleen's as grown-up as it gets—at a mere twenty-four—but just now she had a pleading face on that reminded me of Jen, my eleven-year-old niece.

"Sure, good idea. I'll join you at the library as soon as I can get away. Take a cell phone so you can call me if you get finished before that."

She didn't salute, but I could tell that real detective assignments might warm her more than the Darcy charm ever had.

With that we shut down the office for the evening and braved the elements. Cold but clearing. I climbed into the Horizon and goosed the heater up. Maybe by the time I got to Pho Grand, the little car would be toasty.

CHAPTER THREE

The temperature had dropped, and Pho Grand's plate glass windows were steamy, creating an even cozier feel to the place. I'm getting used to the new location now—I love the walls' mellow bamboo colors, painted to suggest figures emerging from swirling mist. Beautiful Vietnamese stringed musical instruments adorn those walls. The atmosphere is more upscale than the old storefront place, but the basics—low prices, swift service, and great tastes—remain the same.

I was fidgety, but Patrick's animated account of the day's crises at the bookstore was engaging enough that I didn't notice Lindstrom coming up the walk and climbing the stairs to the entrance.

It's always like this. No matter how grumpy I am, no matter how determined I am to stay that way—just the sight of Lindstrom and there's the little flutter in my stomach, the thrilling rush of sweetness through my veins. Even the jagged little scar now embedded in one perfect eyebrow doesn't mar her face. I couldn't help it. By the time she reached our table, I was grinning up at her.

Patrick waggled his eyebrows at me. Was I that obvious? I slouched in my chair and ditched the silly grin.

"Ah, here you are. How've you been, Patrick?" she asked.

"Well, the phones aren't fixed, yet. I may have to join the twenty-first century and get a cell," he said. "How goes your current case, Sarah?"

"Pretty well. About a year after the murder Harper was charged with another kidnapping in the city, but not convicted. I suspect Harper may be my man."

"How do you find leads that the cops who worked the case couldn't find?" Patrick asked.

"Mostly because so much time has passed. Often cases aren't solved because someone who knows something won't tell. Over time, their reasons for not talking change. Loyalties shift or some witnesses are no longer afraid of the perp—he's gone to prison for something else or drifted out of the area. In this case my new source is no longer the perp's sister-in-law. She'd never have come forward to volunteer the information, but when I re-interviewed her, she spilled it pretty casually. Like 'everyone knows he did it.' I'm pretty sure I've got the one who actually killed the baby. It will be a capital case."

How could such a beautiful woman be delighted by the thought of an execution? I tried to formulate my first volley, but our spring rolls arrived, and I decided my attention was better spent on them than on lecturing Lindstrom on state-sponsored murder.

"How are things at Miller Security? Working any hot cases?" she asked, blithely unaware of the political harangue she'd narrowly escaped.

"Walter got the security contract at the Galleria. So I'm hip deep in hiring, and then next week we'll be training. Leaving time only for a family case for a niece of one of Walter's buddies."

"Divorce?" A little surprised. She knew Walter's aversion to those cases.

"Sort of—preparing for divorce anyway. They have an adopted daughter and the mom suspects there was something fishy about the adoption. She wants to make sure if she leaves she won't lose her daughter." I gave her a brief sketch of Diane Mann's case, omitting names.

Lindstrom asked the same question I'd asked Diane. "If the adoption wasn't legally correct, won't the wife's custody of the daughter be at risk?"

"Yeah, but the wife thinks just the threat of exposure will cause the husband to back off." I hadn't told Lindstrom the husband was a retired police officer.

"You think that will work?" Patrick asked.

I shrugged. "Maybe, maybe not. But she knows him and thinks it will. He sounds like a bully who deserves standing up to."

"To Meg Darcy, Injustice Righter!" Patrick said, waving his glass of chablis.

Lindstrom arched a brow. I changed the subject, and we discussed a couple of police officers who had applied for the Galleria openings as their second jobs.

Just as I slurped the last of my soup down, Lindstrom started pulling out her wallet. "I've got to run. I'm meeting a realtor on South Thirteenth in a few minutes."

I looked down. I would not ask to go with her. Why hadn't it occurred to her to invite me? Things had been decidedly weird since she moved out of my apartment.

"In Soulard?" Patrick was curious. He loved Soulard but her previous house had been there—the one where her ex-lover had been murdered.

"Yes, sort of—just west of I-55. In fact, I'm worried about it being that close to the interstate. I'll have to see how much noise and vibration it gets."

I knew that Lindstrom wanted to buy a house. She had listed her previous home a month ago—had cleaned it out and stored most of her furniture. I'd entertained the idea she'd just stay with me while she looked for a house, but she'd been like a cat in a cage at my place—unable to settle down and too cramped to pace. So she'd moved into an apartment building she now co-owned on McPherson.

"Want to come along?" she asked casually.

She's losing weight, I noticed irrelevantly. Skipping too many meals to prove she could solve even impossible cases faster than the average crossword puzzle champ. Now that I'd been invited, I wasn't sure. If I went along, I'd certainly have an opinion about the house, but...but.... "Okay. Let me drop the Horizon off at my place."

The house was nice, but the bathrooms hadn't been renovated and Lindstrom hadn't shared the realtor's excitement about redoing them.

The ride back to Arsenal was silent. I used the time to admire Christmas lights. My invitation in for a cup of tea was tepid; I had given up hope for any real connection this evening. To my surprise, she accepted.

She prowled around the apartment while I heated two cups of water in the microwave and opened a plastic container of peanut butter cookies. I slopped some milk into my tea and carried both mugs and the cookies into the living room. The windows on the front of my building face Tower Grove Park. Henry Shaw imagined this as a Victorian walking park, and that is what Patrick and I do there most Sundays. Just now, I could see only a silhouette of the top of the Chinese pagoda in the dark.

Lindstrom seemed to be pacing back from the bathroom. She had one of her towels in her hand. I'd have to go back to using my old threadbare ones or break down and spend money on new ones. Neither option appealed, so I was irritated that she was taking it. It wasn't as if she needed that towel. Perhaps she wanted to have all signs of her habitation removed. No signs that she'd been at home in my place. Although, if I were honest with myself, she never did feel at home here—able to stay only because she couldn't go home. She still didn't have the house she wanted, but at least her sojourn here was over. She was reasonably comfortable in the apartment building that Colin Lanier and Viv, her ex, had co-owned. I cursed myself for having done the laundry yesterday and washed the stupid towel. Probably every other time she'd been here since moving, it had been dirty.

"Here's your tea. And Patrick baked cookies for Food Outreach and left some here," I said.

"Thanks, Meg." She tossed the towel on the coffee table and sat down beside me on the couch.

"Ben called this morning," she said.

I took a second to rummage around the mental attic where I kept Lindstrom's family. Since I'd never met them, her four brothers—two older and two younger—tended to merge. Luke was next-to-youngest, the only one still single. Matt was the oldest. Ben was the youngest, a farmer with two sons of his own.

"What's up with Ben?"

"He wanted to know if I'm coming home for Christmas. He and his wife are doing the dinner this year so Mom doesn't have to. They've got the space."

"You're going to Nebraska for Christmas?" Why hadn't I assumed this?

"Oh, sure. I always do."

I pondered that. "How long will you be gone?"

"Oh, three weeks or so." She undercut it with a wicked grin. "Will you miss me?"

"I doubt it. I often go weeks without seeing you now—you're always at work."

She sighed.

"So how are things going at the station?" I asked.

"Not well. Almost everyone treats me differently now that they know."

"Not Neely." She and Neely had talked about Viv's murder and Lindstrom's subsequent outing months ago over beer and grilled burgers at Neely's house. He'd told her that he had known she was gay for years, that he'd liked Viv and mourned her loss. He encouraged Lindstrom to seek out a support group. Neely advised her not to duck the issue at work, but to tough it out and insist on the respect she had already earned.

"No, not Neely. And not the Lieutenant. But lots of others. And working cold cases isn't helping either. Some think I'm trying to show people up, prove they didn't work these cases hard enough to begin with. So that resentment fuels the homophobia."

This was the first time I'd heard her use the word except to deny its presence, mocking me as paranoid. Except, of course, she still wasn't interested in the social context, just her own discomfort. She was miserable being loathed by people who had once respected her.

"What's happened, exactly?"

"Little things, mostly. Some don't speak to me as I come in. Some go out of their way to recount the latest fight at a gay bar, or call one another 'faggot' in front of me. Someone left a dildo on my chair."

"A dildo on your chair?" I could hardly believe she hadn't told me. "Did you report that? That's clearly harassment—creating a hostile environment."

"I don't think reporting stuff or whining 'no fair' is the way I want to handle this. If I want to continue working in the department, I've got to tough it out—laugh it off. But I thought things would be getting better by now. It's been nearly five months since Viv's death. Maybe they intend to keep it up until they hound me out."

"Have you talked to anyone at the union?"

"The PBA? No. One of the guys who is always saying 'faggot' is the vice president of the PBA."

My heart hurt for her. Lindstrom's whole identity was being a cop. And not only a cop, but a driven, successful, respected detective. Surely in this day and age she could be all those things and an out lesbian, too. "Is there any way of confronting it?"

She tilted her head forward and grinned, just a little. "I taped the dildo to the door of the locker room and put a sign over it, 'Homophobia makes you look like a dick.'"

I laughed. "Lindstrom, that's terrific! How did they react?"

"I don't really know. Someone took it down a couple hours later. But the guys talked about it all day. Some thought it was my dildo, but Neely made sure they all knew I had found it on my chair."

"Wow, that was just perfect. Maybe you should wage a guerrilla campaign for enlightenment."

"A war with an army of one?"

"Not a war. A campaign. And I know you aren't the only queer in the St. Louis Police Department."

"No, but we aren't exactly organized. It's more like hunker down alone and hope it will all blow over soon."

"Hanging up that dildo doesn't sound like hunkering down."

"I just want to do my job."

"Exactly. And a hostile work environment undermines that. So they have to be encouraged to grow up. How about 'straight but not narrow' bumper stickers on everyone's car?"

"Darcy, I cannot be caught pasting bumper stickers on cars, and neither can you and Patrick, so forget it. But maybe I'll try to have lunch with Billingsly next week. He tried to get some of us to march together in the Pride parade a few years back."

"Is he a detective?"

"No, Bill hurt his back years ago. He's been in records for a decade. I don't know—it all makes me think maybe I shouldn't have worked so many eighty-hour weeks when Viv and I were together."

I was quiet. What could I say? That I was grateful Viv had felt ignored and had dumped Lindstrom for the attentive but drunken Kathleen?

"So what did the dildo look like?"

"You wouldn't have liked it. An exact replica of a penis, but huge. Some four-incher's fantasy." She arched a brow; our eyes locked.

I ran my hand up her thigh, and she put down her teacup.

"Silly boys," I said, my voice thickening.

"You think?" Her own voice was syrup pouring straight into my veins.

Didn't matter that I'd invited her to the dance. Within seconds she took the lead, her fingers unsnapping and unzipping, her tongue seeking out my soft spots. I struggled to stay in charge. But my fingers were clumsy working the buttons on her shirt while she propelled me backward to my bedroom. Subversive elements undermined me. My soft spots rose up to greet her as to a liberating force. My legs clasped her tightly, smearing myself against her silken thigh.

"Ah, you like that, do you?" she gloated, as she pressed into me with her thumb, lifted and flung me into space.

But I was already shuddering, collapsing in on myself, reduced to one thimble of flesh made all.

I stopped everything else: no nuzzles, no endearments, just desperate seeking.

"Ah, yes—" she said, her words choked.

"Damn you, damn you," I said in prayer.

I bucked and tossed. With a mighty heave I rolled us over and pushed down harder, harder and came and came till the core of me spilled over her hands. Her face was lit with a sheen of sweat and pride.

I slithered down her long blonde length, not lingering. I put the tip of my tongue in her—one flick, two—felt the rough jerking response, heard her "yes, yes" as a distant cry. She clutched my head with her hands and thighs while my tongue finished its work.

We lay tangled and wet and silent a long time before shivers sent us scrambling for covers. I think she slept. I lay and considered the shadows on my ceiling. We'd gone someplace new, but I had no words to describe it: rougher, needier. Now we stayed spooned in an innocent embrace—emptied? filled?

I didn't know she'd slipped back into waking till she started laughing.

"What?"

"Think I'll ask those boys to bring in a dildo once a week."

CHAPTER FOUR

I struggled through a tickling mesh of vines and spider webs brushing my face. No matter how I thrashed I couldn't get clear of the wispy thicket. A plaintive mew broke through the dream. Harvey was kneading my chest in his Meow Mix stomp, his white whiskers feathering my chin and cheeks. A glance at my clock told the story: I'd slept through my alarm. Lindstrom had gotten up to go at ten-thirty last night. I'd walked her to the door, then returned to my warm cocoon, sated and not unhappy to have the bed to myself. Now I dressed in a rush but remembered to check my phone on the way out the door. The reassuring dial tone had come home.

The Wednesday, December third, that greeted me outside was drizzly and cold. A fine spitting rain accompanied me all the way down Gravois to Miller. Our neighbor's agency van was the only vehicle in the lot behind our brick building. My short scamper to the back door made me glad for the extra layers.

Inside seemed unnaturally quiet without Walter and Mikie and Colleen. As usual, Colleen had turned the furnace down to sixty when we left; I kicked it up. Before shucking my coat, I made a pot of coffee. I'd resisted the notion of buying some sticky rolls or bagels. A job interviewee doesn't want to juggle that extra etiquette problem while struggling to make a good impression. But on a morning like this a simple cup of coffee was a humanitarian gesture.

While the coffee brewed, I gathered the two files I'd need from Walter's office and unlocked the front door. I had ten minutes before the first applicant was to arrive. Neither candidate was a standout, but in forty minutes I'd discovered they'd both do. Now we had over half of our positions filled.

Ten minutes later I was back in the Horizon, heading toward the library. The mist was finer, but the clouds still looked like dirty slush piles. I experienced an urban miracle and found a parking spot right in front of the Main Public Library at Thirteenth and Olive.

As a working private investigator/security consultant, I'm more likely to draw my library card than my .38 snubbie. So this fine old building was no stranger, but I still felt a little tingle of delight in its marble and polished wood and echoey stairwells. Colleen would be in its bowels, and that's where I found her, her head bent over a microfiche machine. I touched her shoulder, and she gave a start, followed by a quick grin.

"Three down," she said and handed me those pages. She'd gleaned nothing new on Tawnese Johnson, Janice Holmes, or Jenetta Wilcox.

So I was there for the big discovery. When she checked the *Post* files for the days surrounding Teresa Rushing's obituary, the headline popped up MURDERED TEEN FOUND. The story had two paragraphs on page one and finished on ten. On December 23 eight years ago two young boys—eight and nine—had been out "exploring" and had stumbled onto the body. The young woman had been found in the backyard of an empty house, one of several hunkered in a mostly defunct neighborhood near I-55 toward the south end of the city. I recognized the address because Miller Security had installed an alarm system in a business not far from there.

Colleen, whom I never think of as one inclined toward casual physical contact, scooted over so I could share her chair and her view, each of us taking turns reading through the text. I played fair and let her take the lead scrolling forward.

On Christmas a headline on page three identified the mysterious young woman as Teresa Rushing. Police were actively investigating the case, but a Detective Vernon Cole was quoted as saying the homicide squad had no strong leads at present. A small picture of Rushing appeared with the story—a high school yearbook photo no doubt—which the police hoped might help them locate who had last seen the victim alive. The following day her obituary appeared.

When I finished the last text, our eyes met. Murder has a smell. It invites suspicion.

Colleen is not given to emotional displays. Now she clenched my nearest forearm and said—quite exuberantly for the library—"Meg!"

"Yeah—well, we still need to check out the others." Improbably I was cast as the mature voice of reason.

"Where are the phone directories?" Colleen asked, not pausing to take in my restraining tone.

That was a question easy for me to answer since I frequently used the library's directories for research.

We relocated and began. Janice Holmes of Ferguson and Jenetta Wilcox of U. City had surviving spouses listed in their obituaries. We found a Frank Holmes in Ferguson but too many Wilcoxes in U. City. I jotted down those addresses and numbers. Tawnese Johnson's murderous boyfriend was presumably serving time. We'd have to check with the Circuit Attorney's office. One of the underling prosecutors owed me a favor. We found an address for Teresa Rushing's mother, but not for her brother.

"What next?" Colleen asked.

"I'm hungry. I rolled out of bed too late for breakfast. All I've had is coffee."

She gave me a look, one that easily matched Lindstrom's for scorn.

"I'm sorry, I'm starving," I said.

She sighed and let her shoulders rise and fall with it. "Okay. After we stuff a burger in your mouth, then what?"

"We'll pick up something on the way back to Miller. We need to use phones for part two."

That appeased her, and we adjourned to our separate cars. The mist had been driven off by a blustery wind, probably ten degrees colder than the morning's. I had volunteered to pick up the burgers on the way to the office, and by the time I got back to Miller, the Horizon was puffing out modest heat. Inside, Colleen had the coffee brewing again and her desk cleared for action.

I unloaded the burgers and fries and cole slaws and the single side of onion rings for sharing. Colleen lifted a brow but made no comment. While we ate, I talked tactics.

"I'll call Jeb Becker at the Circuit Attorney's office and the Holmes'. You see if you can reach Rushing's mother and start on the various Wilcoxes." I was being generous with the Rushing lead because Colleen had found it.

"No, you have more experience, Meg. You'd better take the Rushing number." Her objection sounded more than perfunctory.

"Okay, but I'll make that call out here from your phone so you can at least listen in to my end of it." I rummaged around in the fast food bag. "They never put in enough ketchup," I said.

Colleen popped up and disappeared down the hallway, coming back from our office kitchen with a tall squeeze bottle of my favorite sauce. I took it as a measure of how much she was enjoying a day away from billing and into sleuthing.

As it turned out, Lorena Rushing's number had been disconnected, and we were left with that familiar sense of deflation as our hopes seeped away. Familiar to me, anyhow. "Hey, it's just part of the process," I said encouragingly

She shrugged. "I'll start calling Wilcoxes."

In my own office I dialed Jeb Becker. Jeb is a twenty-something twelve-year-old who has a law degree from Wash. U. and is serving time as a prosecutor in the Circuit Attorney's office until he can move up and become Governor, President, and Master of the Universe. The past summer he had been charged with interviewing me following a murder case I'd solved (to the city's embarrassment), but he was grateful. Jeb didn't owe me the sort of blood debt that required him to hand over his firstborn or even Cards' playoff tickets, but I had a certain reservoir of good will with him, and I intended to tap it.

I didn't want to hit him with the whole laundry list, so I avoided the Teresa Rushing case. I wanted to talk with her mother first. But the Tawnese Johnson case sounded relatively tidy. I wanted to know if we could ask the incarcerated boyfriend if he knew what had happened to the baby and if Johnson had any surviving adult relatives who could tell me what had happened to her kids.

Jeb, like all prosecutors pursuing truth and justice, always has a full plate. But he didn't snarl at my requests, although he said—not surprisingly—it would take time to get an answer from Tawnese Johnson's boyfriend, if this fella could and would answer. Jeb was pretty sure there were several relatives who'd been questioned or volunteered statements after Johnson's murder, and he'd have the file pulled and get back to me pronto. I thanked him.

Next, I phoned Frank Holmes. I didn't expect too much because if he had a nine-to-five job and the kids were in school—but a woman picked up on the third ring and said, "Holmes residence."

She had a rich alto.

I identified myself and asked to speak to Frank Holmes.

"He's not home. This is Mrs. Holmes. Maybe I can help you?"

The rich voice was still friendly.

But the next part was tricky. I wasn't really surprised. Eight years is not exactly unseemly haste for a widower.

I cleared my throat. "Mrs. Holmes, this is an awkward subject, but I'm tracing an adopted child. I know that Mr. Holmes lost his wife shortly after she gave birth to a baby girl. Did Mr. Holmes give that baby up for adoption?"

Thank God for Oprah and Sally Jesse before her. We all know

about birth mothers searching for kids and kids searching for birth mothers and that probably removed some of the sting. Even so, the voice tightened a little.

"No, of course not. Oh, it was hard for a while, but he had help from family and neighbors, and Frank did a marvelous job"—the voiced warmed again—"till we got married. That was five years ago. Mandy's eight now—a beautiful child." I liked the tone which matched the praise. "And," she added, "we have a lovely daughter who's three. Mandy loves her to pieces."

I apologized for troubling her and said that I was glad such a sad beginning had become a happier story for the little girl. Generously, she wished me luck in tracing the adopted baby.

I walked out to Colleen's desk to report and found that she'd located a Wilcox who was an uncle to Jenetta's husband. Daddy Wilcox had moved away, taking his baby girl with him. Daddy and daughter now lived in Ohio—a single father making out just fine, thank you. More good luck wishes.

Before we were deep into further strategy, Jeb Becker's secretary called with the name of Tawnese Johnson's grandmother who had testified at the trial. Colleen reached the grandmother, who quickly supplied the answer. The orphaned children, including the baby, were living with her and were doing fine. Well, the oldest boy was a handful, but he had an uncle who tried to do the daddy stuff. That helped. But the little girl was fine—eight now—pretty and growing like a weed. Colleen is good at making crisp calls, but even she had difficulty detaching herself from a woman who was glad to tell her story.

In less than an hour we'd eliminated three possible answers to our question: who was Jessica's mother?

"Is it always this easy?" Colleen asked.

I didn't hit her because I believe nonviolence is better. I did say sharply, "Don't jinx us. We ain't there yet. Teresa Rushing may have nothing—I stress nothing—to do with this case."

She looked so abashed I mumbled an apology. "Get your coat," I added.

"Should we both leave?"

"Walter will be back in an hour. We'll leave the answering machine on." I was pulling on my own parka. "We're going to see if we can find Lorena Rushing."

Osceola is a street of small, squat houses; today they looked hunkered down against the cold with no sheltering trees or shrubs to spare them. The address we had for Lorena Rushing took us to a tiny gray house. Nothing softened its shabby appearance. Tufts of brown might become grass next spring, but the postage stamp yard was made up of frozen mud ruts. Peeling paint and broken sidewalk were the points of interest; the grim, gray facade of the house gave nothing else away: no shutters, no trim, no flower boxes. Plain white window shades—once white anyway—offered blank eyes to whoever came prying.

I found myself hoping we wouldn't find Teresa Rushing's baby here, being raised by grandma.

My shallowness was exposed as soon as our sharp knocks rousted her. Lorena Rushing was a dumpling of a woman, younger than my mother, much younger probably, but without a lick of style or pretension. She had the fine wispy hair of a natural blonde and a pouter-pigeon chest, covered now by a worn smock-apron whose print design was obscured by old stains and recent flour. She had small hands and feet; the latter showed trim ankles but sloshed inside too large terry-cloth house shoes.

She ushered us inside immediately without knowing more than our names, a cheery lilt to her voice. Earlier in the day she'd put on some lipstick and had overshot her lips on one corner. Only that pale orange spot remained. It didn't spoil her broad, welcoming smile. She urged us to take a seat.

Even in the dim light I could see the furnishings were sparse and something cheaper than the Early Attic that decorated my apartment on Arsenal. This looked more like Curbside Reclamation. But Colleen and I are just folks, too, and we sank into overstuffed chairs. Lorena Rushing stepped through a small archway and brought back a kitchen chair, once white, now speckled with nicks and popped paint blisters. She pulled it close to me and sat down, still wearing her smile.

"Do you live here by yourself, Mrs. Rushing?" I asked. Even though the room lacked clutter, still the place was claustrophobic. I couldn't imagine much besides the kitchen, a tiny bath, a bedroom, maybe two if each was closet-sized. My own apartment seemed spacious by contrast.

"Oh, yes, neither cat nor canary," she said agreeably.

"I thought maybe your son still lived with you."

"Oh no, he's out of town." Her smile widened.

"Mrs. Rushing, we're trying to trace an adopted child. I hate to bring up such a sad topic, but we wanted to ask you a few questions about the time around your daughter's death."

She was looking at me alertly, like the kid in the first row just waiting for the teacher to finish the question. She kept the look for a moment more, at first not realizing she should erase the smile that seemed to be a permanent fixture. Finally, she nodded me on.

"We wondered if your daughter had perhaps given her baby up for adoption—before your daughter was killed."

"Or if the baby had been given up afterwards," Colleen interjected. I'm sure I sent her a surprised look. No matter who it is I take along on my investigations, that one always has to put an oar in.

Lorena Rushing looked at us serenely while she absorbed the question. Then a pucker formed between her eyebrows. Her china blue eyes clouded. "Her boyfriend gave her money for an abortion," she said.

Colleen and I exchanged a look. "But she had the baby. The *Post* announced its birth—a baby girl," I said.

"But she didn't have it," Lorena Rushing went on tranquilly, as though I hadn't spoken. For a moment I was bewildered. Hadn't had the baby?

"Instead, she went to Our Lady's Inn, but there was some problem. She wouldn't keep to the rules." She looked at each of us with an apologetic smile and a shrug. "Teresa had her own mind."

"So she had the baby?" I prompted.

"Oh, yes. I never got to see it, though. Teresa went to stay with a girlfriend. She took her to the hospital when the time came."

I wanted to ask questions. Had mother and daughter quarreled? Who was the girlfriend? Instead, I nodded in encouragement.

"Then she was killed." For just a moment the wide mouth drooped. "She wasn't a bad girl. Not really. Just a teenager. She liked to laugh and have a good time."

I kept my eyes away from Colleen's. Lorena Rushing didn't seem the sort to have lectured her daughter on life's being a grim round of responsibilities.

Even now, her face was resuming its wide smile. "So the baby was adopted, after all. It turned out all right."

I had to scramble. Her daughter had been brutally murdered—bludgeoned to death, according to the newspaper account—how could this woman make such a pronouncement?

But I wasn't there to chide her. "Who were the parents—the people who adopted her?"

"Oh, he arranged it all. I wouldn't know." A tiny hand waved the issue away.

"Who did?" I asked.

"The man who arranged the adoption. I don't remember. He found the baby and he found the parents—the ones who took her." She smiled and added with emphasis. "And that was that."

"What do you mean when you say he found the baby?" Colleen asked. I could hear her attempt to strain out the sharpness in her tone. Colleen is not reluctant to make judgments, but she knew about catching flies with honey.

"He took the baby. From Teresa."

I was definitely lost. I felt certain the *Post* would have reported the fact if a baby had been found with the mother's body.

But I had to ask. "The baby was found with Teresa?" I guess my tone cued her.

She, too, looked distressed and corrected herself. "Maybe he found her where Teresa had been staying. Some girlfriend."

Colleen actually sighed.

"What was the man's name?" I asked.

Lorena Rushing looked into the middle distance for several seconds. "I don't know. He was a tall man and thin. A fine man."

"Did you write down his name somewhere?" I pressed.

"Oh no," she said, as if I'd asked whether she juggled machetes.

"Do you know where Teresa had been staying in the days before her death?"

Lorena Rushing shook her head. "Teresa didn't have a lot of friends."

Wouldn't that make it easier? I took a breath and asked, "Do you remember the names of some of them?"

Her smile this time was an entreaty. "They drifted in and out, you know. First this one, then that. Teresa didn't like girls much." All of this was delivered apologetically, for Teresa's shortcomings, for her. Would we, could we understand?

"How about her boyfriend, the one who paid for the abortion? Do you know his name?" Colleen asked, not doing a fine job of concealing her impatience.

But Lorena Rushing merely shook her head again. "I couldn't tell you that."

"Had you and Teresa quarreled?" I asked. I felt as though I were oppressing the helpless, but maybe something would come out.

Her eyes sent another plea—to me, to Colleen. "She wanted to keep the baby. But we couldn't afford it." She looked around the small house. "Her brother was living here then. He didn't have a job." She shrugged. "It costs money to keep a baby."

"But Teresa wanted to keep the baby?" I spoke gently.

She nodded. "She said the father would change his mind and marry her when he saw how sweet she was."

"The baby?" Colleen asked, softening her own tone.

She nodded. "And I bet she would have won him over. I never got to see her." Only then did her voice wobble a bit, but she pulled deep breath and managed a smile. "If you find her, tell her—" she paused dramatically, "tell her that her grandma loves her!" She beamed at us.

It was anticlimactic, but I had to push the point anyway. Sometimes siblings confide in one another things they won't share with parents. "Mrs. Rushing, do you know how we can reach your son?"

"Oh no. He moves around a lot. He just calls now and then." Her smile collapsed. "They shut off the phone. Maybe he'll send a postcard when he can't reach me."

I looked at Colleen. She shrugged. I stood and thanked Lorena Rushing for her time. We were starting toward the door when Colleen turned and asked, "What high school did your daughter go to?"

The woman actually blushed as though we might be truant officers about to rake up old records. "Roosevelt," she said meekly.

"Thanks. Thanks a lot," Colleen added.

Outside the cold smacked against my face. Shabby or not, the little house had been tight enough to hold heat.

"Was she on Prozac?" I asked when we climbed back into the Horizon.

"Try an IQ of eighty," Colleen said dryly. Despite her fine education with the nuns, she sometimes has difficulty empathizing with the least among us.

"Well, you see the detective's life isn't all smooth roads."

"Let's go to Roosevelt," she said, interrupting my philosophical sharing.

I looked my question.

"Maybe someone there noticed Teresa Rushing," she explained. "Which is more than her mother did," she muttered into the faux fur ringing her parka hood.

Colleen is closer to the high school experience than I am, so she took the lead, threading us through the needles of tightened security and bureaucratic indifference till we found a counselor who had worked there eight years before and had, indeed, known Teresa Rushing.

Margo Pound was a tall woman with mahogany skin, a lush alto, and a dramatic sense of style. She politely requested that the clerk in the reception area of the guidance department dig up Teresa Rushing's record from the inactive files.

The office she ushered us into was a cramped cubbyhole, but despite overflowing stacks of manila folders and computer printouts, she'd used posters, photos of students and swoops of ivy spilling over ceramic pots to put her stamp on the space.

"Might I ask why you are inquiring about Teresa Rushing?"

"We've been hired to search for the birth mother of an adopted child. Teresa's baby was born at the right time," Colleen said.

Margo nodded. "Well, what I have can't hurt poor Teresa now. Maybe it will help the child."

We were all squeezed together, she behind her desk and shoved against a window, the two of us knee to knee in orange plastic bucket chairs before her desk. Colleen had to list toward me to see around one stack of files.

"Almost anything would help, but specifically the names of any friends she had, the kids she ran around with," Colleen said.

"Mmm-huh." She fluttered polished nails on the oversized calendar that served as her desk blotter. "That might be hard. Teresa was more absent than here, and something of a loner when she was here."

We nodded and looked hopeful.

"Have you talked with her mother?" she asked,

We nodded.

A shrug. "Then you know Teresa didn't get much support from home. Not that Mrs. Rushing didn't care—she was—maybe overwhelmed?"

"Sometimes school's a substitute for home," I said. Ornery as I am, even the rules hadn't kept me from liking the parts of school that made me feel good about myself.

"I wish I could say that was true about Teresa, but I don't think she found much here. She had a fair number of run-ins with the law."

We probably looked alarmed.

"Sorry," she said, with an ingratiating grin. "With school rules. Lots of absences, lots of tardies, a couple of suspensions for fighting." She shook her head. "Some trouble with integration. Some sassing teachers. Sadly, not so unusual." She tapped one forefinger on the calendar. "But I don't think she was a bad kid. She was angry, not mean. And, like a lot of girls, lookin' for love in all the wrong places. Maybe she found it."

The young woman from the outer office tapped on the door, entered at Margo Pound's request, and placed a folder on the desk.

Margo Pound opened it and skimmed a page. "She stopped attending maybe two months before her death—that was in December, wasn't it? We don't have that in the file, but of course, her murder was a big shock here."

"Even though no one knew her?" Colleen asked, not tactfully.

The counselor noted the barb, made a moue. "Yep. She was still one of ours."

"So you knew she had found love—she was seven months pregnant when she quit," Colleen said.

Margo Pound threw up her shapely hands. They were large but womanly and adorned with colorful, enameled rings. "I didn't see much of her just before she dropped out. I hadn't noticed. I'm sure her teachers did. But it wouldn't have mattered. She could attend while pregnant."

"Is there anyone here who might know more, any teacher who had her in class?" I asked.

"Dana McCullough, one of Teresa's English teachers, used to take an interest. I think she stood up for Teresa a few times. Maybe Teresa confided in her."

"Does she still teach here?"

An apologetic shrug. "She quit to raise her own babies. But I'll ask Debbie to call her for permission to give you her phone number."

"How about other students? Can you think of anyone at all that she maybe hung out with, here or outside school?"

She took a minute to think about it, scanned the papers in front of her. I wasn't hopeful. But at last she nodded and looked up. "I'd forgotten. Maybe Twyla Sharp." She laughed, a small, private joke laugh. "They met in detention."

"How might we get in touch with Twyla Sharp?"

"You're the detective." She laughed. "Sorry. Twyla isn't the sort to attend class reunions. She didn't graduate, and she didn't much care for us while she was here. Maybe we have her parents' address." She picked up the phone and gave further instructions to the clerk.

"Do you know if Teresa had boyfriends?" Colleen asked.

Margo Pound nodded. "That I do know. Her freshman and sophomore year she had lots of boyfriends—a revolving door of them. I didn't like what that signaled to me. But that slacked off—and I think maybe she had just one man she was deeply fond of for her last year and a half here."

"Man?"

"Yep. Not sure why I have that impression. But many of our pregnant ones are going with older guys—even late twenties, early thirties." Her tone said what she thought of it.

"But you don't have a name?"

"No, that's one you couldn't pry out of her."

She followed us out and instructed Debbie to make the call to Dana McCullough. Margo Pound wished us luck and returned to her office. The McCullough's phone line was busy, but I'd watched Debbie punch in the phone number.

CHAPTER FIVE

Outside a puny sun peaked through ragged clouds. A gusty wind tugged my hair. I smelled snow in the air. We hustled to the Horizon, trying to shrink into our parkas like turtles retreating into their shells.

I started the engine and optimistically switched on the heater, but the cold had sapped any leftover heat from the drive over. We were starting from scratch.

I was about to apologize to Colleen for the Horizon. But she was into the chase. "I brought a cell phone. We could try Dana McCullough again," she said.

I dialed and got a live human voice. Dana McCullough was now home minding her baby. I identified myself and asked if she recalled her former student Teresa Rushing.

"Poor Teresa—" Her tone reflected a genuine sadness. "She really didn't get a chance to start her life."

I made appropriate murmurs of empathetic agreement and waited.

"They've never found who killed her, have they?" she added.

"No, I don't think so." I would have to ask Lindstrom. Would Lorena Rushing have mentioned it? Not necessarily.

We tsk-tsked through another round about the waste and tragedy of a young life cut short.

Then I moved toward my point. "I'm really calling in an effort to find out what happened to Teresa's baby." I fudged a bit—said an adoptive mother was concerned about her child's medical history and was trying to find out if her baby was Teresa's.

"Wouldn't Teresa's family know?" she asked reasonably.

"Mrs. Rushing is a bit vague about the circumstances."

A slight pause. "She would be, I imagine. I remember talking to her once while Teresa was my student." She was choosing her words carefully, trying not to be hurtful.

"I know this is personal, but I wonder if you could tell me if Teresa ever considered an abortion." I wasn't sure of the relevancy myself, but

I was just trying to feel my way inside Teresa Rushing's mind.

She thought about it. "Maybe right at first—you know—'Oh, God, what am I going to do?' But pretty early on she was thinking she'd keep the baby. She hinted she and the father were going to get married."

"Was that likely?"

She sighed. "I hate to sound cynical. I hate to be cynical. But we have a lot of young ladies who miscalculate about the degree of their swain's commitment."

Swain? Well, she was an English teacher. "Did she say who the father was?" I asked.

"No, she was coy about that. Maybe wary is the better word. That's not unusual either."

"Do you have any notion of who the father was?"

A longer pause. I interrupted it. "Ms. McCullough, I'm not just interested in old gossip here. I'm trying to find anyone who can help me trace Teresa's baby."

"It's not that I'm protecting anyone—even Teresa. But she wasn't that forthcoming."

"Did you get the idea it was somebody at Roosevelt?"

"No—the opposite. But that's not so rare. Kids nowadays meet at the mall; they aren't so loyal to their own neighborhoods."

"Margo Pound thought he might have been older. Did you pick up on that?"

"No." She sounded unsure. "In fact, I would have guessed the opposite. But I can't remember why I thought so."

I glanced at Colleen. I saw a shrug under her parka. I thanked Dana McCullough. For a second I was taken aback when she wished me luck finding the baby's medical history. A good fibber needs to keep track of the details, but my quick creation hadn't stuck. I made a recovery and thanked my way out of the conversation.

"You liar," Colleen said, probably confirming her long suspicions.

I grinned. "Subterfuge is a necessary tool in the trade."

She gave me a dismissive look. "Are we going to Twyla Sharp's parents' house?"

I considered it. Maybe seven times out of ten I prefer an unannounced visit, so interviewees don't get a chance to concoct a story. But sometimes a little civility is a better strategy—like honesty is the best policy.

I thought about it. "You know, Twyla Sharp is close to your age. Maybe we could tell her parents that you're a former classmate trying to find her."

Funny thing. The face that was so disdainful about my little fib now lighted up as though I'd offered her an Oscar-worthy role. "Good idea, Meg!"

I called information and struck it lucky; a family of Sharps who lived near Roosevelt was listed.

Twyla Sharp's mother was home and rather pleased that an old classmate was seeking out her daughter. She wasn't at all surprised that Colleen's name was one she didn't know—whether this was because Twyla had so many friends or parental vagueness was more epidemic than we knew I couldn't guess.

The mother provided us with two sets of addresses and phone numbers, work and home. Colleen asked another question and learned that Twyla worked until seven on Wednesdays at the Chez Paree Salon.

When she pushed END on the cell phone, Colleen gave me a wondering look. "People will just tell everything about their private lives."

"Depends," I said. "Sometimes they clam up like someone guarding national security secrets. I think it has more to do with individual temperament than the actual circumstances."

She nodded. "I guess so. Joey never gives any personal information over the phone. He just slams down the receiver."

Joey, her long-time boyfriend—her fiancé, to be accurate—is not a lad I admire much. Surly hang-ups exactly fit my view of him. I pressed my lips together to seal in my opinion.

But she wasn't paying attention. "I did some telemarketing before coming to Miller. It's a tough life. I try be polite when I'm refusing," she said.

"Yeah. I just lie and say Meg Darcy isn't home and ask if I can take a message. That usually works."

She laughed.

"I wonder if it would be better to talk to Twyla after work?" she added. "If she's busy, she won't want to talk in front of customers and other beauticians in the shop."

"I thought beauty shops were hotbeds of gossip."

She smiled without friendliness. "And you a feminist!"

I sailed past it. "Won't she get an afternoon break?"

Colleen shrugged. "Not necessarily. She might have a full afternoon of appointments without even a fifteen-minute breather." She paused. "Maybe we should call for an appointment?"

I laughed. I saw Colleen going in for a haircut and trying to work the casual chat around to Teresa Rushing and her baby.

She understood my amusement. "No, just to reserve a slot—we could pay her for her time."

I started to say that Miller Security didn't operate like some movie version of a detective agency, then closed my mouth. Sometimes we did.

We decided calling ahead might get us more cooperation. Colleen made the call but didn't pretend to be anyone's old buddy, simply someone who wanted to talk to someone who had known Teresa Rushing. Afterwards she recounted the conversation.

"We're set. Twyla was busy, and she sounded distracted and a little abrupt—you could hear lots of shop noises behind her. But she's okay with our coming by right at closing time."

That left us with the afternoon. Reluctantly we headed back to Miller. While I drove, Colleen quizzed me about our morning. How did I plan to sort out the different versions of what we'd heard—for example, was Teresa's boyfriend a fellow teenager or an older man?

"We just keep gathering facts. Besides, he won't matter to us if we get a better lead on what happened to Teresa's baby. Who cares who the father was?"

"Yeah, but aren't you hooked? Don't you want to know?"

I pulled myself up behind the wheel and struck my best mentoring pose. "Sure, it's easy to get caught up in the sideshow but you gotta keep your eye on the main issue. In this case, who was Jessica's real mother?"

She didn't look convinced.

Back at Miller we found Walter and Mikie at work reviewing the interview files. Walter was grumbling and chewing on a cigar, clear signs that he wanted a bit of soothing. I volunteered to help him evaluate the candidates, and Colleen started returning calls left on our answering machine. Soon Walter and I were locked in a tug-of-war over one of the interviewee's suitability for training, a debate that could have been settled by a coin flip but which afforded us both some entertainment as an intra-family pissing contest. I'm young and quick, but Walter is old and sly.

I let him win.

On a normal day—when we have one— Colleen's quitting time is five-ish. At ten of, Colleen appeared in the door and asked to see me. This was so formal and out of character that Walter lifted his scraggly brows, but he didn't press it. Walter, like many males of his generation, is always wary lest he be oppressed by unwanted information on some "female problem."

I followed her down the hall.

"Do you want to meet at Chez Paree?" she asked, nearly whispering.

I saw her problem.

"I could stick around and do some billing if you wanted to go together from here," she added, trying to give me plenty of room.

"Do you have plans?"

"I'll call Mom and tell her I won't be home for dinner." She still lived with her much-loved and very Catholic parents, and everyone involved pretended that she wasn't sleeping with Joey. She was an old-fashioned gal who sustained such a pretense in part by spending a lot of hours with mom and dad.

I had hoped Lindstrom would call. But her name wasn't among the phone messages. "Great. Let's work another thirty minutes, grab some dinner, and go see Twyla Sharp," I said.

Walter and I wound up our discussion of two more candidates and sketched out a training schedule. We had our usual back and forth over who would do what. The older he gets, the more reluctant he is to "speechify," yet he's a terrific instructor, especially for all the would-be tough guys. As Patrick says, Walter's butch quotient is in the triple digits. When Walter Miller lectures them on using their brains before they draw their weapons, he has great boy credibility. My involvement in some headline-making murder cases has brought me some credibility, too, but still there's always a boy or two in the group who doesn't want to learn anything from a girl. It's not my feminist duty to avoid all practical short cuts like using Walter to advantage.

My mother Betty says Walter is grooming me to take over at Miller. I know in my heart she's right, and it scares me sometimes—what it would be like if Miller Security meant me.

I shoved that thought to the back of my mind, opened the Diane Mann case file on my Mac, and typed in a hasty summary of the interviews Colleen and I had done. Only then did I shuffle through some of the paperwork Walter and I had generated.

I was only half a mind into my work when Colleen entered in her parka and asked, "Ready?"

I shut down the Mac, pulled on my own coat, and we stepped out into the cold night.

Once in the car, we had a brief discussion of where to eat. Colleen vetoed fast food. I wasn't in the mood for Mexican. I persuaded her that MoKaBe's would be fast, cheap, and not out of the way. MoKaBe's is lesbian-owned and gay friendly. But its patrons include generous dollops of Wash U and SLU students and leftover hippy-dippies of vague persuasions with a sprinkling of GAP-clad yuppies. Like all South Grand establishments, MoKaBe's attracts a UN of ethnicities.

We bellied up to the bar and put in our orders for Colleen's quiche and mocha latté and my sandwich and hazelnut cappuccino. Two dykes were playing video poker in the back, a black male cop was sitting at the counter chatting up one of the owners, and an apparently het couple were huddled over hot chocolate and their calculus texts. Maybe it was the reassuring sight of the latter or the officer's presence, but Colleen, after an initial wary survey of the establishment, took a deep breath and managed to relax. Even without Joey at her side, she was not in imminent danger of a dyke attack.

I was disappointed that my being there wasn't security enough. After all these years—four, anyhow—didn't she trust me?

Before I could mope about that, she started talking about what we'd be asking Twyla Sharp, and by the time we'd received and eaten our food, it was time to reenter the cold.

I couldn't resist. "How'd you like MoKaBe's?"

"Not very busy," she said neutrally.

"It's a weeknight," I said, and let it go. I wanted to explain that in summer its patio is bursting with people, that customers bring their dogs and get water bowls served to the pooches, that students can sit for hours scribbling in their notebooks. But I decided not to play Gay Defender. If she wasn't impressed, she wasn't.

I turned us back toward Gravois and Chez Paree. The shop was on a corner across from a small bank branch and next to a tux rental shop. Only Chez Paree was lit up for late evening business. The broad plate glass windows gave complete visual access to the front of the shop— the row of driers, the three lift chairs, the two shampoo chairs toward the rear. Inside, the women looked vulnerable to the night. Anybody could be staring in at them. I wondered if this bothered the women who worked there.

Just now, one woman was sitting under a drier, and another was being combed out by a tall, slender brunette who was talking her customer's ear off. Toward the rear a somewhat older woman was wiping out the sinks. I pulled to the curb across the street. Traffic was slow at seven twenty-nine. I put the Horizon into gear, moved forward a bit, made one of my famous U-turns in the intersection, and parked us right in front of the shop. Colleen shook her head just like Lindstrom—only Patrick and Jen enjoy my U-turns—but kept her counsel. She was going to do nothing to make herself unwelcome on this jaunt.

By the time we got to the door and entered, the older woman had come forward and was saying "We're closed. I should have locked that."

"They're here to see me," the tall brunette said. She caught Colleen's eye. "I'm Twyla Sharp." She glanced at me, then nodded toward the empty drier chairs. "Have a seat."

The older woman shrugged and moved toward the back, found a broom, and began sweeping. Colleen and I put our bottoms to the stuffed vinyl and waited. The smell of perming solutions and hairspray was acute—like that hospital smell that always sets off my alarm system. Too many ethers in the air.

I tried to watch without staring as Twyla finished combing the customer's hair. Twyla's own hair was curly, cut medium-short, and tousled at the end of this day. She had marvelous dark eyes and sharp features under pale skin that in the fluorescent glare of the shop seemed gray despite her youth. She and her customer resumed their conversation but were lowering their voices as though Ted and Mandy's excellent adventures might interest us. Twyla, however, couldn't maintain that level. She had a piercing Missouri twang and the self-confidence to magnify it. She made pronouncements, not suggestions.

I did some calculations. If Teresa Rushing had been seventeen eight years ago, then our Twyla was probably twenty-five, give or take a year to allow for variation in a student's birthday or pass-fail rate. I was afraid she'd made a snap judgment as we entered the shop, liking the look of Colleen, not so amiably inclined toward me. All of Betty's years of warning me to use honey to catch flies have had their effect. I leaned over and whispered to Colleen, "You do the talking."

She was ready for it, not an "ah shucks" in her. Just a nod that she'd heard.

Soon Twyla had finished with her customer, offering her last advice that Mandy "just give up on Ted" in exchange for a five-dollar tip. Meanwhile, the older woman—maybe in her early forties—had stopped sweeping to release the other customer from the drier and was combing her out in the farthest chair. Twyla ushered her customer out, locked the door behind her, and walked toward us, fishing out a pack of cigarettes. Wordlessly she offered the pack to us, and our refusals brought an exasperated sigh. She struck me as a woman impatient about many things.

"Long day?" Colleen asked sympathetically.

I sat up and noticed. This was Colleen away from our shop, away from even the surely gentle hierarchy of Miller Security.

"Ain't they all?" Twyla said, not at all intimidated by the older woman's presence. Maybe she was not the boss. Maybe Twyla didn't care. She took a deep pull on her mentholated cigarette and generously shared its smoke with us as she exhaled. I wondered if it was especially dangerous to smoke in at atmosphere so heavy with ether and its friends, but Twyla was complacent.

Colleen nodded and smiled, a fellow worker ant. She didn't look at me, and I felt a little hot in my parka. "We're sorry," I began, forgetting who the lead was, "to keep you after work, but—"

Twyla blew another puff at us, shrugged elaborately, and looked at Colleen. "Well, we're here now, aren't we?"

It wasn't sexual. But it was high school. Butt my nose out.

Before I could err again, Twyla went on. "So, whatta you want to know about Terry?"

Of course. To her pals Rushing would have ditched Teresa for a more teen-friendly name.

"Whatever you can tell us would help," Colleen said. "You probably knew her better than anyone."

Twyla swallowed it whole. She smiled at both of us and waved her hand in the air to thin the smoke. Unfortunately she used the hand holding the cigarette so the cloud wafted our way. "I was Terry's best friend," she said. I noticed no wobble in her carrying voice. I glanced toward the other beautician and her customer. They were engaged in their own conversation.

Before Colleen offered a comment or question, Twyla added, "Are you trying to find out who killed her?"

Colleen sent me a glance; I did half a head shake. "No," Colleen said. "We're really interested in what happened to Terry's baby."

Twyla shrugged and looked down as though snuffing out the cigarette required careful attention. "Don't know," she said, maybe a little surly to be ignorant despite her best friend status.

Colleen wasn't going to allow that to interfere. "I imagine she was secretive about it. Was her mom upset?"

"Nah, not like you'd think. Terry's mom's a bit dim, you know? But a good heart. No, it's like Terry didn't really live there any more. That wasn't her real life, was it?" She checked Colleen's understanding, or maybe just her age, because then she asked, "Where'd you go to high school?"

Colleen told her, and Twyla sighed, "Catholic, uh?"

For a heartbeat I thought we'd lost her, but she added, "Me, too, but my folks couldn't ever afford the tuition. Just as well—I'm not very religious." Her tone was defiant. If we expected an apology, forget it.

Colleen, who was practically Miss Altar Girl, smiled dismissively. "I know—what a hassle!"

For a moment they bonded over Catholic oppression of the young in the form of catechism classes and early Masses and unearthed the fact that they both had known—slightly—delicious Father Ryan, the stereotypically handsome young priest who'd been a prominent youth minister at some rally they'd both attended. I was patient. I only thought murder. But finally, Colleen came back to the subject. "So Terry wouldn't have considered an abortion?"

Twyla laughed. Her laugh was harsh, like the angles of her face and body. Her eyes were dark, luscious pools, but all the rest of her was sandpapery. I could imagine her in high school—the rebel, the shit stirrer, braying at the foolishness of teachers and suck-ups alike. She'd have been a magnet to those not quite brave enough themselves.

"Terry wasn't Catholic," she said. "Wasn't anything. She thought about an abortion, and her boyfriend paid for it. But she changed her mind and kept the baby." She fished another cigarette from the pack and lit it. Close up her skin looked gritty. If she'd started the day with makeup, it had worn off. With her free hand she reached down to massage a calf muscle. The floor was concrete under the linoleum, and I felt for her.

"Do you know what changed her mind?" Colleen asked, as though this were the current hot gossip.

Twyla laughed again. "Sure. She thought Booth would change his mind and marry her when he saw how sweet the baby was. They'd be one happy family—happier than either of them was in their own family." She was scoffing at this romantic view.

"But Booth wasn't won over?" Colleen asked.

She shrugged. "Don't know if she ever got a chance to test him. She had the baby, then she was out of commission for a while, then she was killed." This time her tone acknowledged the loss of someone she'd been close to.

"What do you mean by 'out of commission'?" I asked.

"Oh, she had the baby and then she was just staying at home for a few days like you would after having a baby. Then she got killed."

"I thought she wasn't staying with her mother," Colleen said. She managed to sound merely puzzled, not contradictory.

"Not home home. She had to stay with Gina." She looked put out. "She couldn't stay with me. I was still living at home. Gina was her second best friend."

We both nodded. "What was Gina's last name?" Colleen asked.

"Trevino. Traharo? Doesn't matter. She's long gone back to Texas," Twyla said, unable to hide her impatience.

Colleen thought a moment and then asked, "Booth must have noticed she was staying pregnant. What did he have to say about that?"

Twyla shook her head. "Well, he broke it off after he gave her the money for the abortion. She was really down about that. But she talked herself out of it—out of being depressed, I mean. Terry had lots of gumption, you know."

"So the baby was a complete surprise to him?" I asked.

She favored me with a glance. "Would have been if he'd known about it. But I think she was killed before she could spring it on him."

"Would seeing the baby have changed his mind?" Colleen asked.

Twyla gave it a moment. "Might have. He was a pretty sweet guy. I think he really loved Terry. But, you know—a guy's a guy." She flicked ash into the ashtray.

"Did he go to your school?" Colleen asked. She'd been following Twyla's lead and pronouncing Booth's name with easy familiarity. This was a slider.

"Are you kidding? The son of a brewery owner?"

For a moment I scrambled frantically, reviewing every scandal about the scions of Anheuser-Busch that I could call up. Colleen's face reflected a similar chase.

"Heitner!" Twyla said with impatient emphasis. "He was a sweet guy, but he was a prince. He wasn't raised to marry a Terry Rushing, cute baby or no cute baby." She spoke with the scorn of the working class for the privileged.

"So what do you think happened to the baby?" Colleen asked.

Twyla shook her head. "I didn't get to talk to Terry's mom at the funeral. And when I talked to Gina, she didn't know either. She thought Booth might have made arrangements, but that was just guessing because Terry hadn't said she'd been able to talk to Booth. Maybe her mom just gave the baby away to a relative or something."

I thought about the contradiction that being a teen is. In some ways you're so independent and ready to take on the world. In other ways you're so dependent and hamstrung. In their separate teen world Twyla and Terry had been buds and free agents. They'd arranged their own sex lives, planned their future. But in dozens of small ways they were tied to childhood. Even a best friend might not be free to follow up with the obvious questions to Mrs. Rushing. She was in another part of Teresa's world.

Colleen had her own thought. "How did Booth take Teresa's death?"

Twyla snuffed out her cigarette with extra vigor. "Can't tell you. He didn't show up for the funeral. I haven't seem him since. He just dropped off the radar screen." She gave a wry smile. "Sometimes I see his name in the papers."

The other beautician and her customer walked between us, and the beautician unlocked and relocked the door. Then she returned to the back of the shop and resumed sweeping.

"I can get that, Sheila," Twyla said, projecting her voice more than necessary.

Sheila shrugged and nodded and put down the broom. "Lock up," she said and disappeared into the back of the shop, presumably to leave by the back way.

Twyla made a face. "As if I've ever forgotten." She shook her head at the dimness of others. Then she smiled at Colleen. "The little girl would be what—eight—now, wouldn't she? I hope she landed with good parents." Somehow it sounded false, conveying only a pretended interest.

"We don't know yet—the little girl in question may not be Terry's," Colleen said. No matter how she said it, this sounded feeble and unsatisfactory. As soon as the question was raised, people wanted to know— Teresa's mother seeming the one interesting exception.

But Twyla had her own issues. "I guess no one's looking for Terry's killer any more." This time her sentiment struck me as real.

I shook my head. "Who do you think might have killed her?" I asked, on a lark.

"Well, at school people figured some nigger did it. But I think it was some geek." She spoke casually, comfortable in our bubble of whiteness. Maybe our faces told her something because she added hastily, "I have lots of black friends."

Colleen was opening her mouth, but I squeezed her forearm. "Well, you've given us lots to think about," I said. "We appreciate your time." I was making other soothing murmurs and pulling Colleen with me.

Twyla's face suggested she thought we might be dykes after all—or that I'd magically transformed Colleen in an instant with my amazing but secret lesbian powers. Twyla seemed uncertain whether Colleen deserved sympathy or enmity.

But she unlocked the door for us and wished us a lukewarm "Good luck" as we stepped into the night.

Colleen wrenched her arm free and said, too loudly, "Why did you shush me? I can't believe you let her get away with that crap." Her eyes were blazing.

I wanted to get her away from Chez Paree. I walked to my side of the car and slid in, leaned over and opened her door to encourage her.

I was feeling more than the decade older I actually am. "We might need her to talk to us again."

"Well, if I do, I definitely have some things to say."

"Not if she finds out you told her mother you were a high school friend." I reached over and patted her arm. A mistake.

"Don't patronize me," she said.

I felt a guilty blush creep up my face. "Sorry. It bugs me, too, that someone her age—your age—could believe such asinine things."

"Your generation doesn't?" She was still plenty hot.

"Not what I meant. I mean I'd like to think younger generations are getting smarter about the race crap—less tribal."

We fell into silence. I drove carefully, even though traffic was light. "Wanna go for a cup of coffee?" I asked after seven blocks.

A long beat. "No, just take me to my car."

"You mad at me?"

Another pause. "Not you." She turned to look out the side window. "You're right. Why aren't we getting smarter?" She turned back to me. "What do you think about Booth being the father?'

"Interesting, if its true."

"You didn't believe her?"

"I think Teresa probably told her that. We'll dig into it."

Colleen nodded absently. We had a truce, but for the rest of the ride we didn't talk about the interview either. We said goodnight, and I waited to see her start her car and drive off.

I felt low—Twyla's assumption that we shared her casual racism had somehow splattered guilt onto Colleen and me. Or maybe Colleen was right. Maybe there was no excuse not to confront Twyla. I wanted to run after Colleen and remind her that Barb Talbot, my best Army buddy, was black. But that was feeble and defensive even in my own ears. Tiredly, I headed north toward Arsenal.

When I got home, Patrick's old MG wasn't in his parking space. I climbed the stairs and was met inside my apartment by a hungry Harvey loudly complaining about the irregularity of his meals. I put down some wet food to atone before I punched my answering machine. Betty had called with a general howdy; I'd had two hangups that probably represented computerized telemarketing. Lindstrom had called with a brisk apology: she was working late and would try to catch me tomorrow, December 4. I noticed that my thirty-plus body was achy and tired. Nobody loved me quite enough, except maybe my mother.

I was in bed, snuggled under the covers with my lonesomeness surrounding me, when Harvey stomped in to nuzzle me and assure me it wasn't so.

CHAPTER SIX

We had agreed to start early on Thursday with the Galleria interviews and make decisions as we went, rather than creating a huge "maybe" pile that buried faces and details. All that had seemed good and straightforward. Thursday at six in the morning, when my alarm went off, I wasn't so sure. Even Harvey wasn't ready for the day. I had to move to reach the alarm clock, and his response was to curl around the other direction and find the crook of my knee. He had a point. It was warm and comfy in here, and out there was the coldest December in the last hundred years.

I tried to look around for bright spots. We were interviewing only two women, so the chances of my meeting another cute lesbian were pretty small. One of them had worked for us before and had quit without notice, but we'd agreed to give her another try because she was a pretty reliable worker and both of us were nervous about finding enough decent guards for this big job. In the end it was that anxiety that propelled me out of bed—not a good start to the day.

I ate a bowl of Cheerios and made a double-size cup of tea in my travel mug. Colleen wasn't in yet when I got to Miller, but Walter was hunched over the resumé file in the kitchen. "Didn't we interview this Raul guy before?" Walter held up a creased and poorly typed letter asking for an interview.

"Not that I remember. Isn't he the guy who works in his brother's restaurant?"

"So he says. We interviewed some Raul for a job about a year ago. He was an idiot. Wouldn't stop talking. Wanted to tell us how he'd got his neck broken—don't you remember?"

"Oh, yeah. Raul. I think maybe this is a different one. If not, we'll get rid of him."

Walter grunted. "You bring donuts?"

"Colleen probably will. She's been pretty happy about working on the Mann case with me."

"What time you guys quit last night?"

"We were done before nine."

"You know we have to give her time off for that. Or pay her over-time. She ain't gonna get the billing done if she's out chasing around with you."

"Maybe we need to hire her some clerical help."

"Why don't you ask one of these gals we're interviewing if they want to sub as a receptionist?"

I counted to five so I wouldn't throttle him. "Maybe I'll make that a general interview question for men and women alike."

Walter's once-red eyebrows rose, but he hadn't yet formulated a reply when the phone rang. I walked out to Colleen's desk to screen the call.

"Meg? This is Diane. Doug's out today, so if you…"

I grabbed it. "Hi, Diane. Thanks for calling me." I had found the rule not to call her more confining than I had expected.

"I just wanted to check on how you were doing. Have you made any progress,yet?"

"Some. I've got a pool of possible mothers, and I've started check-ing on them. Does the name Teresa Rushing mean anything to you?"

"No, I don't know her."

I sighed. "That doesn't mean anything, really. It was just a shot in the dark. I'll keep following up."

"Meg, part of the reason I called was to ask you not to contact Willard Gardner. I'm sure he would tell Doug, and I can't afford for Doug to know I'm looking into this. He'd be furious."

I was quiet a moment. I had avoided Gardner for a similar reason, but I didn't like Diane's shutting the door completely. "At the moment I've got some other leads on these women, but if none of them are Jessica's mom, we may have to revisit the idea of tackling Gardner."

"Just talk to me first, okay? I'm not ready to leave yet, and I can't be here if Doug finds any of this out. He'll kill me."

My friend Donna's frequent assertion that leaving is the most dan-gerous thing a battered woman can do floated into my consciousness. "Diane, do you really believe he might hurt you?"

"No, no. I don't know. What he will try to do is prove I'm an unfit mother and take Jessica. He knows that would kill me."

Maybe it was time for a little more truth or consequences for the client. "How would he try to prove that you are an unfit mother?" There was a long pause. "Diane, I'm like a lawyer—I can only do a good job if I know the facts. What might Doug bring up in a custody battle?"

Another pause, this one with heavier breathing. I could hear Walter's low rumble from the kitchen and chairs scraping. Was the first interview candidate here? Must have come in from the back.

Her voice, when it came, startled me. "My medical records."

"Are you ill?"

"I have been."

Uh-oh. I recognized that tone. Some mental health history here. "Have you been hospitalized?" I asked.

"Twice."

"Against your will?"

"No. I checked myself in the second time—Jewish Hospital."

Enough pussyfooting. "What was your diagnosis?"

"Clinical depression."

"The 'I've got the blues' kind or the 'I can't get out of bed' kind?"

"The 'I can't get out of bed' kind. The first time Doug took me to the hospital I hadn't spoken or moved off the couch for three days. I was in the hospital seven days before I spoke again. The second time I didn't let it get so bad. I checked myself in."

Now I was the one with nothing to say.

"I haven't been in the hospital since we got Jessica. My doctor even decreased my meds this year. Really, it was all about not having a baby. It was just so bleak, and Doug was so frustrated with me. He'd work twelve or sixteen hours every day, and when he got home he wouldn't talk to me. It was just awful."

What a burden on that child, I thought. Perhaps I should meet Jessica before I took this any farther. Maybe I was working for the wrong parent after all. It couldn't be healthy to be your mother's only link to sanity.

"Diane, you should have told me this before."

"Why? So you could decide I'm crazy and that I don't deserve my daughter? That I'm imagining that Doug is hateful and ruthless?"

"No, so that I could make some informed decisions about how to proceed."

"You need to proceed by figuring out how my husband got my daughter and how that will affect my ability to remain her mother. That's what I hired you to do."

I traced the R.J. that someone had carved into my desk before Walter had picked it up at an auction years ago. I tried to think. It wasn't really my job to decide who Jessica got to live with—that was thankfully up to a family court judge. All I had to do was figure out if her beginnings should have any bearing on that decision. Lots of perfectly good parents have some illness in their lives. And I couldn't exactly ask Jessica who she'd rather live with as the girl didn't know her mother was planning to leave yet. So my choices were to continue on or to quit in a snit because my client hadn't told me she'd been hospitalized. Evasive clients are what you get in the PI biz.

"Okay, Diane. But I want you to tell me things. Is there anything else that might be relevant?"

"No, just that. I'm sorry, Meg, but you aren't a mother. You don't have any idea how high the stakes are here. And I am a good mother."

"Have you searched through the house for any papers that Doug might have kept about the adoption?"

"I've looked everywhere. There is nothing here. Nothing."

"I had another thought. Just because it wasn't Marianne's baby doesn't mean the family connection is totally out. You might ask around, see if you can get people talking about unwanted pregnancies within the family. I'll keep working on the leads I've got. And I'd like you to call me at least every other day, in case I have something I need to ask you."

"All right. I'll call tomorrow and then maybe on Sunday when Doug is watching the game."

"That will be good. If I'm not home Sunday, call me on the cell phone." I thought Diane's tone indicated she could do with a bit more reassurance, but that wasn't my job. Not telling me important facts should pinch a little. Maybe she'd be more forthcoming from now on. As I hung up, I decided that perhaps Diane was over her bouts with depression after all—didn't they say depression was anger turned inward? Her tone with me and about Doug, indicated progress toward turning her anger outward, at any rate.

Walter was finishing the first interview when I returned to the kitchen. I could tell it hadn't gone well from his over-hearty "we'll be making the decision in a few days" speech. The candidate didn't get it, though. He pumped Walter's hand too long and then reached for mine before he was introduced. I could have been another candidate for the job, for all he knew. The next three weren't promising either, but I thought we could make do with one of them.

In the afternoon all fifteen showed up and were adequate. So by five-thirty we had a class of thirty-three to train. Probably twenty percent would quit before the training was over—or do something so stupid that we washed him or her out. One time a candidate listened and learned at a fabulous clip during training, but on the last day before we'd sent him out on his own, he'd worn a short sleeve shirt and Walter had spotted his swastika. Sometimes the security business is worse than the police force. You have to scrutinize the kind of people who want the job.

At a quarter to six I drifted out to Colleen's desk. She was clearing the decks before leaving.

"Want to go to check out Booth Heitner?" I asked.

"Tomorrow?"

"I was thinking tonight."

Her face fell. "I can't tonight. It's my sister Megan's birthday. We're having a party."

"Um. How old is she?"

"Nineteen. But I have to be there. She just broke up with her boyfriend and she's been blue. Plus, Joey's coming over."

"How is Joey?" Colleen and Joey had been engaged since we hired her four years ago, but I never really heard about actual wedding plans. I knew Joey wasn't good enough for Colleen from the moment she revealed to me that he told her to go on a diet.

"He's okay. His dad is drinking again, so Joey's thinking about moving out. He wants us to get a place together." She didn't say—but lurking in her tone was a hesitation.

"What would your folks say?"

"They'd be unhappy, but they love Joey. They'd get used to it. I'm just not sure…"

I had a rush of loneliness thinking about Colleen, her family and her in-laws to be. Where was my beloved tonight? Certainly not planning on coming to a family birthday dinner. I tried to remember the last birthday I had celebrated with my siblings, Brian and Nicole. It might have been Nicole's fifteenth—over ten years ago. "Listen. We'll do Booth Heitner tomorrow. We can catch him at the office then."

"That'd be terrific."

"Well, have a good time tonight. Wish Megan a happy birthday from me." I walked out the door feeling little better. Maybe I'd call my mother and treat her to dinner.

Unfortunately, trying to recreate the Waltons didn't work all that well. It was Betty's canasta night. Patrick was working until ten. In desperation I called my eleven-year-old niece and was informed by my sister-in-law that Jen was out at a basketball game with some friend I'd never heard of. I tried Lindstrom both at home and at the office—no luck. I disdained the pager number Neely gave me; it would hurt too much when she didn't return my call.

Instead, I bought two pints of Chunky Monkey and limped home resolving to clean the bathroom. After ice cream and before Comet, I looked up Heitner Associates on the Internet. Since quitting the brewery business, the Heitner empire had diversified. First real estate, then insurance, then stocks and bonds. I was gratified to see the Market Street address. The company had stayed in the city. I spent the rest of the evening typing up my notes. With concentrated effort, I managed not to have time to scrub down the shower after all. At ten I knocked off and tried Lindstrom again. No answer anywhere.

CHAPTER SEVEN

I called Heitner Associates the moment I got into the office the next morning. Booth's secretary assured me she'd return my call as soon as she had an opportunity to see if Mr. Heitner had any free time on his calendar today. I looked at my calendar and saw 'check references.' I wandered out to see Colleen, but the phone kept ringing; she had no time to talk. So I snagged a quick cup of coffee and settled down to my phone work.

Very few references are really all that helpful. They are generally friends or relatives of the potential employee that only want to get off the telephone without saying anything that might hurt the applicant. Occasionally I get an ex-employer who'll tell the truth: 'He's lazy as sin but basically trustworthy' or 'He calls off sick every sunny day.' Mostly I hear that the choices we make were good enough.

Jerry Cross, the thin guy, called at ten. "I was just wondering, ma'am, if you'd made a decision yet on that security job."

"Not yet, Jerry, I'm still checking references. Let me see—I rifled through the yellow legal pad to find Jerry's page. I had talked to an ex-brother-in-law about a summer job mowing lawns but I hadn't gotten a call back from the guy at Burns. "Nope, I haven't got all your references checked yet. I'll be making calls over the next couple of days."

"If I got the job, when would it start?"

I repressed a sigh and reminded myself that interested was vastly preferable to not interested.

"We're doing training next week. We'll hire everyone at once, and all of you will have to attend four days of training." Which reminded me I needed to make sure Colleen called the Holiday Inn to check that we had the large meeting room rented next week.

"Okay. Should I call back on Monday, then?"

"No, Jerry. I'll call you, or Colleen will, and let you know."

"Well, good, then. I won't take my sister to Memphis this weekend. She wanted me to drive her, but she's not comin' back till Tuesday, and it sounds like that would mess this job up, right?"

"If we hire you, you'll need to be in training Tuesday morning, Jerry. We'll call you one way or the other." Strangely, as irritating as he was, I liked him a bit better after this conversation. I called Burns again as soon as I hung up and learned almost nothing about Jerry. But I had to listen to the manager moan about how overworked he was. I scribbled Jerry's name on Colleen's list of people to call and schedule for training.

Colleen buzzed me. Heitner's secretary was on the line. She said I could stop by Mr. Heitner's office at ten-forty-five and catch a brief interview with him. I glanced at my watch. Ten. Good, plenty of time to jot down some notes for questions. I wasn't going to let Colleen handle this one. I buzzed her back.

"We've got an interview with Heitner in forty-five minutes. I'll be ready to leave in twenty."

"I can't go."

"Why not?"

"I've got people coming to fill out W-2 forms and bonding papers."

"Can't Walter see them? We'll only be gone an hour or so."

"No, not if I want them filled out right and I do. Besides, the phone is ringing nonstop, in case you hadn't noticed. And I've got all these calls to make to talk to these people about training. Plus there is a problem with the training lunches." Her voice was growing tighter, and I realized that once more I was going to get to dance off and do the fun part, and Colleen, in spite of her good work earlier, was going to have to stay home, mind the baby and do the dishes.

"What's the problem with lunches? Do you want me to call the caterer?"

"No, they are supposed to call me back. The assistant manager says he has an order for only three days, not four. I'll get it ironed out, but I just can't leave right now."

"Okay, I'll go interview Booth, then tell you how it went, huh?"

She heaved a sigh. "Don't forget to ask him about Gina. She might have been the only one besides Teresa to actually see this baby."

"Okay, and Colleen—thanks for doing all this work on the Galleria thing."

"Tell Walter a raise before Christmas would be welcome—and remind him I'd like some part-time clerical help."

"I promise." I fled before Colleen could hand out the union ballots.

58

Heitner Associates was housed at the 1010 Market Street building, which shared the block with KSDK, St. Louis's NBC affiliate. Parking down here was outrageous, with the civil and criminal courthouses facing one another. I refused to pay eight dollars for the garage, so I was condemned to searching in ever-widening circles. Finally I snagged a meter on Clark almost within the shadow of the Police Department's ugly hulking complex and hotfooted it back to Tenth Street. I stood on the sidewalk outside the building for a moment to catch my breath. From here it looks like the St. Louis Arch straddles Market Street. Just before that is the dome of the old courthouse where the slave Dred Scott discovered that in the land of the free, he was merely chattel in every state, not just those south of the Mason-Dixon line.

Heitner Associates was on the sixth floor, and after a noiseless ride in the mirrored and rosewood elevator, I surveyed what a million cans of lager had wrought. Heitner had all the trimmings—real furniture in the waiting area, a marble woman provocatively draped and an ugly old grandfather clock that probably cost more than my net worth. The real woman, behind the over-large reception table was high quality, too, although at the moment she seemed to be trying to decide between the kitties and the dolphins for her screen saver. I've long suspected the big world of capitalism rests on decisions like these.

Booth must have given some secret signal that he was ready for me because the receptionist turned the megawatt smile on me and even stood so I could get a look at legs that were nearly as long as Lindstrom's and slightly more shapely.

Heitner himself was shapely, too. His clothes were tailored so I'd notice his over-muscled masculinity. I could swear that his abs rippled in a perfect six-pack under white cotton.

He had a warm smile, though, and came out from behind his power desk to greet me. We shook hands and introduced ourselves and assured one another that we were mutually pleased to be sharing this moment. He seated us in the green leather armchairs in front of his desk.

To my right was a beautiful glass-fronted cherrywood china cabinet displaying several generations of bottles and advertising copy from Heitner Brewery. One drawing showed a pink-cheeked young man and his father enjoying a bottle of St. Louis Ale in the backyard under a tree. A rotary mower rested against the trunk. A caption below explained that the top of the family line had been a lager—Koenig. I asked Booth about it.

"Koenig is a family name. My great-great-great-grandfather was a brewer in Stuttgart. His name was Koenig." He smiled charmingly, "As is mine—Booth Koenig Heitner." He paused. "Rachel said you are working on some old adoption case?" A gentle nudge to my purpose there.

"Yes, I'm looking for the birth mother of an eight-year-old girl. She was adopted privately, and I have reason to believe Teresa Rushing may have been her birth mother."

His tone was not quite chilly enough to frost a beer mug. But we were no longer buds. "Surely if it were a private adoption, the adoptive family could help you with that information."

"Unfortunately not. There are some conflicting interests in the matter. I have information that you may have dated Teresa Rushing around that time."

"Oh, Teresa and I might have seen a movie or gone skating with the same group, but we never really dated—"

The door opened and a handsome young woman stepped inside. She looked as if she had just stepped out of a high fashion magazine. She gave me a critical once-over that relegated me to fashion purgatory at best and said to Booth. "Sorry to bother you, sweets, but I'm on my way to mother's and just wanted a goodbye kiss."

Booth made a hurried introduction, "My wife, Leslie... Ms. Darcy..."

Leslie gave her a curt nod and said, after receiving her goodbye kiss, "Don't forget to make the Terry Gross tape for me. I'll need it for my talk Thursday."

Booth nodded and escorted her to the door.

He returned to his desk. "We've just been married a year."

I tried to sound reassuring. "I'm sure she didn't hear."

He flushed slightly. "It wouldn't matter. After all, I barely knew Teresa."

"Twyla Sharp seemed to think you did. She assumed you were the baby's father."

He seemed unruffled by the suggestion of his unacknowledged paternity. "Oh no, I assure you, things never went that far. My dad didn't approve of Teresa."

"That would hardly have made a difference at seventeen, would it?" I remembered my mother's thin lips when she caught me necking with Anne Bettino at that age.

"I know it sounds odd, but Dad's disapproval was enough then. I was just straightening myself up. I'd been a bit of a rebel for a couple of years—then my older brother died in a car accident. Dad was devastated. So that year was difficult. I didn't do anything to rock the boat, didn't want to bring any more grief to my parents, let alone fathering a child. Sorry to disappoint you, but you haven't found the right guy."

"But you do remember running around some with Teresa?"

"Sure, she was even at the house a couple of times. That's how I know Dad didn't like her. But I don't remember Twyla at all. Was she a friend of Teresa's?"

"Her best friend, according to her."

"Could be. I didn't know Teresa that well. But I don't remember her hanging with other girls much. She was usually at the center of a pack of boys."

I stiffened at the not-so-subtle suggestion that Teresa was cheap, so anyone could have fathered her child. "Any boy in particular?"

"Let me think. Those guys weren't really my friends. What were their names?" Booth pulled a concentrating face. "There was a Jim. He had dark hair and drove a yellow pick-up truck. They called one of them Walker. I don't know if that was his name or a nickname."

"You knew Teresa was pregnant?"

"You know, I don't really remember. She wasn't pregnant the last time I saw her, but now that you bring it up, I think I did know. Someone must have told me. I remember I was sad. I liked Teresa. I mean, Dad was right, she was too wild for me, but she was a nice girl under that rough and ready surface."

This man's memories seemed so different from the story Twyla had told. But Twyla hadn't seemed to know anything about Booth directly—just what Teresa had told her. As I looked around Booth's office, it wasn't hard to figure out why Teresa would have wanted to finger the Heitner boy as the father. But was he?

"Did Teresa ask you for help after she was pregnant?"

"No, we had drifted apart. Probably I wasn't as kind to her as I should have been. It was such a terrible year. I was so torn up about my brother's death and really unsure of myself. I was trying to grow up quickly. When Teresa and I were friends, I was headed for trouble. I guess she got pregnant right after I quit seeing those friends. She might have been a little sweet on me, Ms. Darcy, but I didn't get her pregnant."

"You didn't give Teresa money for an abortion?"

"No, I didn't. Although I'd like to believe I would have if that's what she wanted. Would have helped her as a friend. I felt like a shit when she was murdered. Because I had just sort of dumped her. Not as a girlfriend, but like I had my other friends. I just walked away from them after my brother's death. To please my father—to get a hold on myself. I don't have any idea if it hurt her feelings or not."

The selves we shed trying to grow up! It sounded to me like Booth Heitner had been on the way to becoming a useless rich playboy, but his family's tragedy had saved him. Had it? Did he do real work in this fine office? Or was he just filling a son-shaped hole in his daddy's corporation? "Teresa had another friend—Gina. Gina was who Teresa was living with when she gave birth."

"Gina? No, I don't remember a Gina either." Booth's phone buzzed, and he apologized and picked up. "I'm sorry, Ms. Darcy, but I need to take this call."

"Okay, Mr. Heitner. Thanks for your time. Here's my card in case you think of anything that might help." I let myself out of the office. Well, I thought, nodding to the receptionist as I left, Booth Heitner was extraordinarily cooperative, wasn't he? I had a funny feeling that if I did need to see him again, it wouldn't be half so pleasant.

When I got back to Miller, Walter was in his office, bouncing Mikie on one thigh and grunting into the phone. I gave a wave and walked down to reception and Colleen's desk. She was nose deep into her printouts, so I pivoted, walked to my office, shucked my parka, poured two coffees, and walked back. I set the black one on her desk and took the cream-and-sugar one with me to the orange-plaid two-seater couch.

"This thing is too short, too nubby, and too ugly," I said.

"You're just now noticing?" She didn't raise her nose from the printouts.

"I talked to Booth Heitner."

"Hmm." To the untrained ear it was an indifferent hmm, but I knew better.

"So do you want to hear what he had to say?"

"Are you going to tell me?" She looked up and took a sip of her coffee.

I recounted the sparse facts of the interview.

"What do you think?" she asked when I'd finished.

"Like Twyla said, he seems like a nice enough guy. I wonder how nice he was eight years ago when he was running with a wild crowd, a cute and vulnerable rebel."

"So?" she asked. "What's next?" Not impatient, just curious.

"Dunno. Maybe I'll go back to my office and have a good think. Try to route incoming calls to Walter."

She shrugged and returned to her printouts.

Back in my office I entered my meager gleanings from the Booth Heitner interview onto the case file on the Mac. Even typing slowly, that took only five minutes.

What did we have? We'd eliminated three mothers for Jessica. If Teresa Rushing wasn't her biological mother, where did I look next? I thought about all those churches, all those christening records. We could start running personal ads in the *Post* and *Riverfront Times*, but those were always a long shot. Even if the right people saw them, they might choose not to respond. Blech. I played with a pencil. Then with a click pen.

Something about the Booth Heitner interview bothered me. Maybe all the facts we didn't know about Teresa. Maybe the big fact that murder spreads a stain over everything.

What had happened to Teresa's baby? Unless she was Jessica, she seemed to have disappeared into thin air.

I wondered if we could check the courthouse for adoption records for that time period. The thought died like a snowflake on a steamheat radiator. Adoption records are sealed to protect everyone's privacy. As a lesbian, I'm a big advocate of privacy; as a private investigator, I want freedom of information to prevail. Just another tug-of-war in the life of Detective Darcy.

Maybe the tug-of-war image nudged me. Before the last of our leads melted away, I might be able to find out more about what had happened to Teresa Rushing. I dialed the familiar number, asked for the familiar extension.

"Lindstrom here." Also familiar: crisp, alert, crime-fighter.

"Got time for lunch?"

She managed to make her sigh sound rueful rather than exasperated. "Ah, no. I'm deep into it."

"You have to acquire calories to burn to keep that keen intelligence sharp," I said in my best not-easily-dissuaded Darcy pleading.

"I've got one of the Circuit Attorney's assistants coming over for a working lunch. We're trying to decide if we've got enough to take this case to court." Less rueful now. Just her assumption that I would, of course, understand her priorities. "But I'm flattered you asked," she added in a rare stab at diplomacy. Lindstrom is unflatterable—and proud of it.

"Well, then, maybe you could do me a favor?" The trap sprung.

"If I can—" Already wary. Where did the woman acquire all her suspicions anyway? Could Nebraskan Lutheranism really account for such a dark view of humankind?

"This one should be a breeze since you're already messing around in the archives. I'd like to see a file for a murder case—a woman killed in December eight years ago. The victim, Teresa Rushing, was the mother of a baby I'm trying to trace." Of course, I didn't know if the last statement was true. But I could always say, "Oops, sorry," if that didn't pan out.

A beat of silence. "How will that help you?" She has to control everything. She'd decide if I had a need to know.

I answered with my own sigh. "Private investigation is different from police work, Lindstrom. We can't always cut to the chase. We sometimes have to meander a bit, gather facts like lint on a suit."

"You're mixing metaphors, Darcy," she said, amused. There was no point to it except that once again she was in a superior position and eager to criticize me.

"Sue me." I wasn't going to be deflected. "So, can you get it for me?" I have my own crafty ways, my own command of English. *Can* you do it, not *will* you, because *can* involves her ego. Does she have enough punch, pull, clout, wherewithal to get into those musty old files just 'cause she wants to?

"All right. I'll take a look. Give me the name and date again."

I complied, though I knew she probably already had the facts in her memory chip. But she's thorough and careful and "measure twice, cut once" is her everyday rule.

"You know, I'd like a little peek at the paperwork myself," I added, trying not to press too hard.

"Ah, well—" she said, not even bothering to spell out the difficulties, the department policies.

"Do your best," I said, trying the ego route again. "They're going to search the great detective who's solving cold cases right, left, and sideways to see if she's carrying home an old file?"

At least she laughed. "Don't push it," she added, but the warning sounded pro forma.

"So, if the prosecutor cancels, give me a buzz, and I'll run by and take you to lunch. It's cold enough, chili at Crown Candy would be perfect."

I forgot. Bad move. She's still uncomfortable with being outed. Crown Candy is a major cop stop. She wouldn't want to be seen hanging out there with the PI that half of the department knew and everyone else speculated was her sweetie.

She's too honest to fake it. "Maybe someplace else. If the prosecutor cancels."

"You can't keep hiding, Lindstrom. It's too late."

"Don't lecture me, Darcy. You don't work here."

Fair enough. Still, she took one timid step forward, then two or three giant steps back.

But I wasn't putting her into a generous mood. "You're right, I don't. So, good luck with prosecutor boy. Hope your case looks tidy to him."

"Actually today it's prosecutor girl, but thanks." She sounded relieved to be off The Subject.

We said our goodbyes without her promising a return call. I tried not to mind. I knew in the last stages of building a case, she would work late into the evening.

CHAPTER EIGHT

The phone pierced the fog of my sleep. It would have taken a generous interpreter to understand the "hello" in my answering grunt.

"Sue, this is Diane, Diane Mann. You know those wool suits we were looking at last week? Today's paper says they are on sale at Lord & Taylor's. Thirty percent off. I want to get over there this morning. They'll go fast at that price. Could you meet me there?"

It was too much for my sleep-slowed brain, but I understood that it was Diane Mann and concluded that I shouldn't just hang up on her. "Diane, this is Meg Darcy," I explained slowly.

"I know, Sue. But you can bring her along. That red suit looked perfect on you, and you can't beat thirty percent off. I may buy the blue one. Just say you'll meet me at Lord & Taylor's. We'll have lunch after."

"You want me to meet you at Lord & Taylor's?"

"Yes, exactly. We can't miss this sale."

"Where is Lord & Taylor's?"

"There at the Galleria. In the women's department at ten."

"I got it. Lord & Taylor's at the Galleria at ten this morning."

"Great, Sue. Thanks, see you there." She ended as abruptly as she had begun, and I listened to the dial tone for a second. Doug must be there.

Lord & Taylor's certainly wasn't my first choice of rendezvous points, but when we finished, I'd be able to saunter through the Galleria and take some notes for our training next week. It couldn't hurt to have concrete details of the mall's layout fresh in my mind. I rolled over and looked at the clock. Seven-thirty. Did straight women really call one another before eight on Saturday to make plans to shop at Lord & Taylor's?

Just to amuse myself, I looked at some of the racks of clothing as I waited for Diane to appear. I had a hard time imagining people actually buying clothes at a place like this. I ran my hand down the sleeve of a silk blouse. There was a slate blue one that would look terrific on Lindstrom. I imagined her pulling it on and tucking it into wool slacks. Ninety-seven dollars. Damn, did people really pay nearly a hundred dollars for one shirt? Did Lindstrom? I realized I had no idea where she shopped. Only that her clothes always looked perfect—like they were made for her—like this blouse.

"Meg! Thank God you're here. What have you done?" She grabbed my arm.

"Diane—hey. Slow down. What's happened?"

"Doug knows I've hired you. He said if I don't make you stop I'll never see Jessica again. We have to call it all off. I can't do this. God, I don't know what I've done." She put her hand to her mouth.

"Back up, Diane. In fact, let's go sit down somewhere. Is there someplace in this mall we might get some privacy?" Diane looked around, and for an awful moment I was afraid she was going to suggest a dressing room. "Let's go get a cup of coffee and you can tell me everything he said."

She led the way to St. Louis Bread Company where we were greeted by the calming smell of freshly brewed coffee. Christmas shoppers crowded most of the tables with their heavy coats and brightly colored bags. I steered Diane toward an open spot and got us both coffee and a muffin.

"Now, what did Doug actually say?"

"He said I'd better not make trouble if I knew what was good for me. He said I could leave him if I wanted, but I wasn't getting a dime and I'd never see Jessica again."

"He started in like that, just out of the blue?"

"He came home from the station angry. I don't know why he went there, but he was in a rage when he came home. He threw a picture frame at me—it left a dent in the wall. Whatever you've done, he's found out about it. And he'll do it. He'll take Jessica if we don't stop. Or have me put in the hospital again.

My mind raced over what I'd done so far. Margo Pound? Twyla Sharp? Booth Heitner? Booth was the most likely—Doug Mann worked for his family. "You said he came from the police station?"

"He said that interfering bitch wasn't going to find anything on him, and he knows I put you up to it, and he knows I want to take everything he's worked for. He called me a crazy whore and said I'd better get my ass out now."

"That might not be a bad idea, Diane. Is there someplace you could go for a few days until I know more?"

"Don't you understand anything? Now that he knows I've asked questions about Jessica's adoption there will be no getting away. I cannot leave without Jessica, and if I try to take her, he will hunt me down wherever I go. He'll either kill me or get me locked up in the hospital."

"He can't get you committed, Diane. You're not crazy."

"Oh, I'll look crazy enough when he gets done with me. Trust me. He'll tell them anything—that I tried to kill myself—that I tried to hurt Jessica. And there is no place to hide. He has the whole St. Louis Police Department on his side. He'd tell them I kidnapped our daughter. They'd be looking for me in just a few hours."

"We could get you out of the city. My mom lives in Belleville. Or I have friends who live down in the Ozarks if you don't want to go out of state with her."

"No, I can't do that. He'll find me. I just have to convince him that I've changed my mind. That I don't want to leave. So I can't have any more contact with you. Whoever you've talked to, you've got to stop. You can't ask any more questions. I'll just have to find a different way."

"How about a good attorney, Diane? Someone who is experienced in family law. That might be a good place to start. One of the women who might be Jessica's biological mother was murdered shortly after she had her baby girl. I'm looking into that. When Doug said something about an interfering bitch, did he call me by name?"

"No."

"When he said he knew you'd started this, did he say why?" Since he'd been down at Clark Street, I suspected Lindstrom might be the interfering bitch.

"No, he was just screaming at me. He was more angry than I'd ever seen him."

"I think he might have just been fishing. He's heard that some questions are being asked about the Rushing murder, and he must know that Teresa was Jessica's mother. Did you tell him you'd hired me?"

"I just told him I'd stop it. And I have to, Meg. I can't risk it."

I got up and refilled our coffees. "Diane, I'm pretty sure Teresa was Jessica's mother, but I don't yet know how Doug got the baby. I don't think you can afford to let it drop."

"I just don't know any more if this is a good idea."

"It's your decision, Diane. If you want me to drop it, I will." I paused, put my hand on hers for reassurance. "But it sounds to me like you need an ally. And a good attorney. If you want me to, I'll follow up on this murder discreetly—and see if it leads us to anything about Jessica or about your husband."

She stared into my eyes, searching for answers I didn't have. Would Doug win? Could he really manipulate the system to keep her daughter? Would what we found be enough to derail that?

"Please, please, please be careful. And don't trust anyone in the police department. Most of them would do anything for Doug. Including lie. And if something happens to me, make sure he pays for it."

I couldn't think what to say to that. I certainly wasn't some Dirty Harry who was interested in vengeance. I wanted my client and her daughter to be safe.

"Listen, if you change your mind about going out of town, I can help. If you do go somewhere, call me as soon as possible. If you can't get me, you can trust Colleen."

Diane nodded and gathered her purse a little shakily. "Thank you, Meg. I do feel better."

"Good. Do you need to buy something before you go home?"

"Oh, yes, I'll go shop. And I'll call Sue to see if she can meet me here." She pulled out her cell phone. Sue was home and willing to spend the morning at Lord & Taylor's. Evidently I was the odd woman out here.

I couldn't follow through with my plan to prowl the mall though. I had to talk to Lindstrom and see which sleeping bear she had poked when she'd pulled the Rushing file.

When I left Diane Mann, I didn't hesitate. I took Route 40 to Kingshighway. I wanted to ask Lindstrom how Doug Mann knew his wife was my client.

I was taking a chance on Lindstrom's being home. I hadn't brought my cell phone. Somehow I haven't made that gizmo a permanent appendage.

Northeast of Wash U and northwest of Forest Park, McPherson is one of the more attractive streets in the Central West End, but made damned near impossible to get into by concrete planters, five-feet-by-five-feet, set at the mouth of the street. These planters reflect a time when the street's fortunes dipped, and the neighbors wanted to stop would-be troublemakers from racing through the street at top speed. Now the neighborhood is being gentrified into respectability again, but getting into Lindstrom's block of McPherson is like penetrating a maze. That Lindstrom had learned how to do it after one visit never improved my mood.

I made two false passes before I lucked into an entrance that worked and pulled in front of her apartment. Her Toyota was parked two cars down; I was twice lucky.

Like its fellows on the street, Lindstrom's building is a three-story of aged red brick, dignified by tall trees along the sidewalk and ivy on its porch. Once a single-family home, it had been subdivided into six apartments. Viv and her friend Colin Lanier had bought the property cheap and restored it, if not to its former glory, certainly to its late-sixties charm as an apartment building. Lindstrom had inherited her share of the building from Viv and moved in after putting her Soulard house up for sale.

I have a key to the main entrance. I was delighted the day she'd given it to me, as if it were her police academy ring. But with dispiriting regularity I'm reminded it's just pragmatism on Lindstrom's part to give me a key.

The stairs to her second-floor apartment are lined with dark polished wood that show the nicks of usage but smell deliciously of lemon. The new runner on the steps is deep wine.

I knocked—three sharp raps is our signal—on the thick door at the end of the hallway.

She stood there, tall and trim in buff cords with a yellow oxford shirt under a rusty vee-neck sweater, looking good enough to lick. I never get used to the electric surge she sends through me: the sight of her, the promise of more. For a moment I forgot why I'd come.

"Darcy! I'm glad you came by—I was just wanting to talk to you."

That threw me, too. Suddenly it was her agenda.

I stepped in. The apartment is really a grand old place, the ceilings high with an ornate plastered frieze around them; solid oak floors, refinished and glowing; walls thick enough to muffle the sound of bloody murder. Not that I'd ever say that to Lindstrom, given Viv's death in their Soulard home. Lindstrom's bedroom even has windows overlooking a backyard of well-tended shrubs and flower beds. But, despite its obvious charms, this was still just a place to hang her hat. Her furniture hunched here, too blond and too jammed, for its space. Her books were shelved but not organized, her pictures not hung, her personal mementos still boxed.

She motioned me back to the kitchen. Only then did I notice she was padding about in her stocking feet—thick wool socks in heather beige. She disdains any discussion of fashion, yet somehow arises each day and effortlessly dons an ensemble.

"I was just making a pot of tea," she said, nodding toward the kettle on the narrow stovetop.

As usual with Lindstrom, everything was tidy. Leaving a dirty saucer in the sink overnight is an act of wild defiance.

The kettle started to whistle, and Lindstrom pulled down an extra matching mug. I don't know how she avoids the usual assortment of KWMU pledge drive mugs that grace my cabinet.

She flipped open a flat wooden box of assorted teas, strong English blends from Harrods, and offered me a choice. I pointed at Blend #49. She put four bags in a blue porcelain pot to match our mugs.

"I had an unexpected visitor last night," she said, while she set out a pitcher of skim milk and the sugar bowl.

"Mmm?" I said and helped myself to one of her kitchen chairs. The blond wood didn't fit the dark kitchen, but this was, after all, a temporary encampment.

She nodded. "After we talked, I had a little time, so I checked on the case file you wanted."

"Teresa Rushing?"

She nodded again. "Right. I had no trouble finding it, but it was a disorganized mess and rather thin, too, as though some of it were missing." She sounded cross—like maybe I'd filched it.

I shrugged and kept quiet. She peeked inside the pot, swirled the tea bags, and replaced the lid. Then she focused her Norwegian blues on me.

"There didn't seem to be many leads in the case and, except for the usual handful of false tips, the case petered out pretty quickly, considering the circumstances."

"Which were?"

"Well, she was a reasonably pretty white girl found in a vacant lot. It looks as though she was killed elsewhere and dumped there. It's the kind of story the media would run with and turn into a scare-and-shudder story for the sort of white people who believe their streets and homes aren't safe and haven't been since the Eisenhower era."

That was a long speech and quite political for Lindstrom. She poured an experimental stream of tea into her mug, nodded, and filled both. She let me add my own milk and sugar. Then she turned a chair around and straddled it, reaching around its back to pick up her tea.

"O-kaay," I said, trying to match her pensive tone.

"The point is none of that happened. And the investigation stopped within a couple of weeks.

"They don't close murder cases, do they?"

She shook her head, her smooth blonde hair moving slightly, inviting touch. "No. Not officially closed, but it wasn't pursued. And it didn't trickle to a stop. It just stopped. Why was that?"

She waited as though I might offer an explanation. I had none.

"I give," I said.

"Why did you call me about this case?"

"I told you. I'm trying to trace a baby's mother—to find out who the baby's biological mother was. The baby's birthday—December 13—and Teresa Rushing's presumed death date—December 20—would fit."

"Who wants to know this?"

"A client. You know that's confidential."

She gave me a look. It was one of those awkward moments. We sleep together. Not often enough, but I know the silk of her skin, the salt of it. We both know what the rules say, for her, for me.

"Let me tell you that getting this file was not without cost," she said.

I looked back at her. A client's confidentiality does not rate up there with the secrets of the confessional or even lawyer-client privilege. But it's good practice. Plus, following my private code may be my only contribution to keeping the barbarians outside the gates. All this ran quickly through my mind. Alongside, yapping, was a confusing counterpoint that she who offers no back scratching doesn't get her own itches eased. I wasn't clear if the itches were personal or professional.

"How so?" I asked, stalling.

She gave me a thin smile. "Darcy, didn't anyone ever teach you about fair trades?" She sipped from her mug. I sipped, too, and for a minute all we heard was the tick from a handsome grandfather clock she has in the living room. I thought we might be at an impasse.

Her hands are a separate seduction—long-fingered and strong, an athlete's hands, easy to imagine around a basketball or—well, frankly, on my butt. Now she opened them, palms up, as though saying, "look, no secrets."

"I skimmed through the file when I got it," she said. "Then Sally came—Sally Doyle from the Circuit Attorney's office, and we spent the afternoon going over the old kidnapping case I've been working on. We ordered out for sandwiches and went back to work."

So far her recital had been calm, matter-of-fact, typical Lindstrom in reporting mode. But now I noticed a tighter set to her lovely jaw line, a narrowing of her fierce eyes.

"I was still working on the kidnapping case when I had my visitor." She paused for effect. "It was the cop who'd worked the Teresa Rushing case. He's been retired a few years now, but there he was, not three hours after I'd first pulled the file."

"Gee," I said, unable to muster a more adult response. I probably didn't get all the nuances because I'm not in Lindstrom's skin. Ever since she was outed at work—very much against her will—she's been jumpy, and not without reason. Before the dildo incident, there'd been a few crude cartoons. Even worse than the paper taunts, were the averted eyes, the lowered voices when she entered the room, the camaraderie denied. Without her usual partner Neely by her side, she felt even more vulnerable.

"Right. What little bird called him and told him I pulled the file?" Lindstrom's stare challenged me.

"A clerk in the archives?" I was distracted, my mind scrabbling for purchase like a hamster on a wheel.

"Thanks, Sherlock. But I was walking around with the file. I spent some time reading it in the squad room, it was out on my desk—and I probably left it open while I took a pee break before Sally came. I didn't think I had a state secret in my hands." Her voice was tight and hard, a deep anger being tamped down.

"Did you ask the clerk if he'd made the call?"

She looked away. "No, I didn't want to confront him unless I knew for sure." She turned back to meet my gaze. "I don't want to step on more toes than I have to."

I put a sympathetic look on my face, but inside I felt scared for her. Lindstrom is, no bad pun intended, a straightforward sort who lives her life without second-guessing herself. Sometimes her self-assurance is irritating. But just now I felt a kind of panic. How could she operate in the department if she had to tiptoe around as if ordinary give-and-take were a mine field?

But she wasn't pausing for my sympathy. "Anyway, this guy who ran the Rushing investigation comes on smooth as buttercream. He's read about me in the papers and heard through the grapevine that I'm doing a splendid job and have a great future with the department. And he does this with a fine touch—like a coach sparing with his praise."

She fixed me with a look. Was I getting it?

I nodded her on, trying not to show the suspicion I was feeling.

"But then he's telling me that pursuing this old Rushing case could be a waste of my time and department resources. He and his partner had done a thorough job of it, and there just wasn't a case to be made. Why spoil my record by wasting time on a case that wasn't going to get solved—good as I was?" She took a deep breath, let it out slowly. "Pretty slick, eh?"

I nodded again.

"I guess he saw I wasn't convinced because then he went all confidential on me. They had had one suspect—a retarded kid, maybe nineteen, who worked as a kind of night watchman guarding an old abandoned brewery in the neighborhood where Rushing was found. They thought the kid might have done it on impulse, then dumped the body down the street. You know, maybe they made a date and got into a spat—the girl wouldn't go far enough to suit him, whatever. They'd talked to the kid, he was kind of in a panic. But—and here the guy's voice gets soft and philosophical—the kid wasn't some serial killer. He was just a poor unfortunate who'd never had much of a life, a kid living on the margins but trying to support himself. And they didn't have any hard evidence to nail him. So opening the case now would just kick up shit for the kid."

I made playing the violin motions. She nodded.

"Right. Just the view I'd expect from a hard-nosed cop—who, by the way, says he's kept his eye on the kid over the years since then and the kid hasn't had a single smirch on his record—not even a parking ticket." She blew air through pursed lips. "And this guy said I should ask around the department, especially the older guys, to see if he's a stand-up guy—in case I didn't know his rep. He knows how fast glory fades, he says. You're a hero one day, a cow pile the next—especially if you make a misstep." Suddenly she grinned. "Clearly that was for me— you're on top now, little girl, but if you screw up—gotcha!"

"I thought you guys stuck together to a fault," I said.

"Ah well, you know he actually used a phrase that I just don't hear down at Clark Street on a daily basis—'unless you queer your pitch'— does that sound like a warning to you?"

"Which was it—that you're queer or you might mess up by investigating the case?"

"Both." She drummed her long fingers against the chair back and thought. "He said 'You're getting rave reviews, Detective, and that'll continue unless you waste your time on a dead end case or annoy the wrong people or queer your pitch.' That's what he said."

I believed her. I've heard her recite witness testimony verbatim before. "So he's saying that if you rattle the wrong cage, the anti-queer gang could get nastier?"

"Sounded like that to me."

"Is there any chance he was really trying to be helpful?" I didn't believe that, especially if my suspicions were true, but I wanted to test the idea.

"Not a chance. He was smart—it was between the lines, but he didn't leave a warm house on a cold evening to deliver a fan letter."

"And who is this guy who just popped out of nowhere to warn you off like the Ghost of Christmas-Past?"

"Well, he was a big cheese in the department before he retired, and he's still well thought of. Even Neely says his record was good— lots of high profile cases, lots of convictions. Tough but fair. Good relations with most of the African-American cops. Not too biased against African-American perps." She held up a warding off palm. "Don't lecture me, Darcy. I'm not saying any bias is okay. I'm just saying he wasn't a raging racist." She drummed the fingers of her right hand on the tabletop. "You and Walter might have run into him. He's done security work—consulting."

"And his name?" I knew what was coming.

"Doug Mann."

CHAPTER NINE

I told her the details of Diane Mann's story, this time naming names. Lindstrom's eyebrows went up as I related the facts and my suspicions. I didn't give her time to grill me, but launched into my questions.

"Which brewery did this retarded guy work for?"

"Well, it's not an active brewery any more, but they still own the buildings—Heitner."

"And Mann works for Heitner," I said.

I reached for the teapot. I needed the pouring to cover my thinking—and to keep me from cussing out Diane Mann, who hadn't bothered to tell me that her husband had investigated the Rushing case—and had, in fact, concealed it.

"His wife says he moonlighted for the Heitners before he retired. Think he worked there before he caught the Rushing case?" I asked.

"Could be. If he did work for Heitner, that puts a different color on it," she said.

To pick up freelance work as a result of a case was different from working a case that involved someone you were already hired out to.

I pursued the point. "How did he get away with that? Was Mann so holier-than-everybody that he could work a case that touched the Heitners when he was already on their payroll?"

"Neely says there was never a sniff of corruption on him—that Mann, in fact, was a no-mercy guy for cops on the take."

"So what did Neely think about Mann's coming all the way to Clark Street to make his little speech?"

"I didn't tell him Mann had talked to me. I just said Mann was the lead detective on the Rushing case and what did Neely think of him?" She gave me a careful look. "I'll ask Neely Monday. But Darcy, I know him. Neely admires the guy's record, but he didn't like Mann. Not when they were in the force together."

"And you wonder why."

"Yes." She paused to think. "But his wife's hiring you may explain his visit to me. Nothing riles 'em up like the wife packing to leave."

"How did he know his wife hired me?" I mused aloud. "I interviewed Booth Heitner…"

"Who probably didn't like being questioned about an old murder case."

"Enough to sic Mann onto you?"

"Maybe Heitner was just giving him a friendly heads up." She didn't say it ironically.

I didn't want her to fix on that. "Also, Teresa's best friend said the daddy of the baby was Booth Heitner. He denies it, but I'd love to do a DNA match. Coincidences happen, Lindstrom, but this case has two or three layers of them."

For a moment I thought she was going to blow it off. You know how it is—your own interpretations are so much more convincing than anyone else's. But Lindstrom really is a good cop. She'd look at the evidence. "Tell me again why you think Teresa's death connects to your client."

"It's the baby. Did the stork bring her? Doug Mann has told Diane at least one pretty big lie about where the baby came from. And Teresa's mother is the picture you see in the dictionary when you look up *vagueness*. I mean, no one except Doug Mann knows where this kid came from. And the timing is right."

"That could be coincidence."

"Sure it could," I said, for once not sarcastic. I wasn't going to pressure her into my view; I couldn't.

"But it would be Coincidence Number 12, wouldn't it?" She grinned. No matter what, she liked the custody angle as Doug Mann's motive for his surprise visit better than whatever other motives she'd been imagining.

"I think so. So I hope you're not going to stop looking at the Rushing case." I was pressing my luck here. All I'd asked her to do was look at the file—and maybe let me peek, too. Now I was hinting that 'looking at' meant more.

But she was already there. "Who said I'm going to stop? Don't you know me, Darcy? When someone says I can't go there, I'm always curious why." She wasn't smiling.

Two or three quips came to mind, but I sat on them. It's difficult to say which of us has a harder time taking no for an answer, and this once I was glad for her stubbornness. "So what's your next move?"

"Letting you see the file." I must have looked surprised because she grinned and said, "You showed me yours."

"Many times," I muttered to her back because she was already walking toward her den. I tagged along.

Her apartment has two bedrooms, both good-sized. This one she'd turned into a guestroom-den. She bought a narrow daybed just for this space and put her regular guestroom furniture into storage. She has her desk, computer, TV and VCR, her stereo and CDs, and two comfy chairs squeezed into this room. So far it's my favorite room because the night after she moved in we'd put our personal stamp on the narrow bed, and I still blush when I recall the details. I'd have made a fond reference to it, but she was in full work mode, and I really didn't want to deflect her.

She handed me a manila folder which showed the marks of age and use, but was, as she said, pretty thin for a murder file. She nodded me into one of the easy chairs, then perched on its wide arm so that she could read along with me. I did a quick skim first, then a more careful reading.

Doug Mann had been the lead detective. The body had been found December 23rd by some kids playing in the neighborhood. It had been dumped in a lot behind an abandoned house. The autopsy had determined Teresa Rushing had been killed by a blow to the head. No signs of sexual molestation. No mutilations or tortures. She was a healthy seventeen-year-old who'd recently given birth. They'd found no skin or blood under her nails. Some soft yellow fibers were attached to her winter coat. Probably she had been dead for three days. The autopsy couldn't pinpoint the time of death, but interviews with friends who'd last seen her, including Gina Menendez with whom Teresa had been living at the time, suggested that date. Twyla Sharp wasn't mentioned. A staple had been removed from the top of the page suggesting a second page. I rifled through the file. It wasn't here now.

Jimmy Sills and George Fowler, who worked as watchmen at the Heitner Brewery, had been questioned. Folks who lived in the residential part of the neighborhood hadn't seen or heard anything.

No one had seen the body dumped. In fact, no one had seen it lying there for two to three days. Someone, presumably Doug Mann, since the note was in the small, neat script that dominated the folder's handwritten comments, said that the body had perhaps been concealed from view by a pile of trash consisting of old boards and broken concrete chunks. Anything in this pile could have been the murder weapon, but nothing there showed any telltale signs of blood or hair or any other evidence.

The interviews with Jimmy Sills—there seemed to have been three of them, including one trip downtown to Clark Street—weren't helpful. Again pin-pricks at the top of the page suggested another staple had been removed.

"Do you take old stuff out of the folder—like if you change your mind? You know, we've proved that isn't so, now we're putting in the right version?" I asked her.

"Un-uh. You leave it all in. You might scribble a note alongside saying the first version turned out to be bull, see page ten instead. But mostly you want to keep your evidence in one place, as clean as you can make it, and your conclusions elsewhere."

"So pages are missing."

She sighed. "I think so."

"Who's this Vernon Cole?"

"He and Mann were obviously partners at the time."

"Long-time partners?"

"Don't know yet. But he retired before Mann. There's something about his name, though, that's got a buzz to it. I think he made some bad arrests. Something. I'll ask Neely on Monday."

Vernon Cole had handled a lot of the interviews with people living around the crime scene—the dump scene. His writing wasn't neat or even legible, and his comments were curt and uninformative—except in the 'no, seen nothin', heard nothin', done nothin' ' categories of information.

Some forms had been typed and signed off on by one or the other of the detectives. But if Mann had suspected Jimmy Sills of anything, even nose picking, nobody had put it into the file—or someone had taken it out. Trying to guess which part of the file wasn't there was crazy-making. You can plug holes so many different ways.

When I turned over the last page for the second time, Lindstrom asked, "What do you think?"

"Not to be cute, but what do you think? You're the police detective." She was so close I could smell her soap, and now that my nose was out of the file I could notice that.

Maybe she sensed my sniffing wasn't professional. She moved from the chair arm and paced. This shouldn't annoy me since I'm something of a pacer myself, but the space wasn't large enough for it. I settled for scooching deeper into the chair.

"I think the file isn't complete." It was the kind of cautious statement she's trained to make.

She made another trek across the room, annoyed that my feet still stretched too close to her path.

"I'd like to see this scene," I said.

She paused, looked happy.

I glanced at my watch and frowned. "I promised I'd pick up Patrick at the bookstore in twenty minutes. His car's in the garage for another tinker." MGs are notorious for needing their fine-tuned engines tweaked and Patrick's old baby is there more than most. I think the mechanic must be very cute and very butch.

She was no longer happy. She made a face. "Ah well, I'll check it out myself."

"Don't you dare." I tried to make it light, but my voice was caught straddling the tease and the real indignation.

She came to a full halt and towered over me. "Darcy, I can't be hauling you and Patrick around like a caboose full of demented relatives. This is a real investigation."

I didn't even stop to deal with "caboose full of demented relatives." Who knew what that meant? "Real investigation? As though my cute little play investigations haven't saved your real butt at least twice."

"Once."

"Whatever." I stood up and paced away from her. "This is my case, too. I can pick up Patrick and drive there in a separate car, you know. We'll just snoop around on our own—and, if we find something, I may tell you."

Okay, I admit it. Voices were raised.

"Look, don't go rattling around the neighborhood like a loose cannon." She paced to the door.

"The case is eight years old. We aren't going to be stomping over a fresh crime scene."

"Patrick has no standing whatsoever."

"All kinds of people knock on doors and ask questions. Census takers, reporters, the man who wonders if his Aunt Clara used to live there." I don't know why I was arguing for Patrick. I walked toward the bookshelf, gesturing.

When I turned, she was laughing. "Darcy, you're ridiculous. Half the time you're complaining that Patrick's underfoot when you're trying to work a case."

"Yeah, well, you oughta be glad he was there when you needed him."

We both grew quiet. "That's unfair," she said calmly.

I felt the heat climb to my cheeks. I nodded. "You're right. I am glad he was there. I know you are, too."

We were silent for a moment, not comfortable with this old unresolved stuff. I was looking at her, swept again by a fear of losing her to some creep with a gun and a grudge. No wonder her mother Karin wanted to wrap her in Kevlar and cart her back to Nebraska and a lower crime rate.

She was looking away, staring at the day bed. Did its memories move her? She shrugged her broad shoulders and capitulated. "All right. But you cannot be connected with me while I'm working a case."

"We won't be. We'll just be a caboose full of demented census takers." I grinned big to signal no hard feelings.

"Right," she said, but she was already leading me out of the room toward our coats and the great outdoors.

Fifteen minutes later we were outside Patrick's work. I was behind the wheel of her Toyota. The doctor says her left arm is completely healed, but she still needs to do physical therapy to get the muscle tone back. She works at it seriously, but her months of healing have made her a little more willing to be the passenger in her own car.

When Patrick saw us, his face lit up. As he climbed into the back, he said, "Double the pleasure."

I tried not to mind. He's my best bud. For a long time he and Lindstrom irritated me by sniping at one another. Since their shared brush with death, they now annoy me by too much bonding. I want each all to myself, in separate compartments—the lovely bunch one and the best bud one. How's a girl to have any secrets if those two compartments slop over?

Lindstrom and I said our "heys," and he leaned over the seat. "Why the party?"

"We're going detecting," I said.

Maybe he judged Lindstrom's face. He didn't give a delighted squeal but said quietly, "My favorite thing."

CHAPTER TEN

The sulky clouds had retreated. For the first time in days I saw the sun, not that it sent much warmth, but at least the day didn't seem so bleak. We were headed east, toward the Mississippi, crossing Gravois on Sidney Street. Even though we weren't much more than twenty blocks from South Grand—which is stomping ground for Patrick and me—we were into an area less familiar to us than to Lindstrom. We were just west of I-55 where, as Lindstrom had said, there was some mingling of light industry and small businesses, some boarded up, some still thriving, with small clusters of houses in the mix. We made a left and crossed over to Shenandoah.

Approaching from the west, we first saw a long two-story brick building with rows of glass blocks running its length. A lone loading dock ran along three-quarters of this side. Now United Services and Technologies had its offices in a corner of the large building. A small white van sat outside, but their place looked closed for the weekend. We drove past and saw that the abandoned brewery grew taller on the far side, climbing several stories above its west side. Here the red brick was older, the windows tall and narrow and now boarded up, except for one on the second story that was open to the breeze and the birds. Across the street was another abandoned brick brewery building and a metal tower. We came to a dead-end by a vacant lot where a storage company parked its trucks. "At Your Service, Moving and Storage" the sign read—but we saw no one stirring around to provide that service.

I backed up and took us along Lemp, between the brick brewery buildings. The larger section occupied nearly a full block, and we found that one end wall looked as though a truck had driven through it—a huge hole gaped with an uneven border of bricks. Of course, we all got out and peered into the hole. What we saw was a basement level with lots of trash—boards, bricks, metal pieces. Above us was blue sky—a good part of the roof had collapsed.

"I wonder how old this part is?" I asked.

"Probably turn of the century—twentieth century," Patrick said. "St. Louis had dozens of small breweries in the 1800s, but this one got big in the 1890s."

He's a bit of a local history buff, but even from Patrick this information seemed esoteric.

"How do you know that, Healy?" Lindstrom asked.

I wasn't happy to hear her calling him by his last name. For Lindstrom and me it's a kind of endearment. I didn't want her sprinkling it around.

"A friend of mine is a cousin of the Heitners."

Lindstrom and I exchanged looks, but said nothing to Patrick. He was peering up at the ravaged roof, so he hadn't noticed our look. "They minted money from this place. Then they sold out to Anheuser-Busch, and now they make their riches investing the profits they've made."

"Do you know the family?" Lindstrom asked, unable to wait.

He turned around and grinned. "Only Carter—the gay cousin, of course. But I've known him a long time."

I don't know why I was surprised. Patrick seems to have pals from every caste and class in St. Louis's gay community.

Lindstrom nodded, filing it away. "Darcy, let's take a look around the neighborhood."

"Walk or drive?"

"Let's walk it."

The neighborhood was an oddity. Across the street from the main part of the brewery were some narrow red brick residences that looked spruced up. One of the places had vivid magenta trim. Patrick and I rolled our eyes and said "Brothers" in unison, drawing a blank look from Lindstrom. At least one place had a large backyard with a neat chain-link fence around it. Winter had scraped bare most of the trees, but with just a little imagination I could picture a rather pleasant summer garden. We walked up to Victor, the street that ran perpendicular to Lemp. Here was another row of houses that looked alive and well.

We heard the traffic from I-55 roaring by us. Where Victor dead-ended, the highway had been carved out below, so that we could look down on the speeding traffic. No doubt local realtors weren't well pleased.

Turning up Victor, we saw the brewery didn't occupy the entire block after all. A new building, with many shiny new vehicles parked in its lot, claimed to be Monarch, Certified Restoration and

Construction. They looked to be a thriving concern. I wondered if they'd helped scrub up some of their neighbors' houses.

Lindstrom took the lead, and Patrick and I trailed after. I was glad for her long stride because, sunshine or no, the cold was penetrating my parka.

It's funny how neighborhoods turn on a dime. Lindstrom next led us up James, a stubby little street that quit after three or four houses. To our left, we saw plants and shades hanging in the windows that suggested tenants still lived there. These houses had no yards, but butted up to crumbly sidewalks. On our right, one house was clamped tight against the cold and offered few clues to its inhabitants, if any. The next two were long empty. Doorways and windows gaped open, sills and frames were peeling and splintered. Steps listed tiredly.

The end property was circled by a serious chain-link fence five feet high. As we rounded the corner, we saw a rusting dump truck sitting by the side of the house, as though someone had started to strip the house of any valuable components and then had walked off, abandoning the effort and the truck in the yard. *Yard* implied nothing green or growing except small patches of the most determined weeds, now wintry brown. The house's backside looked an invitation to trouble—doors and windows missing, steps tilting. I couldn't imagine trusting the floors.

Lindstrom laced her gloveless fingers into the fence and peered into the yard. "This is where the body was found." She pointed to a corner trash pile. "Behind that."

"Didn't they take that apart to see if any of it could have been the murder weapon?" I asked.

"Supposedly. But when they found nothing with blood or hair on it, they tossed the stuff back." She shrugged. "Crime scenes aren't always worked as meticulously as TV and the movies suggest. Every case doesn't get the full treatment."

"But you said this one started like the kind that would get attention," I reminded her.

She shook her head. "Ah well, maybe if I see Detective Mann again, I'll ask him."

Patrick had been standing nearby. "Do tell," he said to me, knowing I was the likelier blabber mouth.

I glanced at Lindstrom. Her worst suspicion is that I keep no secrets from Patrick. I hate proving her right.

She refused to acknowledge my look. I wouldn't draw her into this.

"It's a big secret, Patrick. But somebody's body was found here eight years ago," I said.

He turned toward Lindstrom. "It's one of your cases then. I swear I don't know how you do it. I was telling Joseph the other evening that you're something else, solving cases that are way over twenty-four hours old." He beamed at her, his baby blues innocent and trusting.

I have to say this for her—she's not easy to flatter. Lindstrom shot me a sour look. "I knew this would get complicated."

I shrugged, though I'm afraid my parka prevented her noticing.

Lindstrom looked past me to Patrick. "Some neighborhood kids found the body, but not till three days after she was last seen alive. I guess that rubbish pile hid her from view." She looked around. "I wonder if the kids lived right around here or farther away?"

Patrick stepped to the plate. "Who owns this property? And isn't it dangerous to leave it like this? It looks like the kind of place that would invite lots of dumped bodies." He looked toward Lindstrom.

She shook her head. "Well, it takes manpower to enforce all the city codes."

"Still, after a murder victim was found here, you'd think someone would want this place cleared away," he said.

"You'd think," she agreed. If I had said it, she'd have been defensive, but today she was cutting him plenty of slack—even if she hadn't wanted him along to begin with.

"So maybe we should adjourn to someplace that serves hot chocolate," I said, stomping my boots against the hard ground in the vain hope of reviving my circulation.

"Maybe I should knock on a few doors, and see if any of these households own the kids who found the body." She looked toward the houses across the alley and then at her watch. "Want to meet me back at the car in an hour? If you want to, you can get your hot cocoa and pick me up on Lemp then."

Patrick started a gentlemanly protest, but I elbowed him. "Good idea. We'll be careful of the time."

She nodded and marched off toward the first house. I pulled Patrick by the arm and headed back toward Lemp. While we walked, I sketched in the basics of the case: Diane Mann, Jessica, Teresa Rushing, Booth Heitner, Doug Mann. It was a lot to absorb quickly, but he'd honed his skills on *One Life to Live* during his adolescent years.

"Okay, Patrick, we're looking for anyone who might have known Jimmy Sills." I decided the best place to start was with Mann's suspect.

"Who?"

"He's the kid who used to work at the brewery—well, this shell of it, sort of as a night watchman, I guess. Some people thought he might have killed Teresa."

"You've left parts out, haven't you?" Patrick said, more in sorrow than in anger.

"Patrick, we don't have time for me to connect all the dots now. We've only got an hour. Just trust me."

"Right." He followed me up the walk to the first house, where, despite a Ford Explorer parked in the driveway, we knocked in vain.

"Who are we supposed to be?" he asked, as we walked to the next house.

"Depends on who answers," I said, sorry we were too late to be the census.

Disappointingly, Magenta Trim didn't answer, but the house around the corner on Victor proved luckier. A buxom woman with a long braid down her back and a paint-smeared smock over her jeans opened the door with a smile. "Sorry. We've changed our minds. It isn't for sale anymore." She gestured toward the splatters on her clothes. "We're just giving it a fresh start."

"Shoot! We were excited about this one!" Patrick said in his most beguiling manner. It isn't just gay men he can charm out of trees.

Her broad face was sympathetic. "You know, someone said the people behind us might be considering selling."

"Really?" Patrick's face brightened. He glanced toward me tenderly. "Meg and I were so hoping we could get settled in before…" He patted my parka front. "Before the stork arrives." He met my look with a beatific smile.

Of course, she was watching his performance, so I had time to deliver my glare before building on his fabrication.

"Since you aren't selling, I wonder if you could tell us what it's really like in this neighborhood," I said. My thespian skills will never match his, but my work gives me a fair amount of practice in basic deception.

Maybe it was the baby. She didn't hesitate. She stepped back and waved us in. "Oh, sure—maybe you'd like to see the house? It's a mess, of course, because we're painting—"

I didn't want to use up that much time. "Oh, we don't want to be so much trouble. I see you have a good yard to play in—and some of the neighbors do, too. But I wondered—you've got that big business across the street—Monarch, is it? And that abandoned building down the street—"

"Monarch's no problem. Their trucks and vans are in and out, but it isn't noisy." She laughed. "Besides, the roar from I-55 would drown them out."

"Is that a problem?" Patrick asked.

"Not for a city girl like me. Jack wasn't happy at first, but he's getting used to it. You know, we're closed up in the winter and run the AC in summer, so we only hear it a few weeks a year. But it's like white noise."

She looked good to go on this topic for fifteen minutes, so I risked an interruption. "I hate to ask this, but wasn't there a murder near here, or a body found over in a vacant lot, or something like that?"

Her face sobered. "Yeah, there was. I don't know the details. We didn't live here then, but I've heard about it."

"I don't want to be…" I paused searching for the word. "My cousin's on the police force. He said a guy who worked at the brewery did it. I mean, I'm thinking about raising a child here. If someone dangerous is working nearby…"

She listened carefully and was a little cooler when she spoke. "Well, you have to be cautious everywhere, don't you? Even in Ladue, I expect—if you have kids, I mean. Here you'd have to watch the kid didn't go exploring down the bluff and fall on his head on I-55. Or even go into the brewery. It's got a big gap in one wall now—and I don't think they have a watchman over there anymore."

"You're right. It's just our first one—and Meg is a worrier," Patrick said, giving me a shoulder hug.

I smiled my little wifey smile at him. "Like you aren't fussing about the baby, Daddy."

He blushed, but it didn't matter—it just made him more adorable and put our hostess in a jollier mood. "I'm sure you'll manage fine. Would you like to see at least the downstairs?"

"We'd love to, but, sweetie, don't we need to meet your folks in ten minutes?" He beamed down at me.

"Yes, of course. We just were driving by and thought we'd chance seeing you."

A few more exchanges extricated us. We started back up Victor when I saw a SUV pulling up and parking back on Lemp. Magenta Trim was home. I tugged Patrick's arm and steered him that way.

We let our target get inside and gave him an extra minute. I took advantage of the time to warn Patrick to be more careful of his cover stories. I didn't think my maternal instincts were up to even imaginary kids.

A minute later and nothing would have persuaded him to pose as a happy heterosexual. The man who opened the door wasn't drop-dead gorgeous, but he had smooth good looks and a square jaw. His deep "Hel-lo"—like warmed honey—nearly melted the snow. I could only imagine the effect on Patrick. I tried to sneak a peek to see if Patrick was already forgetting Joseph, who was far, far away in Oxford. But all I caught was Patrick's profile and half of his standard greeting smile—which is pretty rum buttery itself.

Magenta Trim had had time to peel off his coat. He wore a charcoal vee neck over a creamy turtleneck, crisply pleated stone khakis, and husky hiking boots. I suspected that like his SUV the footwear never got off the concrete streets, but who was I to criticize a man's efforts to keep his toesies warm? Under the outfit were broad shoulders and a trim waist. He was a dark blond, his hairline receding even faster than Patrick's. His eyes were light hazel, and the cleft in his chin was a crevice I'm sure many an innocent had fallen into. He was giving Patrick a steady eyelock.

"You're Pat Healy, aren't you?"

"Patrick," said my boy.

Magenta Trim nodded and stuck out his hand. "I know Mark and Chip. And I saw the headlines this summer. I'm Toby Shaw."

He and Patrick exchanged a manly handshake. Then Shaw looked at me. "And you're Darcy, right? I'm sorry, I've let your first name slip." He offered his hand so we could have a manly shake too. "Boy, you two were really heroic."

I still hadn't adjusted to it—strangers popping out of the woodwork, knowing me because of the ten o'clock news and not knowing me at all. I felt grateful to have survived, to have Patrick and Lindstrom survive. "Heroic" made me itch.

But I gave over my hand and first name without too much resistance. Meanwhile, Patrick was jumping in with his own connect-the-dots to Mark and Chip and Paul and Larry, wasn't it?

"Yes, Larry Brightweiser—he's my partner. It's killer cold out there. How about something to warm us up?"

He led us past the living room, which they'd evidently ordered directly from *Architectural Digest*—open brickwork, a supersized fireplace, and soft leather couches, with warm russets and terra cotta splashed around. The dining room was more formal, but the gleaming table was just right for those intimate little dinner parties for ten or twelve. The kitchen was more of the same. No wonder gay men are stereotyped as rich materialists. This had all the right brand names, hanging copper pots, wine racks, a butcher block, dried herbs, and a small assortment of well-thumbed cookbooks.

Patrick and I perched our bottoms on tall stools around a small stub of counter while Shaw ground some Kona beans. He and Patrick created a short list of guys they knew in common, and Shaw was as gifted as Patrick at including me, so that I wasn't sitting there feeling as though I'd wandered into the wrong class reunion. My work teaches me not to trust first impressions, but it was difficult to stay wary of this one, and I couldn't blame Patrick for flirting a bit.

When Shaw served up our coffee—like Lindstrom, he had matching mugs—he finally asked, "What brings you to our neighborhood on such a cold winter's day?"

Patrick and I exchanged a telltale glance. I saw Shaw noticing, so even before Patrick said, "You tell, Meg," I knew I'd better stick to the truth.

"Eight years ago the body of a murdered teenager was found in a vacant lot near here. We are trying to canvass the neighbors and see if anyone can remember anything about that time."

Shaw was nodding, his hazel eyes thoughtful. "Yeah, I lived here then. Larry's been here fifteen years; I moved in ten years ago." He paused to give Patrick a wry smile. "We're old marrieds." I couldn't deconstruct that one. Was it a come-on or a shut-down?

"What would you like to know?" he asked.

Everything. But sometimes it's best to offer a specific prompt. "There was a young man, developmentally delayed, who worked for the Heitners, a Jimmy Sills. Do you know anything about him?"

Often witnesses wet their pants if they have a chance to give you lots of information. Shaw's look was different—not exactly wary but certainly not eager. "I do," he said in that radio voice. "Just by happenstance I'd gotten to know Jimmy over the summer while he was working over at the brewery."

"Wasn't the brewery long closed by then? What kind of work was he doing?" I asked.

Shaw nodded. "Oh, yeah. Closed for decades. But that summer we had a bad wind storm, and part of the roof collapsed."

Patrick and I nodded. We'd seen the open sky.

"Heitners had Jimmy and an older guy, George something, clearing out the debris. Probably a bigger work crew could have cleared it all in a week, but these two guys were plodding along. I got the idea that they weren't expected to go faster. After the discovery of the body, though, the work just stopped."

"How did you get to know Jimmy?" I asked.

Shaw gave me a considering look, then glanced at Patrick, who shared my inquiring face. "I was often working in the yard when he'd come out and take his lunch break, and we got to talking. He was a shy kid—kind of limited but a nice boy. So we talked a bit. If I was working in the afternoon, when he had a break, I'd offer him lemonade."

"I'm under the impression the police thought he might be a suspect," I said.

"Yeah, that's right. I guess they never found out who did it. I know you can't always tell by looking who's a murderer and who isn't, but I couldn't really imagine Jimmy killing someone. More a victim than a victimizer, I'd say."

I nodded encouragingly.

"At first when I spoke to him, he just scuttled off. But gradually he talked to me. Once he got warmed up, he was really eager to talk." He shrugged. "You know, just the usual— the weather, the Cards."

"So you don't think Jimmy did it…" I let my thoughts trail into an invitation.

"I don't know. But George seemed more the type to me. He was kind of angry, always scowling. I think Jimmy was afraid of him."

"How so?" I asked.

"George was the foreman. You could tell he didn't like Jimmy. He cussed at him sometimes. And I saw George drinking on the job." He grinned. "Not that that makes him a killer."

"Did you ever notice any other teenagers hanging around the building? Maybe the girl or teens her age?"

He shook his head. "Not that I recall."

"Some neighborhood kids found the body," I said.

"Yeah—they were younger and lived behind the brewery over on James Street. That's a whole different world." Snobbish, but also accurate. He lived in House Beautiful, and the James Street houses looked like tenements.

"Did you know them?"

He shook his head. "Nope."

"Sort of a mystery why someone would choose that vacant lot to dump a body," I said.

He nodded. "I guess you could drive around to the industrial sites between Broadway and the river, and there'd be several places that would suit."

The interview wound down. I gave him my business card and requested that he ask Larry if he had any other recollections that might be helpful. He said he'd seen neither Jimmy Sills nor George after the story of Teresa Rushing's murder faded from the *Post*. Shaw and Patrick made some social noises about getting together with Mark and Chip and Paul for dinner at Mag's some evening, this being Magnolia's, a restaurant-bar catering to gay men and staffed by some Big Is Beautiful drag queens. If you like hearty homecooking instead of field greens and fish, it's the place to hit on Monday nights.

I'm always forgetting to take off my coat when I go inside, so when we emerged into the cold I had a layer of sweat to freeze up. The earlier sun had disappeared leaving a slate sky. I was shivering before we reached the sidewalk that transected Shaw's stone walk. I was just opening my mouth to complain to Patrick when I realized that something was missing: Lindstrom's Toyota was no longer parked on Lemp Street.

The first sounds from my throat were not words but a helpless gargle.

We were dead meat.

Not only had we gone investigating against orders, we had lost her car.

I looked to my right, then to my left, just in case I'd forgotten the exact location. But Lemp is a short street. Unless David Copperfield were doing one of his supersized illusions, the Toyota was gone. Maybe aliens had vaporized it. Would she believe aliens?

Patrick caught up with me. "Meg—"

"Let's walk around the block."

We did, pretty much at the pace of those 1930s marathon walkers. I sweated some more, and our breath steamed from our mouths. We passed two Jeeps, a Honda, a sleek Chevy pickup, a flaking old Nissan, but nothing that looked like a Toyota in disguise.

I don't think it was my imagination that the sky darkened—probably another layer of clouds blocking the sun—but I saw nothing reassuringly human as we passed James Street and quick marched around the remainder of the block.

I was increasingly regretting the second cup of Kona, sorrier still that I hadn't asked Toby Shaw to use what was no doubt a perfectly appointed bathroom. I could imagine him and Larry, pink-skinned and frolicsome, in an adjoining hot tub.

"Surely the car hasn't been stolen. She must have gone somewhere," Patrick said helpfully.

I glared at him. Obviously she wasn't here; ergo—

But that wasn't cheering news. Maybe we could use a phone and get a taxi. Or we could wait for her return, using our time to concoct a really good story about why, despite her warnings, we were asking questions that intruded into a police inquiry. Somehow beforehand that overstepping had seemed such a tiny indiscretion. A youthful indiscretion as the politicos say.

I was considering a second dash around the block when Patrick tugged at my sleeve. "We'd better wait, Meg. Otherwise, we could be over there, when she returns here." I realized he meant on the other side of Monarch and the old Heitner Brewery. I nodded glumly and turned to cast a speculative eye at the gaping hole at the end of Heitner's building. Maybe I could lower myself into the basement and find a tall cone of debris to pee behind.

CHAPTER ELEVEN

When Lindstrom pulled up to the broken sidewalk in her Toyota, my sigh of relief was quickly replaced with a surge of anger. Who did she think she was—simply driving off and leaving me stranded without a word?

"Uh—oh, Meg. What's our story gonna be?" Patrick asked.

"Our story?" I huffed. "I'm more interested in what her story is." I jerked open the passenger door and stuck my head in the car. "Where have you been?"

"Following up on some interesting information that was not in the Rushing file. Who've you been talking to?"

Patrick slid into the backseat and closed the door gently.

"So you just dumped us?" I demanded.

"I didn't dump you. I came back to the brewery, hoping to catch you as soon as you got back with your hot chocolate. I was surprised to find the car and not you, but figured you were off doing something you didn't want me to know about, so I obliged you by minding my own business. Get in; let's go get some lunch, and I'll tell you what I've found."

It was clear that I was going to get neither a good fight nor an apology, so I got in, but with little grace.

"Did you guys find out anything?"

I was just about to recount Toby Shaw's version of Jimmy Sills when Patrick began, "We met a man who knew the guys who worked for the brewery." He went on to tell Lindstrom the whole story, with details about the interior of Toby's house sprinkled liberally throughout. I had to correct him once, but he gave a pretty accurate account—ended abruptly by the exclamation, "Hey, look. That guy's putting up a *For Sale* sign. We should stop and look." He pointed to a man pounding a homemade sign into his frozen yard.

"Not now," Lindstrom replied. "Can you get the address?"

"Slow down. No, hang on," Patrick said. Lindstrom handed a

small spiral-bound notebook and a pen back to him.

"Okay, I've got the block number and the street. You'll be able to find it later," he said.

We ended up at MoKaBe's. The Saturday throng formed a double line to order hot drinks. The lovely smell of brewing coffee blended with cigarette smoke. I shoved a twenty into Patrick's hand with instructions to pay and nearly knocked a woman down in my rush to the restroom. When I returned, he handed the bill back with an apologetic shrug as Lindstrom, serving as well as paying, set down three steaming mugs. After we were settled at a table with coffee and soup, Lindstrom recounted her morning.

"I couldn't get anybody to answer the first two doors on the block, so I was down to the last house, that gray one. A teen-aged girl answered my knock, and I figured I wouldn't get anything from an adolescent. Most would rather be tortured than help a police officer, and the ones that don't have bad attitudes barely notice there is a world beyond their noses."

Good thing cops don't stereotype. But I kept that thought to myself.

"She invited me in and even offered me a soda. I told her I was head of the Cold Case Division."

Here I couldn't help but snort; the entire Cold Case Division, Sarah Madeline Lindstrom, merely grinned at me.

"And that I was looking into an old murder case in her neighborhood," she continued. "She remembered it perfectly—she had been friends with the boys who found the body. Evidently she'd been away from home that day, and the boys had been insufferable about their magnificent adventure afterward. They'd recounted the story dozens of times. Both boys had moved out of the neighborhood, but one of the boy's parents remained friends with Justine's parents, and she knew where they lived.

"That's when I hightailed it back to the brewery, hoping that you and Patrick would be back soon. When you weren't there, but the car was, I figured I'd just follow up on this lead and then come back to you."

"So did you find the boy who'd found the body?" I hurried her along.

"By a wonderful stroke of luck, he was home and his mother was happy to have him talk to me. He was surly at first—he's sixteen and surly seems to be the default setting but he relaxed. He was still impressed with himself for having found a dead body, even though it was eight years ago. He assured me that he hadn't gotten sick. Doug Mann interviewed him twice—once at the lot where the body was found and once about twenty-four hours later at Danny's house."

I pulled out my notebook. "Danny?"

"Danny Thurman. His name and the other boy's were in the Rushing file, but no notes on the interview with them. Interestingly enough, the boys knew for sure that the body hadn't been there the day before. The medical examiner's best guesstimate was that death occurred on the 20th, but the boys had played on that same pile of junk on the 22nd and Teresa Rushing's body definitely wasn't there."

"So her body was moved a day or two after she was murdered?" Patrick asked.

"Looks like, and there is nothing in the file about that. Either Doug Mann kept the worst records in the history of the department or someone had rummaged through the file before I got it."

"Mann is a dead end street—he doesn't want you to investigate, and he'll kill Diane if we try to put pressure on. How about tackling Cole? Any chance he'd talk to you without spilling the beans to Mann?" I asked.

"I don't know. I called Neely after I interviewed the boy. Neely said Cole quit under some pressure several years ago. There were allegations that he sexually harassed a witness and a couple of suspects. The rumor mill had it that he was a real bad apple."

"It must have been bad if the St. Louis Police Department dumped him," I said. "Was there a lot of publicity about the sexual harassment?"

"No, the women didn't go to the press. It was all handled within the department. We do work to keep our own nest clean, Darcy. All that stuff about cops protecting their own no matter what is bull. Idiots and assholes wash out of the department all the time."

I said nothing, but maybe my face did.

"You know, we really ought to go back and look at that house—if it is a decent buy, someone will have a reserve deposit on it by tomorrow," Patrick interjected.

"I don't have time for that now. Nor do I have time to sit around and listen to people idly insult the department." She pushed her chair away and took her soup bowl and coffee cup up to the bar, smiling as she brushed against a woman in a crew cut.

"Sorry, Meg. I tried to deflect it."

"I know, Patrick. It's all right. I don't know why she's so defensive about the idiots who are making her life a misery."

"Yes, you do, Meg. She wants to…" Patrick's no doubt sage opinion was interrupted by Lindstrom's sudden return.

"I'm going back to the station house—want me to drop the two of you at Arsenal?"

"No, my car's at your place."

The ride to the Central West End was a quiet one. However, she did lean over and kiss me as we pulled up to the Horizon.

I dropped Patrick at home and wandered down to Miller Security to make sure I didn't have pressing business there. Colleen was hard at work.

"Walter's going to let you have a day off this week?" I asked.

She grimaced. "Joey was being a butt. I just came down to finish this copying—mainly to get away from him. I'm going soon, how about you?"

"My love dumped me on the side of the road." I sighed and meandered to my office.

I had just fired up my Mac when the phone rang. It was my old friend Nina Ripley. After catching me up on her nephew Kyle and his girlfriend Alissa, Nina asked what I was doing that evening. As usual, my social calendar was barren.

"Come to Novak's with me, then."

"You on the prowl for a new girlfriend?" I guess even Nina had given up on our mutual link Barb Talbott's ever coming back from Seattle.

"Actually, Meg, I may have found one. Tonight is her birthday, and she had planned to spend it with a big group of her friends at Novak's. I don't want to be stuck knowing only Jeneece. She'll be the belle of the ball, and I want someone I can talk to. Besides, we haven't really seen one another since the party for Kyle. Bring Sarah, too."

I explained that Sarah was otherwise engaged with ancient crimes and agreed to meet Nina at eight. I was ready to put a little fun into my life.

I liked Jeneece. A medical transcriptionist at Barnes, she had a wicked sense of humor and looked at Nina as if Nina was the reason the sun rose.

Jeneece's friends were a large and noisy group, already into telling embarrassing stories by the time I arrived. Nina would have been fine without me, but I was surprised by how much I enjoyed myself. At midnight, Jeneece decided she had to have a bag of White Castle burgers before she officially gave up on her thirty-fourth year, so those of us who weren't vegetarian, and some who were, descended on the South Grand White Castle to be greeted by the lovely smell of hot grease on the griddle. We laughed some more and bragged about the highest number of Belly Bombers we had ever eaten. The others were going on to Attitudes for a last drink, but I was droopy, so I hugged Nina and told her Jeneece was a keeper, crawled into the Plymouth and made a left toward my bed.

Even in my somewhat alcohol—and grease-soaked condition I knew there was something wrong at home. Patrick's kitchen was dark, but a bar of light shone under my door. Why would Patrick be up in my apartment instead of in bed in his own? I reviewed the other holders of keys to my apartment—my mother Betty would never come over in the middle of the night, Lindstrom was ticked off at me. My friend Barb was in Seattle—I was pretty sure she'd have let me know if she were coming for a visit. Was it a madman with an axe? I briefly entertained the idea of going back down to the car and using my cell phone to rouse Patrick but decided I was just too sleepy. I unlocked the door and threw it open with a bang.

"Hi, Darcy," she called from the living room. "I was just about to give up on you." Damn, she was beautiful. Too bad she was too rich and too difficult to get along with.

"Oh, it's you."

"Live and in person." She gave me a closer look. "Been drinking?"

"Not much. A birthday party at Novak's. No biggie."

"Good thing I don't have a breathalyzer on me—I'd have to make an arrest." She stood—another thing I didn't like about her was the height differential. It was only a few inches, but it often gave her a distinct psychological advantage. I sat.

"What makes you think I drove home? Maybe someone brought me. What would have happened if I didn't come home alone, Lindstrom?"

"We would have had to play a hand of poker for you, I guess." She grinned and straddled me.

"No, really. I'm tired. I just want to brush my teeth and go to bed. I let Jeneece goad me into six White Castles."

"My, my, Meg. Such a life of excess. Come on, I'll tuck you in." She pulled me to my feet and for a few seconds I thought I really would be left in peace. But I had forgotten that she'd made a critical step forward on a case today—my case—so now she was in the mood to celebrate.

I'd like to report that I stuck to my refusal—I was tired and half-drunk, with serious misgivings about our future happiness. But it was only present happiness she was interested in.

And she was persuasive.

Even before I was awake I was aware that she was in my bed. I didn't move or try to touch her, but I could feel her there, radiating heat and energy despite the soundness of her sleep. She was curled away from me, facing the windows. I stretched my legs out, seeking relief from the stiffening of sleep.

What did it mean to have her here this Sunday morning? She seemed to come and go according to some pattern or plan that I wasn't privy to, like the jet stream. You knew from years of being told by Dave, Cindy, Kent—all those weather persons with perfect teeth—that the jet stream came down from Canada, bringing arctic weather horrors with it. But you couldn't just call up and say, Oh, I'd like the jet stream to pass through the Mississippi Valley today. Nor could you say, I'd really like a fall picnic with my friends, so no cold winds whistling through tomorrow afternoon, please. No, you just knew the jet stream was here when you reached for another layer of clothes and took up drinking seven or nine cups of tea a day instead of two or three. The jet stream was here or it wasn't. Like it or not, it didn't seem like a good model for a relationship. But, unlike the jet stream, Lindstrom's wake through my life was compellingly attractive. How to say no to the woman who made the earth tremble and move?

Her breathing changed ever so slightly. I turned on my side toward her and pulled the cover up over her bare shoulder. Then my hand traced the line of her spine, downward into the cleft of my desire. Her breathing quickened again and her legs straightened. My hand slid over the mound of her hip and across her belly, up to her breast. Her nipple tightened immediately to my touch. Was she awake yet? How far could I go before she was conscious of me? My fingers circled her nipple several times and then I tugged at it gently. I heard her breathing stop. A long pause, and then again a rhythm I was more familiar with than her sleeping one. She turned toward me and pressed her breast to my lips. The rest was languorous and slow and completely wordless for many minutes. Her skin against mine, her sleepy smile, her thumb thrusting inside me. She was an irresistible force—something that would sweep through my life without mercy, bring wind chill or rain, snow or clouds, regardless of where I lived or the state of my soul, and I burst against her, coming and coming—and nearly cried out "I love you," but buried my face in her neck just in time.

Later over tea I asked her what she had planned for the day.

"I'm going to talk to Vernon Cole. He'll remember stuff about the case that isn't in that file. You don't forget the unsolved ones, the details rattle around in your mind, looking for a pattern, a place to light. I looked up his home address. He lives here but works in St. Charles on the gambling boat there."

"You need to be careful with him. How will you know whether or not he'll go back to Doug Mann and tell him you are asking questions about the case?"

"I can't control that, Darcy."

"We've got to protect Diane. It could put her in a bad position. She's told Doug that she dropped the investigation."

"I'll be as careful as I can."

I thought about pushing her again because I was pretty sure she wasn't taking it all that seriously, but decided I didn't have to be a total control freak. She finished her toast and banana and said she'd go back to her place and shower. I was thinking of going and getting Patrick for a quick pass through the zoo to do the bears.

Patrick was not free to play with the bears; Joseph was supposed to call at two and my pal was in the mood to clean house and cook until then. I would probably benefit from the leftovers later, so I decided not to nag.

I was at loose ends. I went to the office to avoid any stray house-cleaning vibes that might emanate from Patrick's apartment. The sharp air I pulled into my lungs smelled of oncoming snow from the gray clouds massed overhead. At Miller I talked by phone to two of the guys we'd just hired because they wanted to miss parts of the training for other appointments. I told them there were no excused absences. We lost one of them.

I typed up my notes from Toby Shaw and what Lindstrom had told me about how the body had been found. I thought about Doug Mann and how he might have just stolen Teresa Rushing's baby. Would he have done that? The urge to possess a baby seemed strong enough in some people to justify all sorts of strange behavior. A St. Louis woman was the first to sell her twin babies over the Internet, not once but twice.

But did I believe that Teresa had not made any effort to confront Booth with his responsibility to the child?

I twiddled with the phone cord. Could Lindstrom possibly be home yet? I dialed the familiar number.

"So what happened with Vernon Cole?" I asked when she picked up.

"He wouldn't talk to me."

"Wouldn't talk to you? Not at all?"

"Not a word. My guess is he's bitter about the way he got pushed out of the force, and he nearly spit when I mentioned Doug Mann."

That was encouraging, anyway. Perhaps he wouldn't go directly back to Mann to report that questions were being asked about Teresa Rushing's murder. "Maybe it was because you're a cop. He might open up to me."

"I doubt it, Darcy. There's nothing in it for him, and he's the kind of man that doesn't do anything unless he profits from it. I think we should pursue the Heitner family. Since Mann works for them, probably the old man knows something about it. And it may be a way to get a lead on Jimmy Sills."

"Yeah, Colleen and I will make some kind of contact tomorrow."

"You and Colleen?"

"Sure, she's been with me for several of these interviews. She's getting some experience, and she's pretty good."

"Look, this isn't some kind of game we're playing here. This is an unsolved murder."

"To you it is an unsolved murder; to me it is an effort to help a woman keep her daughter. And I'll handle it so that Diane doesn't get strong-armed again."

"You have to stir up some dirt to get to the truth, Darcy. You can't get at the answers you want if your major goal is not to piss someone off. Especially if that someone is out to hide something shady, which looks like the case here."

"I have managed a couple of investigations, Lindstrom. I don't think I need you to tell me how to do it."

"A couple of cases. I've handled dozens. If Diane wants to know the truth, the stable has to be cleaned. That always means some unpleasant things have to be shoveled."

"Well, this is my case, and I'm going to interview the Heitners."

"Is it now? Or did a certain PI ask that the St. Louis Homicide Cold Case Division pull the file and work the case?"

"Cold Case Division, my ass, Lindstrom. I asked you for a personal favor to see what information you had, not to take my case away from me."

"I'm not taking anything away from you, Darcy. I'm trying to tell you that you can't pussyfoot around with this stuff. People have some pretty strong feelings wrapped up in crimes like murder. If the case were one that would just roll over, it would have been solved eight years ago."

"Not if the cop in charge didn't want it solved."

"But now you're in a position where you can't really move, aren't you? Any rocking the boat will mean that your client will fire you. And this is my job, Darcy. Whether you like it or not, I've pulled this case and am working it. There are at least two reasons why I should be the one to interview Richard Heitner." She paused to draw a slow breath. "He'll be more likely to cooperate with a police officer than some private detective who is certainly working for someone who is hostile to his interests, or hostile to the interests of a long-time employee. And, furthermore, Doug Mann can't get me to quit by threatening to punch Diane. That only works for you."

"Doug knows Diane started this."

"She can't finish it. I can. She's one hundred percent safer with an official investigation through the regular channels than with you, who can be hired and fired. He's a cop, he can make a stink with the licensing agency. I've got the entire city bureaucracy to protect the work I do."

How had this happened?

CHAPTER TWELVE

After I hung up, I hit Star 67 to block my number from caller I.D., then dialed Diane Mann's number. She answered on the third ring.

"Diane? Your aunt Margaret here. Can we talk?"

"I told you—"

"I really need to talk with you."

A pause. Longer than custom allows in our comfort zone. I was about to prod again when she spoke. "Where's the nearest Schnuck's?"

I told her and added, "I'll meet you there, by the sanitary napkins."

"When?"

"I'm leaving now."

She hung up.

I located the correct aisle. She wasn't there. I settled in to wait. I started counting the varieties of sanitary products available to the modern woman—super thin with wings, maxi with super wings...

The squeaky wheel on her cart announced her presence. How clever to be a shopper—she already had Wheat Chex and portabella mushrooms in her cart. My client seemed adept in the arts of deception. Maybe that was a skill that developed naturally from living with a control freak like Detective Doug Mann. Maybe it was something else.

I had to be impressed. If you called me on a wintry Sunday evening, you'd be sure to get faded jeans and even more faded sweatshirts, thickly layered without color coordination. But Diane Mann was pulled together: makeup, hair, neck scarf, gloves, wool slacks, cashmere coat, a faint whiff of expensive perfume. Only her forehead, compressed in thought, portrayed anxiety—what to choose? Wings? No wings?

Before I figured out how to start, she maneuvered the cart out of the main drag and sidled up to me. Staring at the array of personal sanitary choices, she said, in a fierce whisper, "I told you never to call the house."

I ignored that. "Why are we meeting in a grocery store?"

"I had to think of someplace Doug wouldn't see us together—and, if someone else did, it would look innocent." Her tone said she wasn't cooling off.

"I don't think he knows what I look like."

"You think not? Wasn't your face all over the TV and in the papers last summer?"

I keep forgetting. Inside me, my fifteen minutes of fame were over.

She wasn't interested in my reply. She went on. "He's gone to pick Jessica up from a birthday party, but they'll be home soon. I don't have hours to waste here."

I risked a sideways look. Any passerby would see an attractive sub-urbanite, a soccer mom in the flesh. She could pass in Clayton or even Ladue. How did she manage that on a cop's retirement pay? Maybe Heitner paid its security consultants really well.

"Diane, why didn't you tell me Doug investigated the Teresa Rushing murder?"

I wished she were looking at me and not at tampons. I wanted to see her eyes, but even without that crap-detection technique I could see I'd scored a hit. Her face stiffened in defense.

"I didn't know."

"I don't believe you." Not the usual line of Darcy charm, but I was more than a little irked. Did she think me a fool?

For just a flicker, her jaw tightened. Then she turned her eyes on me in a full-court press appeal to pity. I could see how it probably worked for her, gray eyes widening and moist. A slight quiver of the lip. She put a hand on my forearm. "Meg, you don't know how afraid I am of him."

That was true. But her plea sounded packaged.

"It's hard to help if you hide facts from me," I said.

Her next look was more convincing, more exasperated: I'd never understand what she was up against. She looked away, toward the cos-metics, pulled a deep breath. "Am I risking my life so you can scold me?"

I wasn't sure about risking her life. But that was why we were here. She might be.

"Diane, I don't think it was my doing that got Doug riled."

Well, not directly, but why go into the fine points?

She sighed. Were there no limits to my shortcomings?

I pressed on. "A department detective is looking into cold cases. Doug has a buddy who tipped him off the Rushing case was being reinvestigated."

Practiced as she was at concealing her reactions, I thought she was surprised. "Why would they do that?"

I shrugged, not wanting to 'fess up. "The point is the department won't let up just because someone asks them to."

She gave me a considering look, turned away, picked up a purse-sized box of tampons and seemed to read its fine print. "You don't know how much pull Doug has."

"Had."

She gave the tampons a wry smile. I wanted to be moved by the single tear that spilled from her eye and crept down her cheek. I wanted to trust it. I was more convinced by the silence she kept. Even the best words sound so scripted.

"Can you remember anything about that time, Diane? Anything about Doug's working the case—you know, he came home and complained, 'Damn, what a day I had!' and why. Anything."

Her gloved hand wiped away the tear. She put the tampon box back on the shelf. All the while she was shaking her head gently. "You don't understand Doug. He didn't talk about his work. Oh, he complained about lenient judges, the usual police politics. But not the details of cases."

"Does the name Jimmy Sills ring any bells? He was a suspect in the case."

Her eyes locked onto mine. The head shaking, the nos, all coordinated and firm.

"Booth Heitner? A Heitner employee named George? Mann's partner, Vernon Cole?"

No, no, no.

If Doug Mann were half the domestic terrorist she claimed he was, she surely would be good at stonewalling. She no longer trusted me. And why should she?

"We need a safe signal, Diane, so I can get in touch with you—in case something happens so that I can warn you."

"It's already happened, Meg. He knows I want Jessica, he knows I want to leave."

"Knows or guesses?"

"You don't get it, do you? With him, suspicion is fact. If he needs more evidence, he'll just keep digging till he gets it. And it's true, isn't it? I wanted Jessica, and I wanted out. I thought I could make that happen."

I didn't like the tone, the giving up. "A signal, Diane."

She studied the Wheat Chex and mushrooms in her cart. Then she opened her purse, dug out a fat billfold, fished out a business card that read 'SASSY SALLY: Custom Fashions.' "When you call there, say the wool material is in. I'll get back to you." She tried a smile. "It's the best I can do."

I believed that, the halfheartedness of it. I nodded. "And you can still call me to keep abreast of whatever I know."

"Can you find out what the police are doing? About this cold case investigation? You must have some connections—after this summer."

I nodded. I didn't want to go into that. "Have you told Doug you hired me?"

"No. But that doesn't mean he doesn't know."

I wanted to scoff, but the cop shop was a hotbed of gossip about Lindstrom and me. And then there was Booth, who may have called Mann. So he'd have enough to suspect my connection.

"You leave first," she said. "I'll pick up a few more things to justify my being gone in case he and Jessica get home before I do."

At home I headed for a warm shower and dressed in thick sweats. I microwaved a cup of tea and settled on the couch. The only available movie on TV was a summer blockbuster I'd avoided in theaters, but its explosion-driven plot was easier to take without surround sound. Harvey butted his white head into my chest between biscuit-making stomps.

Finally, he settled, and I settled.

I hated to admit it, even in the privacy of my own thoughts, but I was hoping Lindstrom would nudge the case along.

Monday afternoon I could stand the suspense no longer, I put in a call to the Homicide Division. Neely answered the phone, so we had a bit of a chat about the abnormally cold weather and his daughter's recent win in the citywide music competition. He thought he had seen Lindstrom around somewhere after lunch, but she was not at her desk at the moment. And he'd be glad to leave a note affixed to her phone to call me ASAP.

I spun my chair around to look out my dirty window. The sky was not a nice one. Even an optimist would have a difficult time finding something good to say about the weather today. Snow was definitely headed our way. I should have been helping Walter and Colleen with all the last-minute details for tomorrow's training instead of ruminating about the weather, but I'd swung back to annoyance that I had lost control of key components of my case. And Diane wasn't helping either.

I made another cup of tea and pondered Diane Mann and her motives. My phone buzzed.

"Lindstrom on line one," Colleen said sharply.

"Hey, what's happening?"

"I was just talking to one of the detectives about Vernon Cole," she said.

"Find out anything interesting?"

"Some. I'll fill you in later."

"Did you see Heitner?" I asked.

"Yes, I did. When are you going to be finished there?"

"I can leave pretty much anytime. Tomorrow is going to be the difficult day here."

"I'm leaving about four. Meet at my place at four-thirty?"

"No problem. See you then."

At four-fifteen, I said my goodbyes to Colleen and Walter, promising to meet Colleen fifteen minutes early the next day at the Holiday Inn's meeting room to help her get our new staff signed in and settled.

On the way north to the Central West End, Kingshighway was slow and slower. The promised snow was falling steadily, and two to three inches had already accumulated. The traffic around the hospital complex slowed to a complete halt, and I couldn't get over to the right lane until Lindell. Something seemed to be going on at the Chase, too. Where were all these people going on a Monday afternoon? Didn't they have real jobs?

Lindstrom was already changed out of her work clothes by the time I got to her place. The baggy gray sweats and tennis shoes were unusual. "Thinking of working out?"

"As a matter of fact, I am. I thought we'd go down to the Y and ride the bikes."

"Ride bikes?" I repeated.

"Yes, exercise. You remember that—moving your body in a repetitive way to build strength and burn calories."

"Sounds tiring. Couldn't we just sit and have a cup of tea and talk?"

"When was the last time you did anything more ambitious than walk to your car?"

"Oh, last month sometime."

"Can you remember exercising last month?" She paused, and when I didn't answer immediately, she upped the ante. "Exactly what exercise did you do last month?" Her blue eyes held mine. Even though it was tantamount to defeat, I flinched and looked away.

"I thought so. I'll get you a t-shirt and we'll be ready. You can ride in jeans."

"I'm not a member." I thought it worth one more try. I could easily visualize Lindstrom making me ride a stationary bike until I fell over with a heart attack. Didn't I read somewhere that vigorous exercise triggered half of all heart attacks?

"You'll be my guest. It'll cost you a buck, though."

She pulled a sparkling white t-shirt from her bottom drawer and tossed it at me.

The snow must have added an inch since I'd left Miller. I scraped her windows and drove into the blurring whiteness—the city lights bouncing off the snow through the beams of our headlights. Thick flakes pelted down. Lindstrom muttered about Nebraska winters and how they'd prepared her for this piddly snowstorm. Once or twice we fish-tailed, but she only arched a brow and kept silent.

I peddled at about a third of the rate she set. I figured it was the only way I had a hope of staying as long as she would.

"Cole left the force about a year and a half after the Rushing case. He resigned in a deal the department made with a prostitute and a young woman picked up for shoplifting. He had tried to make the same move with both of them in the same month, a blow job for a pass on the charges. God knows how many times he had gotten away with it. And the department would never have gone with just the prostitute, but somehow she met this other girl, the shoplifter, who was an A-student, good family, yada, yada, yada. Anyway they got the ear of an alderman, and the pressure was on. Evidently, Cole was pretty much hated by all the women civilian employees of the department. So the Lieutenant decided he'd had enough grief over Vernon Cole and forced him to resign. The women agreed not to press charges. We were lucky we got rid of him when we did. In that position, he was a major disaster waiting to happen."

Sounded to me as though he was a disaster that had happened. But I didn't say that. Instead I said, "No wonder he didn't want to talk to a cop. What about Richard Heitner?" I tried to talk without panting.

"Heitner was cordial at first, but when I pushed him a little bit about Jimmy Sills, he closed up pretty quick. Told me that I couldn't question Jimmy unless I was ready to charge him and made sure I knew that Jimmy would have the best representation. My guess is that he knows Jimmy's guilty. He figures that they made it through the first round of this investigation eight years ago, no reason to believe that they can't just dig their heels in. He must think Jimmy is the weak link, though, or he wouldn't be opposed to our questioning him."

"Anything about Booth being the father of Teresa's baby?"

"Just flat denial. Says Booth and Teresa were never lovers, that they were only friends for a few weeks. Says Booth was out of town at the time of Rushing's murder. And he doesn't remember George, either. Doesn't deny that a man named George worked at the old brewery building, just doesn't remember him. He has a lot of employees."

"Do you think George still works for Heitner?"

"No way to tell. Maybe you could nose around some on that one."

"You think Jimmy's it?" I was peddling faster in spite of myself.

"It sounded to me like Heitner thinks so. And he's still in a position to protect Jimmy. That may mean that Jimmy still works for him even if George doesn't."

"Jimmy Sills isn't listed in the phone book."

"If the guy's slow, maybe he has a caseworker of some kind." Lindstrom threw a long leg over and abandoned the bike. I was thrilled. Then I saw that instead of the shower we were headed for the treadmills.

"I could try Guardianship and Advocacy. I'm not sure they'll tell me anything," I said.

"I haven't run him through the computer yet, either. Maybe he's been picked up for something."

"Is his old address in the Rushing file? Maybe he's still in the same place."

"No, I checked it. There's an address, but the building's vacant now."

"What did Heitner say about Doug Mann?"

"Good man, very competent cop," Lindstrom said.

"And definitely in his pocket."

"I must admit, I don't like the idea that Mann investigated this case and left this crummy file, then tried to scare me off. Begins to sound suspiciously like he helped Heitner protect Sills." She looked at me. "Are you talkin' or walkin'?"

That didn't deserve even a witty acknowledgment. Besides, I was draped like a limp rag over the handrails while she strode at a brisk pace with her usual erect posture. I peeled off the treadmill and headed to the showers.

When we were both clothed and headed back into the storm, Lindstrom said cheerily, "Look, Darcy, let's not spend an evening at cross purposes. We both have something to celebrate. The kidnapping case is going well—" I could see it coming. "You've survived a thirty-minute workout with me."

I had the snowball scooped and thrown before she could duck.

"Foul! I'm still only one-armed!" But she was already scrabbling with her right hand in the snow.

I tried to run backwards, not my best thing even on dry ground. The snow wasn't packed and slippery, but I skidded anyway. "Truce! Truce!" I cried, hands out defensively, just managing to right myself.

She laughed, of course, but she let the snowball dribble from her hand. Flakes of snow bombarded her face; she squinted into them, hiding her blue eyes. Her cheeks were red and already her right hand looked raw from the snow. "Sure, now you're suing for peace."

We scuffed toward each other. Our lips brushed right outside the Y.

Lindstrom's Toyota, despite its superior heater, doesn't offer the wide range of drying materials available on my Horizon's backseat—t-shirts, sweats, holey towels. So I chaffed her cold fingers, warming my own, while we debated our food choices. Lindstrom won, and thirty minutes later we'd made our way to Zoe's at Euclid and McPherson, kittycornered across from Left Bank Books.

The host greeted us and gave us our choice of tables. A few patrons stood at the bar, but on this snowy night only two tables had diners. Lindstrom chose one of the tables up front so we could look through the windows as the snow slanted down. We ordered glasses of merlot and began to enjoy the coziness of being inside while the outside world filled up with white. Lindstrom ordered the salmon, and I chose the Thai grilled beef.

Right away I made the mistake of asking Lindstrom how soon they'd be going to trial on the kidnapping case she was just finishing up. That garnered me a fifteen-minute recitation on the many virtues of Sally Doyle, the Assistant Circuit Attorney, who was smart, witty, and—surprise, surprise—appreciative of Lindstrom's brains and perseverance.

We'd progressed to nibbling the well-sauced spareribs Lindstrom had ordered as an appetizer, and Lindstrom was peppering me with questions about tomorrow's Galleria training when I saw her. I blinked and peered again. Trudging past the window, her uncovered head bent against the snow, a muffler obscuring her lower face, was my client. She was on the arm of and leaning into a man whose full head of hair was dark. I twisted around for a better stare and for a long moment they actually paused right there, their faces intent—and quite close, as though they whispered not to break the hush of snow.

"Who's that?" I asked.

Lindstrom followed my stare. "Who's who?"

"That man." I leaned forward as they moved again.

"Vernon Cole," Lindstrom said, the mild surprise of coincidence in her voice. "Who's the woman?"

I stood, tossed down my napkin. "Diane Mann." As I passed Lindstrom's back, I touched her shoulders. "She lied to me."

"Where—"

"Right back," I promised as I stepped away from the table. I speed walked through the restaurant, grabbed my parka, cursed the zipper, got it to catch. By the time I was outside they'd passed the lighted windows and were headed into the dark shadowed sidewalk on Euclid.

CHAPTER THIRTEEN

Following them was no problem. The snow was easily over my shoes, and I buried my mouth inside my collar so my little indrawn huffs of breath wouldn't reveal my pursuit. None of us moved fast, but trudged on. Often their heads and shoulders merged into one shadow—conversation, not canoodling, I thought. But what did I know? Diane had denied knowing Doug had worked the Teresa Rushing case, said she knew nothing of Cole.

I trekked on, churning with suspicion. I fantasized confronting her, scripted the cutting remarks. Past Balaban's, past Dressel's. I regretted the dinner I'd left behind, felt the drop in blood sugar—the Y workout, now Nanook of the North.

Maybe confronting Diane wasn't my best bet. I knew she was an inspired extemporaneous liar, her appeal-to-pity skills honed.

The lights on Euclid were fuzzed by the blinding snow. Vernon Cole and Diane Mann walked straight into the pay lot toward an SUV and paused. They stood there while she fumbled in her purse and opened the door with a clicker. Vernon Cole held her elbow, maybe giving her a boost into the SUV. No hugs, no kiss goodbye. He gave a parting nod and stood and watched her back from her parking slot. I stepped behind a van as she passed me.

Cole was slogging back toward the corner when I intercepted him. "Vernon Cole?"

He gave me a cop's considering look. "Who's asking?" His tone was less hostile than his words.

"Meg Darcy."

He was good looking by most standards—the thick black hair had a slight wave, the manly chin a cleft. He was probably in his mid-forties. His parka hid his torso, but he wasn't so tall for a man. Now his mouth formed a smile to remove some of the sting as he said, "The private dick who fucked up things for Diane."

Well, that saved introductions.

"I wouldn't have said it that way," I ventured.

"Forgive the indelicate language. What are you doing out here in this blizzard?" He stomped his feet.

"I want to talk with you," I sidestepped.

"Pretty badly if you're following me around in this crap." He scanned the lot. "Your car here?"

I shook my head. "I was at Zoe's, saw you go by."

"Well, I'm at Llywelyn's, so we might as well head back that way." The bar he named is next to Zoe's.

We started back. As we walked, I skidded. He reached out and caught my elbow. "Fuckin' snow," he said and let my arm go.

The snow was still falling at a brisk clip. We thrashed southward.

"You back?" the bartender at Llywelyn's asked him and sent him a grin when I came into view. I wondered if Cole customarily appeared with a parade of women.

Cole settled us at a table and ordered his usual from the slender young waiter. "Coffee for me, please. Sugar and cream," I said.

"So, Meg Darcy, what makes you think I'll talk to you?"

"I don't know that you will. But Diane is in a pretty tight spot and needs all the help she can get." I didn't start off with a list of the lies she'd told me, including that she didn't even know him. I figured that might put his back up.

"That's true enough," he said amiably. Then he waited.

"I've been trying to find out about her daughter," I said.

"And screwing it up, Diane thinks." He sounded amused rather than angry. I couldn't tell if he were being patronizing or just blunt.

"Yeah, well, that's one version."

He gave a rueful sigh. "There always is—more than one version."

"Does Doug Mann still have the clout Diane thinks he does?"

Cole made a sound, maybe a laugh. "Don't doubt it."

The server reappeared and put a tumbler half-full of pale amber and ice before Cole. "I'm making a fresh pot for you," he said to me.

"So what does Diane want from you?" I asked.

Cole smiled, unzipped his parka. He was wearing a shirt, tie, and sports coat under it. Without the L. L. Bean outerwear, he looked trim. "Why should I tell you?"

"Maybe Diane doesn't know the best way to help herself. Maybe two heads are better than one." I paused a beat. "Why did she come to you for help?"

"She knows I think her husband's an asshole. She doesn't have to convince me of that. She knows I know he's got good connections—in the department, in City Hall. Plus, he works for Heitner, and though they ain't Anheuser-Busch, they still got lots of juice in this town." He shook his head. "She don't have to sell that to me. I know."

The server brought my coffee, steaming hot and black. I stirred in the cream and sugar and wrapped my fingers around the mug, leaning my face over the steam. Only then did Cole sip his drink. I was noticing that he had some nice little ways about him despite his gruff words. He was a shape-changer—sandpaper cop, smooth operator—depending on what he wanted to give or get.

I decided on another tack. "You worked the Rushing case with Doug Mann?"

A long beat while he studied my face. "Yeah. He was the lead detective, but we worked the case together."

"Was it a tough case? The file's pretty thin."

I caught a flicker in his eye, an unguarded moment. "Tough?" He didn't pause for my views. "Any unsolved case is tough." He sipped his drink and asked, "What do you mean the file's thin?"

He wasn't such a great actor after all. I tugged the hook. "Looks like some pages are missing, especially witness interviews. Pages have marks where staples have been taken out. Stuff like that."

He gave a slight nod. In the dim light I couldn't see the color of his eyes, but they had fine wrinkles around them. I could see, just as a matter of analysis, that he was a man—in spite of his past predatory behavior—who would be attractive to a certain kind of woman. Maybe my client's kind.

"When I last saw it, it was a thick file," he said.

He didn't ask me how I'd managed to see a file I wasn't supposed to have seen. He was, I guessed, a man who lived in a world where people didn't stick to the rules.

"Do files get culled—you know, to save space?" I asked.

A gravelly chuckle. "*Au contraire*. You put in every little shred that might help. But I'm not surprised if that bastard removed stuff. I was starting to notice, even back then, that Mr. Righteous Cop was playing loose with some procedures." He gave his chin a thoughtful rub with his thumb. "Mann seemed to know a lot of things on this case but wouldn't say how he found out. I asked him if he was hearing voices. He didn't like that. Before, I'd always acknowledged his greater experience—" He broke off. "Don't you hate whiners?"

I ignored it. "You think there was something funny about the way he was running the investigation?"

"Damn straight. For a guy who was a stickler for procedures—I mean he's a total control freak about details, he used to burn my ass over little things, and I took it because I believed his rep—he's this honest cop." A stifled snort. "Well, I'd got a few hints before then that maybe things ain't what they seemed, but the Rushing case really started me thinking."

"You had a suspect—Jimmy Sills," I said.

"Oh, yeah. The kid who worked for Heitner, the slightly retarded kid. He was at the brewery the afternoon we figured the murder had been done. Heitner had hired him and an older guy to kinda keep an eye on the property. The brewery had been closed for years."

I had a question about that. "How did you guys get from Teresa Rushing to Jimmy Sills? How did you connect the dots?"

"Just the obvious police work, really." He didn't successfully suppress a complacent look. "We sent a team to the nearest neighbors asking if anybody'd seen anything around the brewery."

"And somebody had seen Sills?"

He shook his head. "No. Not especially on the day of the murder, but a couple of neighbors mentioned a retarded guy—and you know how some people are. Any kind of mental problem makes you an ax-wielding maniac."

"But you checked it out?"

He nodded. "Sure." He didn't say "Wouldn't you?" but I understood it—any lead to get a case started.

I nodded back. "And Jimmy Sills knew Teresa Rushing?"

"At least by sight."

"Sills knew Rushing because she was Booth Heitner's girlfriend." I kept my voice light, still connecting dots.

"A friend, Booth said."

I couldn't tell if Cole accepted or doubted that characterization.

"How'd you identify Rushing?" I asked.

"A girlfriend had reported her missing. So she was on file as a missing person when a body showed up. Tab A fit Slot B."

"So, you thought it was Jimmy Sills?"

"We did at first, and for a while Mann was really hot on it. He figured the guy maybe made a date with Teresa, and when he didn't get the sex he wanted, he clubbed her with something."

"The file says nothing about the murder scene. Did you identify where she was killed?"

"Yeah, the cave—the cellar of the brewery where the vats used to be. There were some scuffle marks and traces of her blood."

"Did you find the weapon?"

He shook his head. "Nah. But the place was filled with old debris—boards, bits of pipe, chunks of concrete."

I nodded him on.

"So Heitner's still had a huge tank in a room of the cave. Down in the cave they had a little room for a night watchman, too, with an army cot. I guess at one time someone stayed down there and watched the gauges or whatever you do when you're brewing beer, but it made a place for Jimmy or the older guy, George Fowler, to catch forty winks."

I thought about the December Teresa had died and wondered if the weather had been half as fierce as this night was. "Sounds like an unlikely place for a romantic tryst—in a cold cave."

"They had a space heater down there. Besides, caves aren't as cold as you think. They stay at about sixty-two degrees. So maybe Jimmy took the girl to this little love nest for sex."

Sex on a narrow cot sounded like an invitation to calamity to me, but maybe hets do it differently.

I didn't want to go over that part again. "So Mann thought Jimmy did it."

Cole gave me another of his once-overs. I tried to look earnest and trustworthy.

"Yeah, at first he was hot for Jimmy. We were all over the place, even back into the little side tunnels that run out from the main cave. Then he took the tack that we couldn't prove it, no way, and Jimmy was a sad lad who deserved our protection."

"You weren't buying that?"

"Totally out of character for Mann. We'd had a lot sadder sacks nailed, and he never showed any sympathy. He was the farthest thing from a social worker."

"What about Fowler—where was he when Teresa was murdered?"

Cole's eyes lit up. "That's what I wanted to know. He had an alibi— some buddies in a small bar near where he lived. But the bartender was lukewarm about it. 'He might have been in that night.' I thought that bastard Fowler was lying."

"So it sounds like someone else—a random tramp, some high school kid—could have got in without too much trouble?"

He shrugged. "Not so easily. Jimmy and George had gone around nailing up boards on the windows and fixing locks on the doors."

"What about the Heitners—did any other employees still have keys?"

"Supposedly no one besides Sills and Fowler had been inside in years. Those two had also worked in the building during the summer clearing debris when part of the roof fell in."

"Did you have any evidence that pointed toward Fowler?"

He shook his head, gave me his rueful grin. "Nah. Not really."

"Mann didn't buy Fowler as a suspect?"

"Nope. Jimmy was it, then Jimmy was probably it but we couldn't prove it, so we'll just close the investigation and keep an eye on Jimmy. I suspect the Heitners promised that they would make sure nothing happened."

"That's funny. Wouldn't they be afraid someone—say Teresa's mother—would sue for wrongful death and Mann would have to explain why he hadn't arrested him?"

"You'd think." He leaned closer. "Somethin' else. We lost evidence from the property room. That had happened once before on a case I worked with Mann. That time he raised hell from here to Jeff City. He got a property clerk suspended, nearly fired. You'd think we'd lost a kilo. In the Rushing case he just shrugged it off."

"What was lost?"

"A yellow baby blanket."

"A baby blanket?" I thought of the notation in the case file about yellow fibers on Teresa's clothing.

"Yeah. We didn't find it with the body, but it was back in one of the cave tunnels, all wadded up and off to the side in the shadows. Just dumb luck we found it."

"What did Mann say?"

"He pooh-poohed it, said it had nothing to do with the case. And maybe it didn't, but the blanket looked in good shape, not like it had been rotting there for years."

"You knew Teresa had just had a baby?"

"Not at first. Mann interviewed her mother and got first look at the autopsy results. Then he told me one of Teresa's buddies had taken the baby. The *Post* never got that angle." He rubbed a forefinger over the high polish on our table. "Tell you the truth, I didn't figure the blanket was a big deal. Why would a mother take a newborn baby down in a cave—even a bad young mother? And it didn't prove anything."

"Now that Diane has talked to you—what do you think? Could that baby be Jessica?"

He pressed his lips together into a grimace, took a deep breath through his nose, exhaled slowly. "I dunno. As much as I think Mann is capable of anything, that one stumps me. I mean that baby wasn't left on that vacant lot overnight. So where would Mann have found it?" He shook his head.

"That reminds me. From the *Post* it sounds like the body was moved right after the murder. But the kids who found it said the body wasn't on that lot the day before."

"Yeah, well, you don't still believe everything you read in the papers, do you?" The stereotypical cynical cop.

"Maybe. But what did you think?"

"What the kids said. I don't know why the paper said different."

"Maybe someone wanted to confuse the death date. Someone who gave the reporters the wrong information," I said.

"At first I was confused about why the body was moved. But I guess dumping the body got it away from the place where Jimmy or George would be the only ones that could be guilty. Either one of 'em could have managed to get the body there." His voice had the winding down sound of someone who's feeling his liquor. Probably he'd had a drink or two or more with Diane.

"Jimmy's no longer at the address in the file. Do you know where he's living now?"

"They moved him. A piece of crap place on the North Side." He concentrated a moment but couldn't retrieve the address. "Just around the corner from the Northside Cafe."

I did one last pass. "So, what do you think now about this whole thing?"

"I think if you find a way to get Mann's balls in a wringer, call me to help turn the crank."

I thanked him for his help.

"Try to be of some use to Diane," he said. "Don't trust anyone in the department—even whoever let you see that file."

I asked him if he needed a ride home, but he shooed me off. The bartender gave me a signal that I thought meant he would make sure Cole got home safely. I zipped up my parka and walked outside. Amazing! The snow was still streaming down as though mischievous cherubs had ripped open a feather pillow. A lone car approached in a slow waddle. I ducked back into Zoe's. Just as I was safely off the sidewalk a black Lexus skidded into the side of an old battered Chevy. Both drivers climbed out quickly. Obviously no one was hurt. Inside the restaurant our waiter was going through the closing-down motions. He greeted me. "Your friend had your dinner boxed and took it home for you."

I didn't even know what questions I wanted to ask if I found my tongue. He anticipated one. "Don't worry. She paid the bill." Another smile. I guess I still looked lost. "Can I call a cab for you?"

My ears burned. I shook my head, ducked my chin into my parka. "No thanks, I've got it covered."

Outside I reconsidered. I walked to Llywelyn's and called Patrick. I told him I'd meet him on Kingshighway, so he wouldn't have to deal with the wreck on Euclid. Once more I left Llywelyn's warmth, turned back into the pelting snow and shuffled forward. I hadn't glanced at my watch, and my sense of time was thrown by the lack of traffic. I thrashed on, using the walk to script my next encounter with Lindstrom. I'd show her who had the higher claim to total dedication to a case. I stumbled once where the sidewalk's unevenness was hidden by the snow. I caught myself before doing a total splat.

Patrick hadn't sounded at all surprised that I needed a rescue. I was a little worried that his MG, fresh out of the garage, wouldn't be up for this snow but didn't mention it.

I don't know why I wasn't shocked to see him pull up on Kingshighway, not in the MG but in Lindstrom's Toyota, and to see her pale face through the passenger window. I stepped carefully off the curb. Damned if I'd take a clown's tumble to add to their no doubt vast amusement. Damn him for bringing her. Damn her for the smug look on her face.

"Get lost, did you?" she asked as I climbed into the back.

I slammed the door. Patrick cast me a sympathetic look, but I wasn't receiving it. I stared at the floor like a sullen teenager.

We drove in silence for two blocks. The roads were not at all clear, and it took some time. On any other night I'd have relished the adventure—even though cars were turtling—we saw at least two skid sideways across lanes. The hush of snow smothered every sound.

Lindstrom cleared her throat. "Look, Darcy, there's no use sulking. I admit I was a bit upset being left holding the appetizers, but I've had time to think about it. And Patrick reminded me I'm pretty intense when I'm on a case."

I shot Patrick a smoldering look. Oh, so he was her confidant now? The self-same boy, sensing his life was in danger, hunkered into his parka and kept his eyes on the road. I tightened my lips.

Another block went slowly by. She cleared her throat again. "Ah, well, don't talk."

"How did you expect me to get home—dog sled?"

"Well, you're a resourceful girl, aren't you?"

Somehow that round went to her. I felt a sting of tears behind my eyes. Suddenly I was furious. I was cold, tired, hungry—but damned if I'd get weepy. I'd bite her head off first.

"Listen, Lindstrom—"

Crunch. The black Mustang in the oncoming lane slithered into our left front fender, jolting us all. It took a moment for us to disentangle ourselves from seatbelts, and Patrick and I rushed to Lindstrom's aid, fearing she'd somehow reinjured her left arm.

Her blue eyes were blazing—whether from her car's being crashed into or our unsolicited helpfulness.

The other driver was a black teen, disguised by several layers of oversized clothing, but under that, a short, skinny youth who looked like he expected some authority figure to berate him. He readily revealed his name, rank, serial number, and driver's license and nearly fainted when Lindstrom identified herself as a police officer. But I have to say she was good with him—calm, and while not congratulating him on his ace driving skills, clearly inclined to view the matter as the accident it was. They exchanged insurance cards, and she told him to go home and stay off the streets till the snow stopped.

By the time we were back in the Toyota and resuming our own crawl homeward, I was too whooshed to want to behead her. Besides, the way she'd handled the kid made me want to hug her. I was always jerking her chain about the way cops treated blacks, but, truthfully, Lindstrom, of all people, treated everyone alike: abrupt to the point of rudeness, rigid about rules, surprising in her little spells of kindness and nurturing—like the one she'd just shown. Go figure.

When Patrick had finally shepherded us home to Arsenal, I headed straight for a hot shower while he and Lindstrom fiddled in my kitchen microwaving Zoe's excellent food into some semblance of its original glory. I didn't care. I layered myself into two sweatshirts and extra-heavy sweatpants and tucked in as though I had just come in from the Iditarod. Lindstrom hadn't consumed her whole meal either, and she and Patrick split her leftovers. Patrick supplied us with hot tea and made me a cup of real cocoa after. Nothing more important was discussed than "Pass the salt" and "I bet we're getting seven inches."

"Ah," I sighed over the first sip of the cocoa, stealing Lindstrom's favorite expletive.

"Well," she said to herself, "what did you learn from Diane Mann?"

I explained how I hadn't actually talked to Diane, but summarized my long conversation with Vernon Cole. She listened intently. Patrick was clearing and scraping plates, but his pointed little ears nearly bent double as he strained to listen, too.

"Hmm. Cole was sure willing to blab to you what he was too spiteful to tell me," she said when my recital ended.

So willing to credit me with superior interrogatory skills! But I sipped more cocoa and let it pass. Maybe it was better to let tonight remain a draw—a few points for her, a few for me. She certainly acted willing to let bygones be bygones as far as my dashing off mid-dinner to chase Diane Mann.

As for me, I told her everything—nearly. I emphasized Cole's bitterness toward Mann—that could color Cole's testimony. I mentioned the yellow blanket. I did mention Jimmy Sills, but I guess it just slipped my mind about Jimmy's probable home address.

CHAPTER FOURTEEN

I talked Lindstrom into staying at Arsenal to wait for the blade and salt trucks to do their overnight magic, but that meant she woke me at six on Tuesday. She wanted to be in the office by eight.

Lindstrom had a shovel and salt in her trunk, and with my digging and her spreading salt with her good arm, it took us only a few minutes to get the Toyota out into the narrow, cleared space on the street. The left front fender and headlight were smashed. This looked like a day's bodywork and at least five hundred dollars to me.

At McPherson Lindstrom didn't invite me up to watch her shower, so we simply repeated the digging routine in front of the Horizon.

I walked back into my apartment with a cup of hot tea on my mind, but the phone was ringing. It was Walter with a list of twelve guys I should call to delay this morning's training until the afternoon. I called Colleen at home to advise her not to drive anywhere today, but her mother reported that Joey had picked her up a half an hour ago, and she was probably already at the office. I dialed Miller Security. Sure enough, she answered on the second ring.

"Are you trying for employee of the month?" I asked.

"Around here, I'm the employee of every month. You're not coming in either?"

"No, but I'm working."

"Oh, sure. Which great security feats are you accomplishing from bed?"

I decided not to huff about having been across town already. Truth was, if my car had been where it belonged, I would still be in bed. "I'm working on the Mann case. I'm going to interview Jimmy Sills today."

"You're going to be at the training session at one o'clock?"

"With bells on. You don't have to stay, you know."

"I'm here now. Have you called all your guys yet?"

I admitted that I hadn't even started. She hung up abruptly with instructions to start calling *now*.

Jimmy Sill's neighborhood was the kind that suburbanites think of when they list the reasons why they commute an hour to Chesterfield everyday instead of living in the city. There were only two lived-in buildings on the North Side of the street, and both of these looked like they could be condemned by any fair standard. Neither building had a number visible from the street, so I parked the Plymouth—lots of curb space in this neighborhood—and walked up to the slightly less decrepit one of the pair. As I trudged through the snow, I could feel it getting down into my boots, dooming me to cold, wet feet for the day. There was an unpainted, dirty spot where the number plate used to be.

I faced two front doors, one with a truly awful bright blue paint job and its left hand neighbor, which had mercifully escaped the blue paint and was peeling gray. I banged the side of my fist against the gray one. The glass rattled loosely in the door; I looked behind me. Where were the children? They should be out rolling in this pure white invitation to giddiness. I banged on the door again. Maybe there were no children in these two buildings. I heard a voice, "Yeah?" I looked around, stepped away from the house. The voice again, young and female, "Whatcha need?" This time I could identify the direction—up. An African-American girl had stuck her head out of the window above. She was obviously doing her hair. One third of her head was in tiny, neat braids that hung to her shoulder; the other two thirds of her hair stuck straight out about two inches.

"Hi, I'm looking for Jimmy Sills."

"No Jimmy Sills here. Sorry." She reached up to close the window, knocking snow down on my shoulder.

"Wait! Hey, does he live in this building?"

"Don't think so. There's a couple of guys downstairs, but I don't think none of them's named Jimmy."

"Either of those guys a white guy, a little slow?"

"Retarded you mean?"

"Yeah, retarded." I agreed, not correcting her.

"That guy lives in the building next door."

"Thanks."

She nodded and slammed the window shut, sending another slide of snow down. I stepped out of the way this time. I trudged over the uneven lawns to the next porch.

An attempt had been made here. There was a narrow path scraped across the planks of the porch and down the steps. The front door was closed but not locked so I invited myself in out of the cold. The hallway was dark and smelled, but seemed to have been swept in recent memory. There were four doors on the first floor. I knocked on one to my immediate left and, with the luck that occasionally befalls a PI, a young white man, maybe in his late twenties, answered.

He was thin but with soft edges, a little stooped. His light brown hair was cut fairly short, but still managed to stand straight out from his head on the left. Bed head, I imagined.

"Mr. Sills?" I paused, and he nodded. "My name is Meg Darcy. I am a private investigator trying to help a little girl find her real parents. Could I talk to you for a few minutes?"

He took a few seconds to process the information, squinting at me. I smiled and tried to look friendly. I was about to offer additional reassurance when he rumbled, "Can I see some ID?"

I pulled my PI license out of my wallet and showed it to him.

"You got a driver's license?"

I thought about objecting, but squelched it. "Here." I handed it to him, and he carefully compared the two names and photos. Then he looked up at me.

"No one is going to get in trouble here," I said. "A family just needs some information to help their little girl."

He handed the cards back to me and nodded longer than I thought strictly necessary.

"Could I come in, or would you rather we go out somewhere else to talk?" Another PI trick—skip the question "Can we talk?" and get straight to where it is going to happen.

Jimmy squinted toward the front door. "I ain't been out 'cause of the snow. They said six inches on the TV."

I smiled brightly. "At least six inches, I'd say, maybe more. And it's cold, too. Would you rather just stay in?" That set off another round of nodding, but this time it was accompanied by a shuffling movement into the apartment. Stage one, success.

The living room was small and square with mismatched furniture, but it was all clean. When he had shuffled in front of the couch, he pointed down at it. I assumed I was to sit and did so.

He settled himself in the worn easy chair that faced the portable television.

"I spoke to Booth Heitner the other day. He said you work for Heitner Associates." I tried to project an ease that would disguise the intrusiveness of the implied question.

There was a pause Jimmy obviously didn't feel obligated to fill with a confirmation.

"Have you worked there a long time?" I asked.

"I've worked for Mr. Heitner since I stopped school. My dad used to work at the bottling plant and got me a job."

"What year did you leave school?"

He screwed up his face and frowned at me. "I stopped school when I was fourteen."

"And how old are you now, Jimmy?"

"I'll be twenty-eight on the Fourth of July."

"Fourteen years is a long time. What kind of work do you do?"

"Before the plant shut down, I worked with Mr. Heitner at his office in the plant. I helped with the mail and fixed things. I made copies. Nobody but me could clean Mr. Heitner's office."

"Mr. Heitner, that's Booth's dad, right?"

Jimmy nodded, but this time he stopped after only a half dozen head bobs.

"How long ago did the plant close?"

"I don't remember."

"Since the plant closed, what do you do?"

"I work at the house mostly. Sometimes at the office."

"At Mr. Heitner's house?"

"Un huh and Booth's. I mow in the summer and wash the cars every week. Probably this afternoon somebody'll pick me up so I can shovel the snow at Mr. Heitner's."

"When Booth was still living at home, when he was in high school, did you work at the house then?"

"Yeah, sometimes. Mostly on weekends. Sometimes I'd work in the morning at the office, and Mr. Heitner would take me home for lunch. I'd work in the yard in the afternoon. Mrs. Heitner needed help in her garden."

"It sounds like you're pretty much a part of the family."

Jimmy blinked. Did that signify skepticism or did he merely not respond to anything that wasn't phrased as a question?

"Did you meet any of Booth's friends?" I prodded.

"Some. Don used to piss on the rose bushes. I saw him twice. I told Booth to tell him to stop, but I don't think he did."

"Did Don come to the house a lot?"

This brought only a blank look. Quantities and time lines both seemed to be sinkholes for Jimmy.

"Is he still a friend of Booth's?"

"I don't think so. I don't think Mrs. Booth likes him."

"How about Teresa? Was she a friend of Don's, too?"

"I don't know."

"I sort of got the idea from Booth she was a little wild. Sounds like Booth was running with a rowdy bunch then. Teresa had a baby. Did you ever see the baby?"

"That wasn't Booth's baby."

I peered to see why he made that particular leap, but he avoided my eye. "Did Teresa say it was?"

"She lied about that."

Well, well, well. That seemed to be the family line all the way down to the yard boy. Since things were going so well, I thought I'd take a risk.

"What happened when she showed the baby to Booth?"

"I didn't see it. It was covered with a blanket." Bingo, three cherries. Jimmy shifted; these questions were making him uncomfortable.

"Was Teresa your friend too?"

He blinked several times. "Um, no…no. She was Booth's friend. But then she lied and she wasn't his friend no more."

"Did she tell you that Booth was her baby's father?"

"No, no." He jumped up from the recliner. "I didn't know her. I don't want no more questions."

"But Booth saw Teresa's baby that day, didn't he?" I asked.

"I don't know. I told her he wasn't there, but she went on in anyway. I had to go down to do some work with George."

"George worked at the house, too?"

"No, the old brewery. Look, I'd better get ready for work. Someone will be here soon to pick me up. You can ask Booth about this stuff. He remembers better than me anyway."

Time for another big lie. "Booth said he was there at the brewery that day. He said he saw Teresa's baby."

"I don't know. I don't remember. George and me had work to do. We was unloading some old building stuff. That's all I know. I told her he wasn't there. She went off looking for him. I don't know the rest. You'll have to ask Booth. Are you going to tell Booth I talked to you?" His voice was rising; discomfort was turning to fear.

"I don't have to, Jimmy. We can keep this just between us if you want."

"Better just leave me out of it. I didn't know that girl anyway, and that wasn't Booth's baby. She lied."

"Yeah, Booth said she was a wild one. But I wondered what happened to the baby. Teresa's mother doesn't have her."

"I don't know. I didn't even see it. I don't know about what happened to it. All I did was take that stuff off the truck and put it in the dry part. That's all. You have to go now. I have to get ready for work."

"Do you have a telephone, Jimmy?" I hadn't seen one in the living room.

"I don't want to answer any more questions. You should go now." He stood and flapped his arms, shooing me like an errant duckling toward the door.

"Okay. I didn't mean to bother you. I'll just give you my business card in case you want to call me later." He refused to look at it, so I placed it on the arm of his chair and stepped toward the door.

"Thank you for talking to me, Jimmy. You've backed up what Booth told me, so our conversation can be between us." I watched him carefully. Was he just upset because the Teresa and baby episode was an unhappy one for the Heitners or was he afraid I'd find out he had crushed Teresa's skull? "Call me if you want to talk about anything. I'm in the security business so I can help with different kinds of problems."

"Do you work for Mr. Mann?"

I considered saying yes, just to reassure him, but decided it was too risky. "No, but I know Doug Mann. He was a good cop."

Jimmy nodded distractedly and flapped toward the door again. This time I took the hint.

Eleven-ten. I headed the Horizon back toward Gravois. Even with my driving skills, the trip had the slow-motion quality of a bad Western shoot-out. I was gritting my teeth by the time I slid—literally—along the curb beside Miller. Inside, I ducked into my office to make a call, afraid I'd missed Lindstrom, had she done the unexpected and taken a normal lunch hour.

But no, her brisk "Lindstrom here" greeted me.

"Darcy." I quickly recapped my interview with Jimmy Sills. "Jimmy got very, very nervous talking about that day—and he kept denying that the baby was Booth's," I concluded.

"Why would he deny that?" A knowing question.

"Exactly." I waited for "well done" to drop from her lips.

"That doesn't prove Booth was the baby's father—or that the baby is Jessica Mann, or that Jimmy did or didn't kill Teresa."

"You sure know how to squelch a girl who's taken the initiative."

Why had I imagined she'd throw roses at me?

Maybe the little sound she made was a dignified snort. "Rumor is not DNA, Darcy."

"Yeah, well—" I was torn between screaming in her ear and slamming down the phone.

"But it is interesting," she conceded, all magnanimity, "that Jimmy grew rattled when you asked him about it."

For some reason this concession further irritated me—all her condescending cop air raised my hackles. Before I could get that missile off the ground, she veered toward another topic.

"Call me when you get off work tonight. I've got a little surprise." The inflection she gave to the last word suggested red satin panties at a minimum and was so un-Lindstrom I felt the rush like the first hit of anything that's mood-altering.

"What?—you know I'm not good at waiting."

"Ah, well, we all have our trials." She chuckled and hung up.

I slammed the phone down. "Colleen!" I didn't bellow. I didn't yell. Maybe I gave an emphatic shout.

I strode to the front reception area. No Colleen. A quick check of the kitchen, bathroom, equipment room, Walter's office. No Colleen. Back to my office in case she had invisibly passed me in the hallway. This time I saw the note taped to my computer. "Gone with Walter to the Holiday Inn. See you there. C."

Walter greeted them, gave them the lecture about the role of law in a civilized society and the honorable traditions of Miller Security in particular. He advised twenty-five white men, seven black and two latino, four black women, three white and one latina that by the end of our time together over the next three days, they would be the best group of security guards in St. Louis.

Walter is a blue-collar working stiff in spite of the fact he happens to be a small business owner. He grew up in a family that owed its daily bread to the union, and he has never seen fit to vote anything but a straight Democratic ticket. Sometimes I want to strangle Walter for his barely submerged racism, sexism and homophobia, but watching him talk to these untested new employees with enthusiasm and respect, I was reminded that there are other things I can count on Walter for. I was lucky he'd taken me on and was willing to trust and respect me, too, in spite of our differences.

About six-thirty, Colleen whispered to me that they were predicting two more inches of snow for tonight and tomorrow morning, so after a quick conference we agreed we'd start again tomorrow at one at the Galleria. Meanwhile I'd head back to the office to write up notes.

Miller was both dark and cold. So I marched in, turned on every light and jacked the heat up to eighty degrees, then sat at my desk to call my mother.

Betty was in for a change, and we had a nice talk. My mother likes Sarah Lindstrom, but is smart enough not to defend her until I've sputtered out my complaints. I suspect she hopes Lindstrom and I will settle down into a more conventional lesbian marriage someday, but Betty keeps those fantasies to herself. She reported that my brother Brian and his family weren't coming for Christmas, so I'd need to get presents early enough to send through the mail. After some strategic whining by me, Betty agreed she'd shop for everyone but my niece Jen, who is a joy to buy for. I agreed I'd haul it all to the post office and do the mailing end of the business. Just as we hung up, there was a series of loud knocks on the front door.

When I saw the angry, wind-reddened face I knew who he was in my bones. Had he followed me? Why else show up at this ungodly hour? Briefly I entertained the idea of not opening the door, or at least calling for backup before I did, but in the end, I decided that Doug Mann had no real beef with me, and that like most wife beaters, he was probably a coward at heart and wouldn't do anything that might result in a real fight or arrest.

I let him in but stood leaning against Colleen's desk to keep the conversation there in the reception area. Let him wonder if there were people in all those other lighted offices. I started with pleasant.

"Hi, can I help you?"

"You've already helped too much. Now you just need to tell me where you've hidden my wife and daughter." The words were even and low and freighted with alcohol.

"Perhaps we could start by introducing ourselves. My name is Meg Darcy."

"You know damn well who I am. You and your bitch girlfriend have been investigating me. Telling Diane that she can steal my child. Well, that won't wash, you stupid cunt. How long do you think you'll keep your stupid PI license after you're charged as an accessory to kidnapping, huh? I can have you in lock up tomorrow morning. And it won't take much to get Lindstrom canned, either. You think the two of you are hot shit, but now that everyone knows she's a dyke, it'll only take a little mistake to get her ass fired. And kidnapping is a big mistake. So you'd better tell me where they are and I'll go get them. Then you can mind your own fucking business."

He took a step toward me, not yet right in my face, but definitely more threatening. I had to crane to look up. At a quick guess he was six-foot-two and strong, rangy and muscular with no softness at the edges despite his age. Even drunk, he was sure of himself: his strength, his fitness. A natural leader of men and intimidator of women. My hackles rose.

I consciously took a deep breath. Okay, Diane had done a bunk. Hardly surprising, although the last time we talked she'd dismissed it as the worst of her choices. And Mann had made the jump from Lindstrom's causing his problems to me. I took another deep breath.

"Look, I don't know anything about kidnapping."

"Don't play that with me. Your number is on Diane's cell phone bill, and I know you've helped her snatch my kid. We can do this only two ways—first, you tell me where she is, I find her and, if you stop interfering, you can go snoop in somebody else's life or, second, you find your ass in jail, and when you bond out, I beat you and your girlfriend until one of you tells me where Diane is."

"Mr. Mann, your wife certainly didn't tell me she was taking off. I don't have any idea where she is. I just talked to her in the first place because Teresa Rushing's mother wanted to find the baby. I thought it an odd coincidence that you adopted a newborn the same week Teresa's baby disappeared. That's why she returned my calls. Diane told me the baby was the daughter of some cousin of yours."

"It is none of your fucking business who gave birth to my daughter. Why have you been sniffing around the Heitners?"

"Someone said that Booth might have been the father of Teresa's baby."

"Well, someone doesn't know shit. You can take that to the bank. She just wanted Booth to rescue her skinny ass—give her money for an abortion, but even she said the baby wasn't his. But Booth's daddy had money and that idiot Booth gave it to her. If you know what is good for you, you'll leave the Heitners alone. They have some pretty powerful friends. Things could get very difficult for you and your girlfriend in St. Louis. That is, if you live to see the day I get my daughter back for good. Now where is she?" He closed the distance between us and leaned over me.

I didn't want to put myself in a position where fight was my only option. I shifted my weight forward, just a bit. I hoped not enough to spark a defensive move, but enough to make quick movement possible.

As calmly as possible, I said, "I told you, I didn't know she was taking off, and I have no idea where she might run to. I barely know her, Mann. A couple phone conversations was it. She had nothing to tell me. Have you tried her relatives?"

He turned his head in disgust and ran his long, hard hand over his face.

"How about friends?" I prodded.

"She only has one friend; I've been there, too." He grabbed my upper arm, squeezing tightly enough to be uncomfortable.

"Don't do something that can't be undone, Mann. I don't know where she is. Roughing me up won't change that. Think. You were a cop; she's your wife. Where would she go?" I tapped the hand grasping my bicep so painfully. "You'll find her. If she's gone two weeks, you'll have the whole damn police department looking for a kidnapped child, the FBI even."

"Don't delude yourself. The whole department will be looking for her tomorrow morning. I won't wait two fucking weeks. Kidnapping is kidnapping. I don't give a damn who did it."

I stepped a little to the side and tugged at my arm. He let go but intensified his glare.

"And I'll find out if she contacts you, so you'd be smart to find her and talk her into coming back," he continued, not calming down. "If Jessie's not in her own bed by the weekend, the bitch will never see Jessie again. Tell her that if she calls you. And tell little Teresa's mother that the baby is dead. If you keep showing your ass about that, you'll be sorry. That stupid bitch couldn't raise her own child—"

Then from nowhere his hand slapped my face, and I felt something in my neck pop as I fell backward onto Colleen's desk. Blood gushed out of my nose and over my chin. Mann left the door standing open on his way out. The cold blast felt good. I was much too warm.

CHAPTER FIFTEEN

I staggered to the bathroom, cleaned the blood from my face, and closed down the office. I made it out to the Horizon and drove home slowly. At eight-thirty traffic was light. My mind stayed fully occupied with Doug and Diane Mann.

By the time I made it back to Arsenal, the stairs to my second-story apartment seemed steep to me, and I leaned against the wall. Being slapped made me tired. I felt the pull on all the strings and widgets that hold my head to my shoulders.

As I slogged up the stairs, Patrick appeared at the top. "Who ran over you?"

"Damnit, Patrick, it gets harder, not easier."

"What, sweetie?"

"Violence. When I was in the Army, when I was an MP, I was in some scuffles. I thought I was tough. But I didn't know. Now, every time I get—-" My voice wavered; I couldn't finish, couldn't say "hurt."

He rubbed my shoulders and made soothing noises. He walked with me into my apartment. We settled at my kitchen table, his good face attentive.

"Doug Mann came to see me. He slapped me. Betty never slapped me in my entire life. Not even when I sassed back." I couldn't put into words what the slap meant—that Mann had delivered that most contemptuous of blows.

"Hang on, Meg. This calls for the good stuff." He walked to the kitchen cabinet where I keep a small, pathetic assortment of liquor and returned with a bottle of good brandy he'd given me. He poured us both a slug in the Kraft pimento cheese glasses I use for juice.

"That's very good stuff," I pronounced in ignorance.

"Joseph has very expensive tastes."

"Lindstrom, too. Patrick, I can't keep up with the Joneses. With the Lindstroms. She makes way more than I do." I held out the small glass.

He added a dollop. "That's not what we need to talk about now,

Meg. What happened tonight?"

I told him. First, I took another sip, then breathed deeply. He sat in a chair, too, so his eyes could fix on mine, bore into me, keep me honest.

"I hate getting hit," I concluded. I meant hit, stalked, shot at. Then I felt bad because so far, at least, I'd not come as close to getting killed as Patrick and Lindstrom had last July. Well, maybe that time in the cabin. It was a toss-up.

"Damn right, and we'll figure out a way to discourage him. Ready to call the police?" he asked.

I looked into his blue eyes, so calm and resolute. I looked at my feet. The brandy was helping my poor cold toes.

I shook my head, a mistake. "No, not till I talk to Lindstrom."

"She's called me five times trying to get you on the phone this evening."

"Damn! I was supposed to call her. She had a surprise for me." I stopped, felt a blush.

"Nothing bigger than the one you've got for her," he said, nodding toward my face.

My lip was definitely swelling; when I glanced down toward my chin, there was my lip straining upward toward my nose. I wanted Mann to pay for this.

The pounding on the door scared the hell out of me. My pulse notched up in a nanosecond. "What the—" Patrick said.

"Open up, Meg—it's me." Bright, commanding.

Patrick got the door. She greeted him and breezed past, carrying the smell of fresh wintry air with her. I got a second of that lovely face, lit and triumphant, before she registered mine. Then she was peering down at me through narrowed eyes, studying me as though she'd have to identify me in a lineup. She put the long fingers of one hand on my near wrist, but otherwise didn't touch me.

We looked at each other a long time without saying anything. Her eyes, already a darker blue than Patrick's, darkened more.

That was part of the residual effect of last summer's danger. As a cop, she knew not to create a theory ahead of her facts, but I could see she wasn't guessing that I'd fallen off my scooter.

"Tell me what happened," she said in a quiet voice I hadn't heard before. I couldn't peg it. Was it one of her cop voices? She seemed calm, but not like Patrick's calm.

"Doug Mann came crashing into Miller and hit her," Patrick said.

She paled then. Her jaw tightened. Something came into her eyes—pain maybe, or grief.

"You've got great timing," Patrick continued. "I just told her she needed to call the police."

Our eyes were still locked. "Let's go sit in the living room," she said.

I shuffled to the sofa, and they followed. Lindstrom sat beside me.

"I don't want to call the police," I said then, surprised that my voice was croaky. "I don't want to cause you a problem at work. Mann intends to use me to get at you there." I reached my other hand over to squeeze the long fingers again resting lightly on my wrist. "Don't worry. I won't report this."

She listened to it all stone-faced. Then she said, "I'm only thinking what will happen when I kill him for this."

I know what hyperbole means, and this wasn't it. Patrick looked stricken. Neither of us doubted her.

"No killing," I said and fell back against my pillows. I think my eyelids fluttered.

"Meg—" Her voice, low and worried.

"Don't be daft," I whispered. Why in the world would I want Lindstrom to kill Mann? Who could possibly think that would help?

I opened my eyes and saw the answer frozen in her face. For some reason Lindstrom would. Maybe it was a Nordic thing—berserker rage, blood for blood. Some old Viking vow.

I started laughing. "Lindstrom, for God's sake, don't play John Wayne."

Well, that poked her.

"Darcy, he can't get away with that crap. Besides, you're the one who is always such a hard-ass. You think that big, bad butch act makes everything all right. It doesn't."

I jerked my head around to look at Patrick and caught his grin. I have to give it to him; he did try for a neutral look.

"We've just got to outsmart him, Lindstrom. That's all," I said.

She stood up in one graceful move as though she still rebounded like a teenager. She started pacing across my living room. Five minutes of pacing was required before Lindstrom drew herself up and said, "I swear he won't get away with this, Darcy."

"I know, Lindstrom. Let's just make sure we get him without dragging ourselves down." My head was hurting despite all the good booze. "Can we change the subject now?"

"What?" she said, not achieving the sympathetic tone one wishes from a lovey bunch ready to coddle the wounded.

"Your surprise. What was it?" I glanced at Patrick, hoping he would discreetly sidle away while I heard her whisper a sweet something into my shell-like ear.

"Oh, that." Flat, dismissive.

"Yeah—what—?"

She sighed. "I bought a damn car today."

Of course. Isn't that what we all do when someone has crumpled our fender?

"A car?" Patrick asked.

"An SUV. A Jeep Grand Cherokee, to be exact." She shrugged. "I wanted to take you for a little spin tonight."

I have to say that even though Patrick dragged her over to the window where she pointed out the navy blue vehicle sitting under a streetlight in front of our building, it was clear she no longer exulted over it. She had a mature sense of proportion about things—my being hurt outweighed her new toy as breaking news. A fine sense of proportion. Except about killing people.

I awoke to the sounds of squabbling in my kitchen and padded barefoot to my bedroom door to eavesdrop. Patrick was announcing that he'd taken the day off from the bookshop to follow me around and discourage Doug Mann from any more assaults, verbal or otherwise. Lindstrom was proclaiming—a notch louder—that she was leaving the Jeep Cherokee for me to drive through the snow. Groggy as I was from brandy-induced deep sleep, I couldn't quite identify the point of disagreement since those two things were not mutually exclusive. Then it hit me. They were competing in the take-care-of-Meg contest.

Last night I'd have gladly snuggled into either or both. Though, in fact, Lindstrom had taken me over Mann's surprise visit, word by word, as though I were a prime witness, and Patrick had glowered at her as though she'd been using a rubber hose on same. Just as she had started to go back over it "one more time," I'd excused myself to pee, and after relieving myself, had headed straight for my bed and crashed like a felled tree.

By the time I got up, I realized my neck wasn't permanently whiplashed, my split lip was no longer puffed out so that I could see it from above, but one glance in the mirror told me I'd need a good cover story for the day.

I climbed into the shower and then found warm, heavy clothes. A peek through my bedroom window told me Colleen's prediction was right—another two inches had fallen overnight. The sky was still gray, but a little brighter than the lumpen crankiness of the day before.

By the time I made my grand entrance, Lindstrom and Patrick were sitting at my small kitchen table, sipping coffee and sharing the *Post*. Both checked me out: was I able to stand by myself? walk? talk?

"Hi, there. I think I'll live after all," I said. "He just ruffled my feathers."

They ignored this feeble attempt at belated courage and immediately badgered me with proposals for my care and keeping. No one wins a two-front war—I'm sure I've read that. I caved right away to Patrick's blandishments. Though he's a posterior pain to drag around on a case, on the whole, I can keep him in line and on a leash. But Lindstrom—might as well try to steer a hurricane as control her. So I snubbed her offer of the new Jeep.

I noted that I was feeling an extra satisfaction in rejecting her latest toy. I don't love Lindstrom for her material goods—which of late had been accumulating faster than government debt in the eighties. And I felt a little queasy imagining my poor ol' Horizon parked side by side with the sleek navy SUV.

Eventually we sorted it out—Lindstrom gave me a good hug and a flimsy cheek peck and drove off to Clark Street, her spine stiffened to meet whatever effects Doug Mann's badmouthing might have. I sent Patrick to bundle up while I checked the residential pages of the phone book.

There were two dozen Fowlers in the white pages, one "George," one "G.A." and one "G.D." Patrick laughed when he read out the last, remembering how his mother had always substituted "GD" for "god damn" to avoid cursing in front of the children. I called George first, claiming to be in the personnel department of Heitner Associates with a question about an insurance claim. The woman who answered the phone informed us that her George had died two years ago and was certainly making no claims on insurance. I pressed my luck.

"But isn't this the George Fowler that worked for Heitner Associates?"

No, she explained her George had been a truck driver and then spent the last fifteen years of his life in the pulpit.

There was no answer at the number for "G.A." so we were left with

"G.D." This Fowler lived on the Southside, so we decided we'd just drive to his house and hope to catch him. His address was one half of a brick duplex in a neighborhood that had seen a huge influx of Bosnian refugees in the last few years.

"So what's our story?" Patrick asked.

"Well, whether or not Booth was the father of Teresa's baby seems to be a hot button, but I think to get what we want, we'll have to be looking for the birth parents of a child."

I pulled the Horizon up to the curb. Patrick peeked into the bed of a dirty blue Ford pickup; we walked up the drive.

A faded thin woman answered the door and admitted to being George Fowler's wife. She looked at us doubtfully, but I gave her my best smile and assured her we had only a couple of questions for George.

Finally she nodded sharply and stepped aside as an invitation into her home. She hurried up the stairs, and we were left for several seconds to gaze around at the worn hardwood floor and the dingy white paint over rough plaster. There was nothing on the walls here in the hallway, and the house was so quiet as to make me doubt George's presence. Had Mrs. Fowler gone upstairs to get her ax? Maybe she'd been waiting for years for the perfect strangers to murder, chop and bury in the backyard.

I had just turned to offer this theory to Patrick when George himself came lumbering down. I couldn't tell if it was his bifocals or bad knees, but the stairs seemed treacherous to him. He was a barrel-chested man, bulky with short thick fingers. When he finally arrived at the bottom, he cleared the phlegm from his throat. For half a second I was afraid he was going to spit.

"Now, what's all this about?" he asked.

"Good morning, Mr. Fowler. My name is Meg Darcy. I'm a private investigator and this is my associate, Patrick Healy." I held out my ID. Patrick offered his hand, but Fowler seemed not to notice. "We've been hired to search for a child's birth parents, and I hoped to ask you a few questions."

"You've got the wrong man. I'm not anybody's father."

"No, sir, that was never the question. The child's mother may have been Teresa Rushing. Is there a place where we can sit down?"

He looked skeptical, but led us to the back of the house and into an L-shaped kitchen. Mrs. Fowler followed us and offered to make tea. I opened my mouth to thank her when Fowler said gruffly, "Go on upstairs. This is none of your business."

I stiffened and felt Patrick brush my shoulder. I knew he was encouraging me to ignore my politics and principles for the sake of the interview. Fowler sat himself at the formica-topped table and nodded at the other chairs. From the smell I assumed cabbage was the soup du jour.

"Now, Mr. Fowler," I began, "the time we're concerned about is eight years ago. Booth Heitner was still in high school, and I believe you were working, at least temporarily, at the Heitner Brewery building." I looked at him for confirmation. He narrowed his eyes but nodded.

"Teresa Rushing evidently told some people that Booth Heitner was the baby's father and told others that he was not. But we believe she brought the baby to show Booth one day just after the baby was born. For whatever reason, it seems this took place at the old brewery while you and Jimmy Sills were working there."

"Did Jimmy Sills tell you that?"

"Well, honestly, we've interviewed over a dozen people about this, sir. Everyone contributed a little bit to the picture. Jimmy was pretty vague about the details. He didn't seem to remember much."

"It's all a long time ago," Fowler said.

"But you remember Teresa Rushing?"

"I don't remember her. I didn't pay any attention to Booth's friends. All a bunch of spoiled rich kids that never had to do a lick of work in their lives."

"Booth said he was running with a pretty rough bunch. Then he straightened up," I said.

"I heard something about some gal trying to dump a baby off on Booth. I didn't know her."

"Did you see Teresa and Booth talking the day she brought the baby?"

"Look, lady, I don't know who told you that. I wasn't there the day that girl got killed. I didn't know anything about the Heitner's private business. I just worked for them." His voice kept rising. He seemed to realize it and braked, took a breath. "Jimmy might know more. They had him at the house all the time. He was too stupid to know they just used him."

This was an interesting development. Teresa was killed the same day she brought the baby to see Booth?

"How did they take advantage of Jimmy?" I asked.

"They kept him as a pet. He's not legally an employee of the business. So they don't have to follow the contract with him. They get him to work weekends and all. Just feed him at their house. He acts like that means they love him. Stupid chump."

I pondered. Jimmy had his own place to live, but he was obviously kept about the Heitner's home a good deal of the time.

"For a while the police suspected Jimmy might be involved in Teresa's murder, isn't that right?"

"Yeah, frankly, it wouldn't surprise me a bit. Retards are often violent. The missus used to help take care of a retarded boy. He spit at her and my wife quit."

"Did Jimmy know Teresa?"

"Damned if I know. When he was with me, he was working. I don't know what he did when he hung around the house with them."

Patrick jumped in with a question. "Did Booth ever speak to you about Teresa and the baby?" Patrick asked.

George Fowler looked at Patrick for the first time and distaste puckered Fowler's ugly mouth. "Who are you again?"

"My name is Patrick. I work with Meg."

"Do her interior decorating, do you?" He laughed.

Patrick raised his eyebrows, but otherwise kept his cool. I sent him the same silent message he'd sent me earlier. Fowler would have to get his comeuppance from the universe after we'd completed this interview.

"Patrick's question was referring to what Booth Heitner may have said to you about Teresa and the baby."

"Booth Heitner didn't talk to me at all. I worked for the man who reported to the man who was an assistant department head for his daddy. Booth and I didn't have chats about where he'd hid his sausage."

"In the days after Teresa was killed, when they were questioning Jimmy and you about the murder, did you hear anything about the baby?"

"Nobody talked to me about it. That cop works for Heitner now, you know."

"Doug Mann? Yes, we'd noticed that. When did that happen?"

"I don't know, but after he retired from the cops, he was all over the place—changing this and that."

"What was his relationship to Jimmy like?"

"I don't know. Like I said, when Jimmy was with me, he was

working, not shooting the shit."

"Jimmy doesn't work for you anymore?"

"Nah. I push papers in the distributor's warehouse now."

I knew there was probably more I should be asking George D. Fowler, but I couldn't think what it was. I mainly just wanted away from him. "Thank you, Mr. Fowler, for talking to us. Here's my card in case you think of anything more about Teresa or the baby after we're gone."

He looked at my business card. "This is your home number?"

"No, that's my business number. Miller Security."

We walked toward the front door. "Miller Security. You guys do the security at the big lumberyard by my dad's place."

When we were back in the Horizon I turned to Patrick. "Did you get that? He said he wasn't there the night Teresa was murdered. That means she brought the baby to show to Booth the same day she died. That's pretty suspicious, I'd say."

"Think maybe George did it?" Patrick asked hopefully.

"Can't think why."

Patrick sighed. "The trouble with this detecting business is you have to talk to all those people your mother warned you about."

CHAPTER SIXTEEN

I convinced Patrick I'd be safe from further assaults in the company of Walter, Colleen and forty would-be security guards and that, if I wasn't, I had my cell phone, so Patrick asked me to drop him at St. Louis Bread Company for lunch. I arrived at the Galleria in time to greet and chat, although I noticed Andy, my gorgeous redhead, stayed immersed in conversation with Colleen and then wandered off when I joined them. Hard to get or straight? Who can tell?

I only half-listened as the manager of the mall talked about overall mall security and community relations. Most of it was an advertisement for the Galleria. Instead, I thought about Lindstrom's quick decision to shop for what was surely an expensive SUV. And the houses she was looking at—$200,000 and up. I understood she had to rebuild a life for herself after losing her home and her ex to a deranged stalker. But what kind of life? Not a working-class police officer's life. There had been much complaining and controversy about St. Louis's rule that city cops had to live within the city limits, creating situations in which some in the upper echelons kept apartments in the city while their wives and children lived in Clayton, Ladue, and Webster Groves. I wondered if Lindstrom would be living in the city at all if this rule weren't an obstacle. Rental property, a new SUV—she was beginning to look more like a Chesterfield social climber than a city cop.

What were her values now that she had inherited Viv's wealth? And would I be able to bridge that material gap? Lindstrom had been paying for more and more of our entertainment costs—nice dinners, tickets to the PREP fund raiser last month, the weekend in Augusta. Was I on the slippery slope to being a kept woman? I suspected trying to talk to Lindstrom about it wouldn't help. When I had objected to her paying for the weekend in Augusta, she had dismissed me airily. We wanted to go—she had the money—what could possibly be the problem? It was only money.

Walter's gruff voice broke into my reverie. He was going to give us a short break now, and when we returned in a half an hour, we'd break into small groups for practice following and confronting shoplifters. Colleen was stationed by the door, giving everyone a store to report to as they left the meeting room. Walter found me and told me I was to meet with the group in the women's department of Dillard's. I tried to get over to Colleen to insure that Andy was assigned with me, but I was half a second too late. I heard Colleen tell her group one at the Gap. Walter got her. I was sure he wouldn't appreciate her as I would have.

I spent my break at Bissinger's picking out raspberry creams in semisweet chocolate and caramels in milk chocolate, Patrick's favorite. When I found my platoon of eight white men and two black men standing around uncomfortably among the racks of women's suits, I started with a little pep talk. "Now we'll run through stopping a shoplifter. Who wants to be my thief?"

Jerry Cross stepped forward immediately, and I had a whispered conference with him to set it up. Then I dispatched the other nine to menswear. I gave Cross a two-minute head start, then headed for the ties. His mission was to pick up something small enough to jam in his jeans pocket, and I figured ties would be an easy snatch.

I sauntered around the glass cases that surround the cash register in the men's department and scanned the floor. I spotted five of my men, but Cross wasn't near the ties after all.

I rounded a rack of socks and looked down the aisle. No Cross. Where was the little bugger? I could hear my class shuffling along behind me. Then I saw him. He was already at the entrance, loitering, waiting for me to spot him before he left the store to go into the mall, as instructed. I kept my eye on him and headed his way.

He turned and left the store, forcing me to speed up. When I was ten steps behind him, I spoke aloud. "Excuse me, sir. May I speak to you for a moment?"

He ignored me the first time, as I'd told him to. "Sir, excuse me. I need to speak with you now." Jerry turned as I expected him to and looked mildly surprised. The kid was a good actor. As I approached to within ten inches, just enough to slightly violate his personal space, he grew pale. How did he do that?

"Sir, I'd like you to come with me to the mall office. I'd like to talk to you about the item in your pocket."

The hand he brought to his face trembled a bit. Was he really frightened for some reason? "Officer, I…" His knees buckled, and he toppled toward me. I wasn't fast enough to catch him, and he hit the floor with a loud thud to elbow and head.

"Go call the EMTs," I shouted at my class, and two of them broke for Dillard's. I knelt beside Cross and felt his forehead. "Jerry, Jerry. Are you okay?" No response in his face. I pried open an eyelid, but could see only white. I felt his neck. His pulse was strong and seemed to be about the right speed. "Hey, Jerry." I shook his shoulder. No response. Jesus. The kid was way too thin. Maybe he was ill. I stood and turned to look for the two trainees who had gone to call for help. I couldn't see them. The other eight stood around looking stricken. I caught the eye of the oldest, a thirty-something black guy who looked like he'd keep his head. "Hey, stay with him, will you? I'm going to make sure the EMTs are on the way." He nodded.

Someone from the back muttered that we shouldn't have made them all leave their cell phones at home during training. I ignored him. I ran back toward the store. As I raced in, I heard a hoot of laughter from behind me. I turned in time to see Jerry Cross running full speed on impossibly long, thin legs toward the nearest exit. I knew before I started that I'd never catch him. I grunted as I tried to get from zero to sixty.

"Tell them we don't need an ambulance," I shouted as I dashed past my laughing group. I could hear that two or three of them were chasing behind me anxious to see the student outsmart, then outrun, the teacher. When I got my hands on his turkey neck, I'd make him both sorry and soprano.

Jerry Cross stopped dead in his tracks as soon as he made it through the doors of the mall into a side parking lot. He turned and grinned at me like a puppy expecting a treat. My panting created a cloud of condensation around me. I put my hands on my knees and lowered my head, as much to give myself time to decide whether or not to kill him as to recover from the sprint. When I looked up, Jerry was handing me the leather wallet he'd shoplifted from Dillard's.

"Thanks," I said as I took the wallet, wondering how I was going to return it to Dillard's and save face. "Good job, there."

As soon as I said it, the laughter started up again. I realized the group had been holding its breath, waiting to see if Jerry was going to get creamed for showing me up. I grabbed his skinny arm and pulled him toward me. "Come on, let's go get a cup of coffee. It's on me." Over coffee I talked to them about things they could and could not say to a suspected shoplifter and listed de-escalation techniques. Then it was time to return to the larger group.

Walter had planned a field trip to the local cop shop at the end of the day. I begged off. Seen one police station, seen them all was my motto. He could manage that end of things.

Harvey Milk greeted me at the door with a complaining meow and twined himself around my ankles.

"Did I forget your kibble?"

A quick check showed a full bowl. I headed for the couch and fell into the nest of pillows and afghans left from last night. Harvey immediately hopped up for some nose-to-nose confidences and his belly stomp dance. I took a moment to absorb his purring song, for once fighting off my usual impatience with his repeated circling before he settled into my lap. Just me and my cat. I took some deep breaths, hoping the day's busyness would roll away. My best efforts to stay focused on Harvey, breathing in, breathing out with him, ran against all the puzzles Diane Mann had brought into my life.

With a sincere apology to Harve, I pulled myself up and walked over to my desk. I could look out the windows into Tower Grove Park and its deep blanket of snow. The answering machine showed five calls.

Lindstrom needed only a New York minute to tell me she was working late, see me tomorrow. No more and no less than I'd been hearing for months when she was in her nose-to-grindstone mode. I wondered if Doug Mann had started to put into effect his campaign to make her life more difficult. Couldn't tell from her tone. She certainly wasn't hinting she wanted me to call so she could confide her troubles. Nor was she asking me if my split lip had healed enough to resume kissing.

The next call was from Booth Heitner. And the next. And the next. Each time he'd said it was urgent that I return his call, and the only difference was that the last time he'd left his home phone instead of his office number, along with instructions not to mind however late it was. I dialed his number.

A pleasant, mature female voice announced the Heitner residence had been reached. I gave my name and explained I was returning Mr. Heitner's call. "Booth? I'll get him." Still pleasant. I thought I recognized his wife's voice.

I waited long enough for her to have retrieved him from the family room or kitchen. "Ms. Darcy? Thanks for calling. I need to talk to you." He paused.

I waited.

"You talked with Jimmy, Jimmy Sills." Not a question. Again I left the space for him to fill. He cleared his throat. "Well, we can't reach Jimmy. He isn't at his home, didn't show up for work today. I thought you might know what happened to him."

The thought that Jimmy was his responsibility, not mine, flitted though my mind. I shooed it back.

"I haven't a clue, Mr. Heitner."

"You didn't advise him to disappear for a while?" His voice teetered on the edge between outright accusation and still-struggling-to-be-polite insinuation.

"No. Why would I do that?"

That stopped him. A long beat. "Doug Mann talked with Jimmy. Doug thinks Jimmy was upset about your questioning him."

"Mann talked to Jimmy yesterday?"

"I believe so."

He damn well knew. But I ignored that fight. "Well, that might have scared Jimmy away. Mr. Mann was not in a pleasant mood yesterday."

Another pause. I assumed he was picking which thread he wanted to follow. Finally, he said, "I'm sure Mr. Mann was upset for family reasons. But that's no reason for Jimmy to take off. I don't know if you realized it when you talked to him, but Jimmy needs a little help in getting along in this world. My family has tried to look after him over the years. And we're just worried about his safety." This sounded like a speech he'd rehearsed, and all of it was delivered sincerely.

"Me, too—now that I hear he's missing. But I didn't know about that until this conversation," I said.

"You didn't tell him to hide?" Not so polite now, though a long way from Mann's confrontational style.

"Why would I? What interest would I have in hiding Jimmy Sills?"

I guessed he couldn't afford an honest answer to that. He shifted. "You know, Jimmy gets flustered when people question him. He's not used to it. He's really a shy kind of guy."

"I hope you warned Doug Mann about that. His interrogational style can be pretty intimidating." I touched my upper lip. Not quite so tender, but I wouldn't soon forget Mann's methods.

"Jimmy knows Doug well. He wouldn't be afraid of him."

I didn't respond.

"I won't have Jimmy harassed, Ms. Darcy." His voice had an artificial harrumph in it—Booth Heitner imitates his powerful father was my guess.

I admit it. I have a deep prejudice against being harrumphed at by privileged white men who imagine themselves powerful.

"I'm glad to hear that, Mr. Heitner. And just to put your mind at ease, I'll repeat this: I haven't a clue as to where Jimmy is. Or Diane Mann either. It's downright embarrassing to me, my being a private investigator and all. And it's curious how many people connected to the Teresa Rushing case are leaving St. Louis."

Only a slight pause. "Don't overreach, Darcy." An angry rasp in his voice.

"That's still Ms. Darcy to you," I said, but to the empty hum of a dead line. He'd hung up. I tsk-tsked. I thought it curious that Booth Heitner believed I might be hiding Jimmy from him. What would make him think that? Did Doug think Jimmy knew something that would help me help Diane?

The last call was from Toby Shaw, the man who'd befriended Jimmy Sills when Jimmy had been working at the old brewery. Toby wanted to tell me that Jimmy had come to Toby's house and asked for money. Jimmy refused to stay or to explain the problem. So in the end Toby had just given him thirty bucks. I called him back, got his machine, and asked Toby to call me right away if he saw Jimmy again and gave him my cell number.

I had too much to process: my client hiding, Doug Mann rampaging, Jerry Cross outsmarting me. Now Jimmy Sills was on the lam.

Doug Mann's motives seemed murkier and murkier to me. I resolved to find out more about that as soon as I could.

"Nothing to do for now but sleep on it, Harve."

No quarrel from him. He followed me right to bed.

CHAPTER SEVENTEEN

Thursday morning the Horizon wheezed like a heavy smoker, then coughed into life. Along the curb all the plowing and shoveling had piled snow high. But the weather forecast had said no more snow today, so Walter and I had decided the training would proceed eight to five, as originally scheduled.

By now city drivers had had a quick review in snow driving, and traffic moved along at a steady pace. No sideways slides or headers into ditches. Walter and the full complement of trainees met me in the Holiday Inn conference room, and the day proceeded as planned. The sort of folks who want to wear uniforms and guns are not necessarily the sort who enjoy a good three-day workshop—I'm not sure who's in that second group. But our trainees had got an extra buzz from yesterday's practicum at the Galleria, especially the part where Jerry Cross had outfoxed the dyke. So everyone was staying tuned just in case something else outrageous entertained them.

As for the boy himself, Jerry Cross managed not to gloat in my presence, though I saw a couple of the men offer him high fives. Well, we'd see who wore the pants when the job started. I thought the redhead was performing well, too, and would have told her so, but she managed to avoid any one-to-one encounters. At the afternoon break, I grabbed Jerry Cross by the arm.

"Wait a sec. Hang around after class this evening. I want to give you an extra-credit assignment. And don't tell anyone else I want to see you."

He pursed his lips but nodded, keeping his doubts to himself.

By five Walter ended the training with a final inspirational speech about the duties and rewards of security work with Miller and instructions about when to report for their first shifts. The trainees, eyes glazed over and bottoms numbed, melted away with packets and free ballpoint pens. Andy, the redhead, stopped by to shake my hand formally and to say the training had been great and she was excited about working with me. The little flutter this caused at various pulse points answered my earlier query as to "What's the harm in a little flirting?"

Lindstrom would have me for lunch. Wouldn't she?

Would she?

In all our off-again, on-again journey she'd never once shown even a speck of jealousy. Did that mean she didn't care? That she thought no one else would want my sorry ass? That she wouldn't notice if I were gone?

These interesting philosophical questions would have further occupied me, but Jerry was hanging around awkwardly. I asked him if he wanted to do a tailing job for me before starting at the Galleria. He was delighted.

So Friday, Jerry and I spent most of the day outside Doug Mann's house. I picked a couple of good spots on Doug's street where Jerry could see the driveway, but wouldn't be too obvious. I gave him the basics of one-man surveillance. Then I showed him how to keep his logbook. At the end of the day I took him back to Miller and gave him one of our cell phones. I told him I wanted him on Doug Mann until further notice. Jerry took it all in, a solemn, choirboy look on his face. After his Artful Dodger routine at the mall, I didn't trust the innocence to be more than skin deep.

I called the detective agency next door to Miller. They specialize in divorce and custody cases and have a posse of operatives who can tail like a shadow. I made arrangements for a pair of their operatives to work the other two shifts with Jerry, and briefed them all.

I put tails on Mann because I wanted to know what he was up to. I was also afraid of what he might do if he found his wife. And I had to wonder why Mann and the Heitners were so intent on finding Jimmy. I wanted one of our guys to be there if Mann caught up with either his wife or Jimmy.

On the way home I noticed gray slush freezing to stone hardness at the tattered edges of snow piles along the streets. I let my mind wander to ice used as a murder weapon that would melt away—once upon a time that had been an original idea. Maybe enterprising cavemen had used it—just grabbing the nearest thing. I was tired and a little ditzy and a lot hungry.

Lindstrom's smart new Jeep, only a little splattered from slush and street salt, was parked right in front of Arsenal. Maybe it was because I can never depend on seeing her, but my blood throbbed up a notch just knowing that in a minute I'd be seeing her face, maybe nuzzling her, maybe letting appetite rule.

I sprinted up the stairs and found her in my kitchen, hunched down with Harvey. A look at her face, pale and tight, told me she hadn't had a good day.

"What's up?" I asked.

She stood in the easy glide that amazes me. We're about the same age; why can't I do that? She unfolds like a cat.

She didn't hug me. Instead, she stepped back to lean against my short kitchen counter. "Mann must have burned up his fax machine getting the word out to the troops. I've been getting snubs all day."

I bit my lip to stop my impulse to tell her a dozen ways to fix it or to make my own noisy threats to Mann and his minions. Listen up first.

I nodded, stripped off two outer layers, heated mugs of tea in the microwave, all the while keeping my eyes on her.

"Anything else?" I prodded.

She gave me a funny, shit-eating grin. "You should ask. I discovered a bloody tampon in my middle desk drawer."

"That old gag?"

Her chuckle sounded genuine. "Can't you see them going on midnight raids of the ladies' and poking through the little sanitary bins to retrieve these prizes?"

"Any clue?"

"Actually, yes. Neely whispered in my ear the name of the biggest oaf in the lot, and I made sure I stopped by his desk later to thank him for the sex toy." She gave me her authentic wicked smile then, the one that reveals a free-spirited farm girl inside the straitlaced cop, the one who had all that exposure to manure and birthings which protected her from junior-high level grossouts.

"You're sure it's Mann behind this?" I thought of the steady undercurrent of homophobia flowing through the force since she was outed.

"Pretty damn sure. Some guys like Tampon Man will jump in at any cue. But part of what I'm picking up is that Mann's accusing me of messing with his wife—and of helping her hide his child away as part of a custody dispute. You know how cops feel about that."

"They think you're making out with Diane?" I heard my own disbelief.

She shrugged, a seductive sight, one that always distracts me in easier circumstances. "Come on, Meg, you know how this stuff works. Logic, even probability, isn't part of it. Mann gets results by stirring up what they're already scared of."

"Well, I certainly would rather have you tickle my fancy than—ugh—Doug Mann. Maybe if that choice occurred to Diane, she'd prefer it, too."

She tightened her brows into a frown. "Is there a weak compliment buried in that?"

My turn to shrug. "Why don't you come fancy tickling and find out?" I took a step toward her.

She put her palms against my chest to hold me off. This did not have the entirely discouraging effect she'd intended.

"Darcy, get serious. I have to do something about this."

"You could race through the department crying 'I'm coming, I'm coming. Lock up your wives or they'll be coming, too.' Maybe you could wear a blue cape." I stood on tiptoes and leaned over her forearms and started neck-nuzzling.

She pushed me back. Her expression showed she was fence-straddling. Maybe she was thinking, What harm can a little canoodling do? But that side lost. She pushed harder.

"Damnit, they aren't going to drive me off this case, if that's what Mann intends. I'm just tired of their adolescent pranks."

Lindstrom's blue eyes were charged with enough righteous indignation to stun a cow. I'd seen her depressed into passivity by the department's shun-the-dyke stunts in the past, but starting with the dildo caper, she'd been looking less like a doped-up inmate of the St. Louis State Hospital and more like a comic book Wonder Woman.

I flashed on a headline: CRAZED AMAZON COP RIPS NEW ASS-HOLES FOR JERKS IN BLUE. Inspirational, but right now my immediate prospects for hot sex bumped into her granite determination.

I backed away and fussed with the tea mugs. "All right. Work first, pleasure later."

To console me, she ordered a pizza and made it a thin crust.

We sat down at the kitchen table, and this time I coughed up every grain I'd so far gathered on the Diane Mann-Teresa Rushing case. I reviewed my chats with Vernon Cole and George Fowler as well as my calls to Booth Heitner and Toby Shaw. I underlined, emphasized, and italicized my belief that Booth was Jessica's daddy. How to prove it?

"I saw a TV show where the detective got the suspect to drink from a glass, then they got the DNA off the glass," I offered.

She rewarded that with a squelching look. "Maybe I could get Teresa's body exhumed."

"How would that help?"

"We could use her DNA to prove she's Jessica's mother."

That's what had started the case—Diane Mann's wanting to know who her child's biological mother was.

Still, exhumation seemed a big step. "Couldn't we just get Teresa's mom, Lorena, to donate a drop of blood?"

Lindstrom's turn to think. "Maybe."

"Won't we have to get Rushing's mother to agree to have her daughter's body exhumed?" I asked.

"Not necessarily."

"Won't it take a long time to get all the legal stuff done?"

She shrugged. "I'll ask Sally Doyle." The ever-so-bright-and-witty assistant Circuit Attorney Lindstrom had been huddling with for weeks.

"And more delay before getting the results back," I added glumly.

She used a long finger to wipe a dribble of pizza sauce off my chin, then smiled and stuck the finger in her mouth and sucked it clean. She gave me a cheerful wink. Not exactly the oyster sucking scene in *Tom Jones* but an encouragement nonetheless.

I struggled with my conscience. Did my luck depend on my caving now and agreeing her way was the right way?

"A long time," I said, maybe less determined than before.

"Doesn't matter whose blood we test—the results will take awhile."

"I mean the legal stuff beforehand."

"Ah, well—the murder is eight years old. You have to keep your perspective in cold case work." She used a napkin on her own chin. "Besides, the big thing is the formal request for an exhumation will have a more dramatic effect, don't you think?"

I guess I looked dim.

"On Mann, Darcy. Imagine how that will rattle his cage."

I did just that and then joined her in her grin. We slapped palms midair.

I was stuffing another triangle of pizza into my mouth when Lindstrom pointed out the biggest spoiler. "Of course, we don't have anything to compare anyone's blood to. Where's Jessica?"

Indeed.

Saturday morning began harmoniously. Lindstrom had stayed over, and in a burst of domesticity I'd made toast in the toaster she'd bought me a month before. Afterwards I'd stepped into my bedroom to dress.

When I returned, Lindstrom had found the houses for sale ads and had settled in to read them. She perused them for several minutes. Then she looked over the paper at me.

"You know, Darcy, I should have given the Toyota to you instead of trading it in. Your old clunker's reluctant to start."

I was offended on several levels by Lindstrom's casual slur, but I tried to shrug it off. "I'm reluctant to start in this cold."

"Ha."

"All it needs is a tune-up. Soon as I get a little cash put by—"

"Damnit, Darcy." From behind the newspaper.

"What?"

"You and Walter must be raking it in by the bushels. You just got the Galleria contract. Security firms are flourishing. Everyone is convinced they're about to be attacked by terrorists. You poor-mouth as bad as farmers." She came to a full stop, rustled the paper for a better look at something. "And, believe me, I know poor-mouthing farmers."

My blush didn't build slowly but raced up my face. I was ready to spit. Or kick the cat. Not Harve. Some obnoxious other cat. I searched for words. Before I found any, she rattled the damn paper again.

"If Walter isn't paying you enough, you ought to ask him for a raise. Or tell him it's time he made you a full partner."

I closed my mouth, cheeks burning hotter. Just because I couldn't keep up with her scale of spending. Now she was making it my fault. And all of this proceeded from her mouth quite calmly as though we were discussing the Cards' spring prospects. Calmer, in fact. I took a double deep breath. Some sense told me that if I didn't watch my words now I'd crash through the ice.

But she was on to the next thing. "Look, here's a perfectly good house in Soulard for $257,000. Same thing in Clayton would be $750,000 easily."

I closed my eyes and hoped it would all go away. No. I walked to the kitchen and drew a glass of water from the tap. By the time I swallowed the last inch, my blood pressure had fallen—I was almost sure.

"Ah, here's another one. You know I don't want to get too close to Michellene." Her old house in Soulard, the one where her ex had been killed. "But I don't want to give up on the whole neighborhood."

Maybe she noticed I hadn't responded for ten minutes.

"Darcy, are you there? What do you think?"

I thought I'd throw the empty glass at her. If I got down on my knees and begged, I couldn't get Walter to match her police pay, rental apartments on McPherson, half-million cash, and brand new Jeep Grand Cherokee. How could she imagine I might?

Her ex had been a successful closeted corporate attorney. Well, I was an out, blue-collar, hardworking PI, whose normal cases kept me busy in lumberyards and construction sites. I graduated from Belleville Area Community College and SIU-E, not Wash U. Maybe Lindstrom had picked the wrong gal out of the line up.

But I didn't want to talk about that now. I heard her moving toward the kitchen.

"I hate house-hunting," I said.

"Ah, well—you don't want me to shop alone, do you?"

Now that was interesting. The bright shard of it pierced my fog. Did it mean something? Sometimes Lindstrom's pronouncements tantalizingly sounded as though they meant something. Then I'd refer to them later and she'd look stumped. What I thought of as a rune was no more than a casually discarded and quite ordinary rock.

Why couldn't Lindstrom be consistent—like me?

Before Lindstrom contributed further to my confusion, she excused herself, claiming a full schedule of errands. That suited me. I headed for north St. Louis.

No one had cleared a path across Jimmy's front porch this time. I looked up at the sullen sky. One inch or seven? No answers from the gray, brooding clouds. I walked through the front entrance and banged loudly on Jimmy's door. Maybe I would startle him into answering. I waited a minute and banged even louder, hurting the side of my hand. Nothing.

What was it with this case? Nothing could go right. And I had the feeling that even if I tied up all the loose ends with a bow, Diane Mann still wouldn't be appreciative. I pulled my set of picklocks out of my coat pocket. Might as well get arrested for breaking and entering as anything else at this point. I was slow with the picklocks; I always was. It's hard for me to feel the subtle pressure that means partial success. Even harder when my fingers are frozen. Luckily I had five minutes without traffic in the hall and finally managed to outsmart the doorknob. I closed the door quietly behind me and reached for the light switch. Even though it was still early morning, the sullen skies and dirty blinds made for a murky interior.

The living room was just as I'd remembered it—nothing upended or cut open, no signs of violence. The kitchen was tidy, too. A cereal bowl half full of milky water rested in the old aluminum sink.

Jimmy's bedroom was small and musky, smelling of a man's sweat. His bed was unmade, but so was mine. I stepped over a towel and a dirty shirt and stood in front of the open closet. Pants, shirts, a couple of light jackets. No winter coat that I could see. I sat down on the end of Jimmy's bed. Where would you run, Jimmy, and are you hiding from me? Or from Mann?

Parents didn't seem to be part of the equation. Friends? Co-workers?

I rifled the drawers in the bedroom first, then the ones in the kitchen. Flatware, kitchen towels, the third drawer down was the junk drawer. Stubby pencils, an old pocket knife, a dog collar, some flower seed packets and receipts. There were several dozen cash register receipts. I glanced at a few. Over half of these seemed to be from the Northside Cafe. Had Mrs. Heitner told Jimmy to save his receipts in an attempt to teach him to budget, or was this his idea? A record of his days, a prompt to memory less labor intensive than a journal? Someone at the Northside Cafe would surely know Jimmy.

The diner was one of two still-functioning businesses on the block. The other was a small convenience store specializing in malt liquor if the lighted signs were any indication. I pushed open the front door of the cafe and was greeted with the smell of frying bacon and fresh coffee. I took a quick look around and chose one of the stools at the worn formica counter. There was a good breakfast trade, all black men, looking like they were on their way to work. They sat around four-top tables and in three booths along the south wall of the small diner. I looked through an open door into the kitchen. An elderly black woman expertly broke two eggs onto the grill and scooped up four others onto two plates. The waitress, a forty-something thin woman with red hair, stopped across the counter from me. She was a light-skinned black woman with freckles to match the red hair. She raised the coffee pot in her right hand.

"Coffee?"

"Yes, please."

She reached under the counter, pulled out a mug, and filled it. "I'll be back in a minute."

Why couldn't all relationships work so smoothly? I reminded myself I was not going to think about what Lindstrom's problem was

153

this morning. The waitress took plates of eggs and potatoes over to one of the booths and then came back to ask me what I wanted to eat.

"Two eggs over easy, American fries, and wheat toast."

"Onions in the potatoes?"

"Yes, please." She flashed me a smile and disappeared before I could question her about Jimmy Sills. Best to wait until the breakfast rush was over anyway.

The eggs were good, but the potatoes were a work of art, and I rued the fact that the Northside Cafe was miles off my path from home to work. One of the men called out "Tyrise" and the waitress responded. Tyrise...tie-reece; good. I repeated it to myself four times so I'd remember it.

"More coffee?"

"Thanks, Tyrise." I looked around. About half the customers were gone, but the others were finishing up and would be crowding around the register soon.

"When you get a minute, I'd like to talk to you."

She looked at me speculatively but didn't commit herself. I heard the front door and felt a blast of cold air on my back. Tyrise's eyes narrowed, but I didn't turn around. I figured it was some troublesome customer of hers. I didn't hear his footsteps, so when his hand landed on my shoulder, I jumped.

"What the hell are you doing here, Darcy?" His long, splayed fingers pressed into my collarbone before he lifted his hand. Now why was he here—was he following me again or here because he knew it was Jimmy's hang-out? And where was Jerry Cross—just outside, I hoped.

I caught my breath before I spoke. "Same thing you are, Mann—looking for Jimmy."

"Shouldn't have scared him off, then. Stirring up old shit that is none of your business."

"I don't think Jimmy is scared of me."

"What's that supposed to mean?" He lifted his thin haunch onto the stool next to me, but leaned over into my space.

"Jimmy has no reason to be frightened of me. I suspect it's you or the Heitners he is afraid of." I gave him a steady look. "Why are you looking so hard for Jimmy, anyway?" I asked.

"You know nothing about it, Darcy. He needs taking care of. The Heitners have always looked after him."

"Obviously he doesn't want them taking care of him now, or he'd

154

be at work as usual."

"Listen to me. You don't want to make an enemy of Richard Heitner. If you mess with Jimmy or Diane, that's exactly what you'll do." I was intrigued. He was a tough cop threatening to call in Big Daddy.

"Looks to me like keeping Heitner secrets is pretty lucrative, Mann. Is finding Jimmy a high priority security job for Heitner?" Or is it you who wants a lid on Sills, I wondered.

Tyrise approached him, pot of hot coffee held aloft. An excellent defensive weapon, I thought.

"No, no coffee," Mann said to her. "I just wanted to know if you'd seen Jimmy Sills in the last couple of days. A retarded white guy. He eats supper here a lot."

"Jimmy hasn't been in, must be a few days now. I don't work Thursdays and Fridays, though."

"Could you leave this by the cash register?" Mann handed her a card. "Tell the other waitresses that if Jimmy comes in, they should call me right away. We're worried about him down where he works."

I studied his raw-boned face. It seemed to me that you could see the meanness in his eyes and in the way he held his jaw. Mann was always looking for a fight. But he underestimated me. He thought because he'd got away with slapping me, I was as frightened of him as his wife was.

Now he turned his attention back to me. "Darcy, you are stirring up more trouble than you can swallow. And if I don't find Diane in the next day or so, I'll be back to find you." And he strode off on some boy business known only to himself.

"You looking for Jimmy, too?" Tyrise asked me.

I turned back toward the counter. "I am. And I'm beginning to think I'd better find him before that guy does."

"You want to leave me a card, too?"

"You going to throw both of them away as soon as I leave?"

"Yep."

"Then I'll content myself with this. Someone did something wrong eight years ago, and a young woman ended up dead. All the same people are stirred up again. I'm trying to protect the dead woman's daughter and her adoptive mother. And Jimmy, if I can. My name is Meg Darcy, and if you decide that I can help Jimmy, call me at Miller Security."

"Miller Security?"

"Yeah, it is my uncle's business. I work for him. We're on Gravois." I figured a woman who made a living remembering how people wanted their eggs cooked wouldn't have any trouble remembering Miller Security.

"Jimmy meets a white girl here. She's slow, too. Her name's Janet. She might know something," Tyrise said.

"Any idea where she lives?"

"Around here close, she eats here a lot. She comes in for breakfast most weekdays—between nine and ten."

"Thanks."

"I hear you hurt Jimmy, I'll send my cousin after you. He just got out of prison for busting a guy's head open with a pipe."

I squinted at her face. "You're just making that up."

"You sure about that?" She couldn't help herself, she grinned at me.

"Yes, I'm sure. Miller Security. Don't forget. And if anything happens to Jimmy, you send a bad man with a pipe after Doug Mann. Just keep that card so you'll know where to find him."

"I don't know no man with a pipe. But I could get a gun myself if I wanted."

"I don't doubt it, Tyrise." I handed her a worn ten dollar bill. "Thanks."

CHAPTER EIGHTEEN

Early in our friendship, Patrick and I started having Sunday brunches together if we didn't have sleepover dates. I provided the Sunday *Post*, and he provided Eggs Benedict—or whatever other scrumptious dish he concocted and served up with real starched napkins and fresh flowers when seasonable. He said it helped keep him sharp for impressing the "real boy" when he came along. Since his Joseph had been in Oxford and Lindstrom had been married to her cold case files, we'd fallen back into that cozy arrangement.

On Sundays like this, December 14th, when Lindstrom had indeed slept over, he set another plate. We'd reached the second-cup-of-coffee stage of the meal; Lindstrom was attacking the house ads with a thick red marker and intermittent little under-her-breath grunts that Patrick and I interpreted as signs of interest. Patrick's Siamese boys, Oscar and Quentin, were stretched across the back of his leather couch, from which vantage point they kept a blinking, sloe-eyed watch on the human entertainment.

"You know that taking Meg along will be like dragging a reluctant five-year-old shoe shopping?" Patrick offered helpfully.

"Ah, well." Lindstrom shrugged.

I smiled sweetly.

"She has no idea of the kind of questions that need to be asked about a house. No interest in storage space or light sources," he continued.

Lindstrom's head was still bent over her work. I stuck out my crumb-coated tongue. He made a disgusted face.

"Well, I want to know if she likes it," Lindstrom said.

I felt a swell of pleasure.

"She can tell you if she likes the colors in the bathroom," he added in a tone that said I-can-agree-with-this-much, "but"—quietly italicized—"she can't give you an opinion on whether the whole thing needs redone."

Lindstrom stopped marking. "Suppose not." She scanned a column, wielded the marker again. "Ah—" she said. She smiled a brilliant, persuasive smile. "I don't suppose you have the day free."

He smiled back.

"Why don't you two just go without me?" I said around my last bite of stollen.

"Oh, no, I still want to know if you like the bathroom colors," she said.

I was feeling more and more like that sullen five-year-old being press-ganged into shoe shopping. I took my coffee cup and strolled to Patrick's living room windows, which, like mine, look out on Tower Grove Park. The snow fairy had decided that the accumulated mounds were looking too dingy and was sending down a gentle drift of flurries to freshen up the landscape.

By the time I finished my coffee, the two of them were bent over the ads and reviewing her marked selections. "Oh, yes, I know this one. I know the guys who owned that. Good taste. You wouldn't have much to fix up," Patrick was saying.

I skulked over and sat down to pet his boys. They loved their old Aunt Meg. Soon each wound his sinuous way down to my lap where they cuddled in a companionable purring lump while my best pal and my love charted the order in which we would examine various properties.

Lindstrom and Patrick had winnowed twelve places down to six, but that still meant a full day. With heaps of snow everywhere parking was a problem. Soulard's Federalist redbricks hadn't been built with three-car families in mind. When we got out to walk, the snow piling up curbside and spilling over onto the narrow strip of grass or brick between curb and sidewalk added another barrier. The three of us slipped and slid and helped each other along like drunken revelers at Soulard's February Mardi Gras.

Christmas was only eleven shopping days away. Nearly every house had decorations on windows or doors or both.

Lindstrom snapped into her methodical mode and carried a notebook with little codes she'd written down to indicate the owners' answers to a list of questions she and Patrick had composed. Patrick was our designated charmer and carried the weight of social niceties. I was the speech and hearing impaired mad cousin just visiting from Milwaukee and trailing along behind.

After the fourth house factoids blurred: Was that the $198,000 house with the extra-deep closet under the stairway? Or the $250,000 house with the all-black bathroom and the skylight in the master bedroom? Was the second one the gay men with the puppies or the thirtysomething hets expecting a second child and yearning for the country? How did you like the kitchen with those tall old kitchen cabinets, the kind where the scullery maid had to get a ladder to bring down the silver trays and ladles for the formal dinners? No, I liked the redone kitchen, all modern and blond with the butcher's block smack dab in the middle. Did you see that antique clock on the mantle of the second one? No, that was number three, the one owned by the cute orthodontist.

Cute orthodontist?

I suggested we stop for lunch.

Lindstrom looked at her watch and pronounced that we had to press on if we wanted to see the other two houses. Patrick and I rolled our eyes, and I felt a gush of warmth for him. Lindstrom lives her life in boxes: Now I'm a cop. Now I'm a dutiful daughter of solid Norwegian farm stock. Now I'm a house hunter.

My life was consisting more and more of waiting around for a crazed lesbian lover to appear in the cycle.

The fifth house on the list was smack in Soulard, on Claude Street, one of those narrow streets where every redbrick house snuggles up to the front sidewalk—or at most has a decorative ribbon of lawn and herbaceous border. The house itself was narrow with two stories and dark blue shutters, the trim and front door freshly painted the same blue and a shiny brass door knocker adding a final touch. I have to admit that Patrick and I exchanged a look as we drove by that said "Wow!" Lindstrom found a parking space half a block down. She glanced at the Jeep's clock. "Gotta hurry. This one's an open house. The realtor may want to close up shop early." She fast-marched us back to the house. I admired her grit. Some of the neighbors weren't holding up their end in walk-shoveling, and we again had to scuttle and slide over little mounds of packed snow.

The realtor in question was indeed outside locking the door as we raced up.

"Don't close," Lindstrom said, more an order than an entreaty. "We got here as fast as we could."

The realtor was wrapped in parka and wool scarf. She had a round, pretty face, but just now we were pushing her right over the edge of distress. "Oh, my gosh, I was just closing. Slow day. The weather." The words came puffing out as though she'd run to the door or was hiding a corpse inside the house.

"I'm a police detective. It's really hard for me to come during the peak hours." Shameless. Her tone dripped sincerity; her blue eyes holding steady. Lindstrom stuck out her gloved hand for shaking. "I'm Sarah Lindstrom, and these are my friends. They're helping me pick out my next house." Then the brilliant smile, sealing the deal as she shook the realtor's ungloved hand.

"I'm Lauren Kolunski."

Lindstrom upped the wattage on her smile. "I'm really sorry, Ms. Kolunski, but I'd love to have a chance to see this house today."

"Sure," the realtor agreed, turning the key and reopening the door. "Let me step in first and find the lights."

Patrick's blue eyes were alight as we followed in Ms. Kolunski's wake and listened to her spiel. As usual, Lindstrom had a litany of questions—what about plug-ins per room, heating costs, taxes. The smell of fresh paint pervaded the whole downstairs, and the pastel walls—pale greens, light grays—showed the result. The den boasted a restored hardwood floor, saved from carpet, restained and buffed to a honeyed gleam. Built-in bookshelves flanked a working fireplace. Patrick nearly swooned.

Lindstrom, so charmingly intent on seeing the place, had, after getting her way, immediately assumed a cop's poker face, as though showing any hint of pleasure or even curiosity that departed from her set list of questions would hike the asking price.

The kitchen and downstairs half-bath had been remodeled. In fact, I was standing in the kitchen, admiring the clean blond wood of the cabinets and counters when I interpreted the slight uneasy tug I was experiencing. The slow trek upstairs to two bedrooms, a full bath, and a generous storage closet confirmed it—this place nearly matched the home Lindstrom had so recently sold on Michellene.

Oh, there were points of difference, of course. Probably the walls were a different color. This place had found more space for built-in shelves. These differences seemed superficial to me. Could Lindstrom look at these rooms and not be reminded of Viv? I didn't know what I'd expected. Probably a good number of Soulard's old Federalist houses had a similar plan with many of the same decorative features—from mansard roofs to the characteristic metal stars affixed to the outside walls.

I grabbed Patrick by his parka and asked my sixty-four-dollar question: "Is it too like her Michellene house?"

His blue eyes darkened. He got it right away. "Oh, Meg—think so?"

Ms. Kolunski and Lindstrom were huddled in the master bedroom. I lifted my shoulders in a shrug that tilted toward the pessimistic.

He shook his head. "It's such a great place," he said, just a whisker from whining. Living in Soulard tops his wish list.

I heard Lindstrom say, "Excuse me." She walked over to us. She gave us both a half-smile and asked, "What do you think?"

Although she addressed us both, she let her eyes linger on me. I admit it—just for a moment something like pride of possession fluttered through me. My opinion counted more, even though we all knew Patrick's judgment about houses was sounder. But the cloud that I'd cast over the house kept us silent a little bit too long.

"What is it?" she asked.

I shrugged, trying for neutral. If she hadn't caught the resemblance, I didn't want to plant it in her mind. On the other hand, suppose I said nothing, then she bought the house, and then six months later, having noticed the similarities, suddenly hated this new place. For a second I hesitated.

Patrick leapt into the pause. "Well, I think it's lovely. Somebody poured some big bucks into this beauty. Only thing, is it too much like your other house? Do you want a change?"

No doubt about it. The boy has all the tact I didn't get.

Lindstrom gave a small hmm. "I loved that house. I really want one identical to it. I just didn't want to live where Viv—" She didn't have to finish.

"The similarity won't make you sad?" I blurted it out.

I'll say this for her—she took a minute to think about it. "No. Viv didn't die in this house. The rest is wood and paint." As usual, she didn't straddle a fence.

I wondered about a relationship in which one partner was always more certain than the other, where one partner was much better off financially, where one partner called the shots. I was about to ask myself if that thumbnail sketch fitted any couple I knew, when she turned her dark blue eyes on me. "Do you like it?"

"Patrick's right—it's a lovely house." That did not quite answer her question, but she smiled as though it had.

"I'll get the information. I think I'll make a bid on it," she said.

"Just like that?" I couldn't fathom it.

"Why dither? The price is within reason. I've got the cash. I can get on with my life." She ticked off these points as if they were mundane items—and all equal. I wanted an explanation of "get on with my life" but realized I'd have to wait.

Patrick was straining to look nonchalant. Some of his buds in the gay community were used to buying, selling, trading at the six-figure level, but he never pretended that was where he lived.

Lindstrom excused herself and walked back for a huddle with the realtor who suggested we all go downstairs. She and Lindstrom leaned on the kitchen counter to fill out preliminary paperwork. Ms. Kolunski was now glowing. Her unpromising Open House had just earned her a Christmas bonus.

Midway through dinner, Lindstrom interrupted her laughter at Patrick's latest witticism and noticed my silence. We were the only customers at Yemanja Brazil at Missouri Avenue and Pestalozzi, and instead of booting us back into the cold and hanging up the "Closed" sign, they'd started us off with hot buttered rum and lavished two servers and the chef on us, pressing us to try a variety of side dishes that were otherwise going to waste that evening. Lindstrom had ordered an eighty-dollar bottle of wine to follow the rum and when that disappeared I think she went up a notch on the list and invited the waitstaff to join us in a glass. Patrick knew both servers from other contexts, and—amazingly—Lindstrom knew the chef. Maybe from her life with Viv. I didn't pry. Officially we were celebrating her decision to make a bid on the house.

So when she leaned into me and whispered into my ear, "What's wrong?" I shook my head.

"Nothing. I'm not used to so much wine." No way was I going to tell her that I disapproved of this splurge, that I harbored misgivings about the house.

She seemed to believe my excuse. "Ah! And you a noted Army drinker!" She put an arm around my shoulders and gave me a hearty squeeze. Her own eyes were bright with the wine and the general jolliness.

Patrick certainly had swung over to the festive camp. Whatever reservations he'd so recently had about Lindstrom's decision to buy had melted in the camaraderie of this moment: they were serving us a fabulous meal and we were providing them with appreciative customers on one of the coldest, darkest nights of the year when saner folks were home in bed.

I bestirred myself to make nice. I kept my wine consumption down to well-spaced sips. Crying in my beer isn't my style, and I didn't like the melancholy tug this rich red was inducing. I told myself I was relieved that Lindstrom, while not ignoring me, was not paying me close attention. I could fake grins and laughs, and I didn't have to pretend about the food—it was melt-in-the mouth fabulous.

I tried not to notice the bills she was peeling off a thick roll to cover the meal and the tip. Even with the freebies thrown in, she'd spent enough to make a car payment. Maybe I'd always cramp her style—a penny-pinching Silas Marner over in the corner, calculating every coin spent and begrudging it. That didn't suit my own self-image. I was a give-you-the-shirt-off-her-back kind of gal, wasn't I?

More than half the anger rolling around inside was my own irritation at not knowing exactly what was rubbing me the wrong way—except, in a general way, Lindstrom and her new-found wealth. How could she enjoy something that had come to her because of Viv's death? How could she forget where that money came from? Didn't that make Lindstrom crass? I wanted her to move past Viv and on to loving me. But— I didn't like it that I couldn't afford to match her generosity, meal for meal, buck for buck. No matter how many raises Walter gave me, I'd never catch up.

By the time Patrick hugged us both good night, I was looking forward to crashing in my bed. True, Lindstrom would stay over. We were getting more snow, and she'd had way too much wine to drive. But I had firm intentions of ignoring her.

As soon as we closed the door, those firm intentions ran against hers. She was onto me like a randy teenager and, despite our winter layers, she soon had us both stripped to our thermal underwear. I was disheartened to discover anew that Lindstrom in her long johns is as fetching a sight as many a platinum star in some diaphanous gown. My intentions were growing squishier by the second. By the time her fingers had infiltrated the fly on my steel-blue bottoms, my flesh was yelling louder than my crotchety old spirit. But the message was all encouragement. My blood was pounding so loudly in my ears that I must have sounded like a car with a throbbing bass that pulls up next to you in traffic—and even in winter sets your own car vibrating with its huge noise. Surely she heard my pulse drumming through me. I heard nothing else—not even the phone, not on the first two rings. On the third I pulled back.

"Ignore it," Lindstrom muttered into my neck. Her fingers were already warm. And wet.

The answering machine clicked on. My own voice droned in the background. Yes, just there, I was thinking.

"Meg? Diane." But I recognized her voice.

"Damn," Lindstrom said, but I'd already wrenched myself away. We were half on the sofa, half on the floor, and I hobbled to the phone, tangling in my fallen clothes.

"Diane!"

"Caught you at a bad time?" Her voice wasn't as friendly as her words.

"Just came in, up the stairs," I gasped. Why was I apologetic? This woman had been nothing but aggravation. When I'd suggested her going into hiding, she wouldn't even consider it. I wasn't going to let her off that easy. "What changed your mind about taking Jessica away?"

"Doug was so angry he would have hurt me. Ever since he found out that the police department was investigating that old case he just got angrier and angrier. I was afraid he'd put me in the hospital again."

"Where are you?"

"Someplace safe."

"I need to talk to you."

"Do you have anything to report? Anything on Doug?"

Pure acid etched the questions. Without a single profane word she dismissed my efforts, gave a scathing assessment of my abilities. I was at a loss for a defense. I pondered what to tell her. She said she'd known nothing about Doug's police work. Had he been equally tightlipped about the Heitner's business?

"Jimmy Sills is missing," I said.

"What do you mean, missing?"

"Gone. Not at home. Not at work. Not at the Heitners'."

"Why would Jimmy run away?" she asked.

"I hoped you might know."

"What does that have to do with me?"

"I'm not certain, but your husband is pretty intent on finding him. You said you didn't know Jimmy."

"Sometimes he was at the Heitners' when we would go there."

So, she had lied about that too, and—surprise—there had been social contact between the Manns and the Heitners.

"Why is Doug so interested in Jimmy Sills?" I asked.

"Probably because the Heitners are interested in finding him. Doug would do whatever Richard asks."

"How does Jimmy tie in?"

"Not at all with me and Jessica. I imagine the Heitners want to maintain control of him. Richard's very big on control. One of the reasons that Doug thinks Richard walks on water is that Richard has so much control over people and money and events."

She paused. I had to wonder if it was to makeup more lies.

"If you could find Jimmy, he could probably tell you where all the Heitner skeletons are buried," she said.

If he understood what was going on. A big "if" in my mind.

"Did Booth or Richard take a special interest in Jessica?" I asked.

"No, why?"

"I suspect that Booth is Jessica's biological father." I hadn't planned to dump it on her like that, but I was impatient with her disappearance, impatient with her withholding information.

I heard her sharp intake of breath. "No, that's not possible."

"If Teresa Rushing was Jessica's mother, I think so. The chances are very good that Booth got Teresa pregnant."

"Well, if he did, neither Booth nor Richard knew it because they never showed the slightest interest in Jessica. Never asked after her. In fact, Booth could never remember her name. He called her Jennifer."

I thought about that for a few seconds.

"In order to prove who the biological parents are, we'll need a blood test. Can we make arrangements to draw blood from Jessica?"

"No, the Heitners might be able to find out about a blood test. If there is any chance that Booth is her father, they mustn't find out. Doug is frightening enough. I can't possibly fight the Heitners. Just find out what went on. Something we can use against Doug."

"Is there a number where I can call you?"

"I'll call you." The line buzzed in my ear.

I rearranged my bottoms, walked to my Tower Grove windows, and pressed my nose against the cold glass. The streetlights were only fuzzy blurs against the dark night, but every now and then, like a thin laser beam, I saw a razor-edged slash of snow angling down.

I thought of Teresa Rushing, dead at seventeen. Thus far no one had cared much about her unavenged murder. I promised myself then that I would do my best for her—even though I was beginning to hate the one who had brought her into my life. Diane Mann had sounded snug and warm. Maybe she was safe for a while. But was Jimmy?

I turned around and headed toward my couch. Lindstrom had retired to the bedroom and fallen fast asleep with Harvey snuggled up behind the curve of her butt. He opened one appraising eye, then dismissed me.

CHAPTER NINETEEN

Monday morning she lifted herself on one elbow and pulled aside the bedroom curtain. The movement and the light stole my last delicious moments of sleeping warm. I squinted at the red numbers of my alarm clock—six-ten. Right then I gave up my fantasy of living with this creature full-time, unless she had moved into the class of people that can afford separate suites. She could have the east one and get up with the sun.

"Look, Meg, it's snowing again."

I moaned, thoroughly tired of cold, wet feet, and nerve-fraying commutes. Would it never end? I pulled her pillow over my head. Lindstrom rolled back toward me and snaked her hand under my sweatshirt. She twiddled my nipple.

"Ahh—good morning, my little pretty one," she mumbled into her pillow.

I lifted the pillow just slightly. "Are you going to jump up and go to work in twenty minutes?"

"Yes, I've got to go to work today."

"Then forget it. It's going to take me more than twenty minutes to become human, let alone romantic."

She pulled at my nipple harder. "Oh, I'm not so sure about that, Darcy. Seems like some parts of you are awake already. I need only ten minutes of your time and attention. Then you can go back to sleep."

Ten minutes. Now was that an insult or a challenge? An hour or two of post-coital sleep might just makeup for the added accumulation of snow outside. What did I care if Lindstrom slept beside me? Let her go out and slay dragons. I could stay warm and snuggly. On the other hand, if either of us took just a moment or two too long to respond, this could be an exercise in futility. What to do?

"Are you going back to sleep in there?" Her hand slid downward, and I made a decision. I pushed the pillow from my face and kissed her. It was fast and furious, and, as advertised, we were both sated in fifteen minutes. But I wasn't ready for sleep.

I couldn't shrug off Diane Mann's phone call. Her cynicism about my efforts nettled me. She was safe but the question of Jimmy's whereabouts suddenly came into sharper focus. Everyone connected to this case was looking for Jimmy.

As Lindstrom dressed, I tried to think about where a man with the mentality of an eight-year-old would try to hide. He had only thirty dollars from Toby. So surely he would go to someone he knew, someone he trusted. But obviously not the Heitners. What about George Fowler? Even though I thought Fowler an odious cretin, Jimmy might trust him. I ought to at least try talking to Janet. If Tyrise was right, Janet might be Jimmy's only friend not connected to the Heitners.

"Sleep?" Lindstrom asked.

"Er, what?" I asked, realizing I'd missed part of what she'd said. She stood at the side of the bed, combed and tucked and ready for parade inspection. I ran my hand over my sticking-up-everywhere hair.

"I said, are you going back to sleep?"

"No, I'm going to find Jimmy Sills today."

"If you're going to be driving around the city, you should take the Jeep. I can take your Plymouth. I'll be at the Clark Street Station all day."

"No, thanks. I'll be fine. The Plymouth is pretty reliable."

She made a face. "Have you given any thought to telling Walter you need more money?"

Sarah Lindstrom was, without a doubt, the most pigheaded woman in St. Louis. "The problem isn't lack of money, Lindstrom, it's excess of greed."

She frowned at me. "Oh, Darcy, he can afford to pay you more. Just tell him you need more money. Or get over it. Money doesn't have to be a problem between us, you know."

"I can see it isn't a problem for you. New cars, new houses. What's next? A boat?" I rolled out of bed for a fairer fight.

"Yes, I bought a car. And yes, I hope to buy that house. I want to be settled, Meg. And I want to share it with you. But you won't let it be. You're always fighting some damn war with me that I don't understand. I should be out at work. I shouldn't pay for the things we do together. I shouldn't buy things." She shrugged. "What do you want from me, Meg?"

"I want to know you care about something other than things, Lindstrom."

"Do you?" Her eyes pierced me like a shard of ice. "You've always made sure that there is a joke between us. Only so far and no farther."

She paused, added more softly, "Maybe I've contributed to it. I was thrown for a loop when Viv was murdered. But I've never doubted for a moment that we'd be together."

I stepped toward her, but she put up a hand to signal stop. "You have to grow up, Darcy. I do love you, but I'm not some fantasy lover. I'm a real person. Sarah Lindstrom." She turned and left the apartment quietly.

None of that made any sense. Well, maybe I understood the part about loving me, about wanting to be together. But the rest. Grow up? What planet was that from? I resolved not to think about any of it. Not even the "I do love you" part.

Janet was plowing her way through a stack of pancakes when I arrived at the Northside. Tyrise indicated my subject with a short jerk of her head. Janet was a short and plump white woman in an ancient red sweater unraveling at the neck. As I approached from behind her, I noticed her short hair was cut badly, like she'd gone at it herself with the coupon-cutting scissors. I put my hand on the back of the chair to her left.

"Hi, Janet. My name is Meg Darcy. Mind if I join you?" She looked startled, caught with three triangular pieces of pancake, dripping syrup, halfway to her mouth.

"Tyrise told me you are a good friend of Jimmy's, and I'd like to talk to you about him," I said.

She crammed the bite of pancake into her mouth and chewed, eyes wide and locked onto mine. I waited. Clearly Janet needed some time to think, and I steeled myself to stand quietly while she did so. Finally, Janet blinked and swallowed.

"Are you from the government?"

Now I paused to think. I was pretty sure that the truth was the right answer in this case. "No, I'm not from the government."

"This ain't about my check?"

"Nope, nothing to do with your check. I'm just worried about Jimmy."

"Jimmy ain't on the government."

I paused again. I had the sense that there was probably no short-cut through this minefield. Janet had her own way of establishing trust.

"Mind if I sit down?" I asked.

"Sure," she nodded.

"You mean that Jimmy doesn't get a check from the government?"

"Yeah, he ain't on the government."

"Jimmy told me that he's got a regular job. So he doesn't need a government check, I guess. I don't have anything to do with the government, honest."

"I got a letter. Are they going to take my check away?"

"Who sent you a letter?"

"Social Security." This, indignant, as if I should have known.

"I don't think they'll take your check away, Janet."

"Will you read it?" She began rummaging around in the cloth bag on the floor by her chair.

I let a small sigh escape. Clearly the business of the check would have to be put to rest before my more mundane concerns about a missing friend could be addressed. After several handfuls of papers, lipsticks, and a prescription bottle came out of the bag, she found the letter. It was in a folded business-sized white envelope addressed to Janet Seavers from the Social Security Administration. I pulled out the letter and scanned it quickly, then reread the first paragraph. Janet resumed bolting her pancakes. I glanced up at the top of her head. Her hair was dirty and very dry. "It says here that you have to be recertified for SSI. You have to go to your doctor so he can fill out a form saying you are disabled and need your SSI check to live on."

"What doctor?"

"The doctor that said you weren't able to work. Don't you take medicine?"

"The doctor that got me disabled?"

I took a chance that she meant diagnosed her disability. "Yes. When you started getting your check from the government."

"In the hospital?"

How on earth was I supposed to know? "Yes."

"I got no way to Detroit."

I frowned at her. "You don't have a doctor here in St. Louis?"

"I go to the clinic."

"Well, then, take this letter to the clinic and show it to the receptionist. She will help you with it."

"I shouldn't give it to the doctor?"

"You can give it to the doctor if you want."

"I showed it to her already." She grinned triumphantly at me, lips glistening with syrup.

I wondered if she had deliberately set me up to see if I would help her or if she just needed random reassurance from strangers that her income wasn't about to be summarily terminated.

"Good. You did the right thing. I'm sure the doctor will take care of the paperwork. How long has it been since you've seen Jimmy?"

Her smile dimmed.

"He's not at home," I said, "and he hasn't been to work the last few days. Have you seen him since last Tuesday?"

She looked puzzled. "Jimmy's not at his house?"

"No. And he hasn't come to work. I think he is scared of someone. Maybe Jimmy is hiding. Do you know anyone who might help him?"

"Scooter might. He's my ex. You got a car?"

"Yes. Can you tell me Scooter's address?"

"No, but I can take you there."

For a brief, shining moment, I'd thought I could be left to do my job in peace. "Okay, let's go."

"We're gonna go in your car, right?"

"Yes, it's right outside. A Plymouth." Now I was speaking in non sequiturs.

Janet didn't know any of the street names, but she mumbled "left" and "right" in good enough time for me to negotiate the still snowy streets. The north side of the city doesn't get as much attention from the plows and salt trucks as Soulard and the Central West End.

Finally, she picked James Cool Papa Bell Avenue, off Jefferson, as "Scooter's street." I pulled up to the curb in front of the sagging apartment building Janet had pointed out. Whatever caused the paranoia seemed to interfere with Janet's balance as well. She walked like she'd had a few too many.

The hallway was dark and smelled worse than any other human habitation I'd been in. There were three large bags of trash in the hallway. One had fallen over and split and looked as if something had rummaged through it as well.

"Scooter's place is in the back." She pushed into the deepening gloom of the long hall. We picked our way carefully through the garbage and around the empty 40-ounce Busch cans. The farther we went, the more overpowering the smell of urine. Janet stopped and touched my arm when she reached an open door on our left. She gestured toward it.

"That is where Scooter lives?" I asked.

I felt rather than saw her nod.

I stepped into the apartment, just a room really. It was square with a narrow door that I hoped led to a bathroom. The small refrigerator door was standing open and a pile of clothing graced the middle of the torn linoleum floor. A white aluminum cabinet stood open, too, and cockroaches skittered across the stove, oblivious to the daylight and our footsteps. The dirty blue mini-blinds from the room's only window were tossed on the floor beside the clothes pile. Janet stepped in beside me and surveyed the scene. "I wonder if the cops ever found Jimmy's laundry."

"What?" I asked.

"Jimmy said some nut took his dirty clothes. He was scared of him."

"He got mugged at the laundromat?"

"I dunno." The sound of heavy boots startled me from my dismay. I turned and tensed, ready for anything in that environment.

"Hey, whatcha doin' in here?" He was lanky, but strong-looking, over six feet tall. His long brown hair was pulled into a ponytail, exposing the black spider tattoo on the side of his neck.

"We were looking for Scooter," I said.

"The guy who lived here?"

Janet nodded dumbly.

"Didn't pay his rent. Got evicted last Friday. Left this damn mess for me to clean up."

"You evicted him?" I asked.

"Me and two deputies."

"Was he alone?"

"Nah, he had some retarded guy with him."

"Did the guy nod a lot?" I asked.

"Yeah, real nervous. Kept nodding."

"Thanks for the info," I said, sliding around him into the hall.

"Hey, what's your name?"

"Jennifer Slater."

"Tell the asshole he owes Burt five hundred dollars."

"Okay, if we find him, we will."

I grabbed Janet's arm and walked away from Ponytail. She started to speak, but I shushed her and hurried out to the fresh, cold air and the glare of the morning sun off the snow. I felt cleaner immediately.

"You lied," Janet said.

"Yeah, I didn't particularly want him looking me up. I don't think he would be a good friend for me or for Scooter, do you?"

"No, but you shouldn't lie."

"You're probably right. It was a shortcut I didn't need to take. I'm sorry, okay?"

"Okay. But you won't lie to me 'cause we're friends, right?"

"Right." I hoped I wouldn't lie to her. Perhaps if I were able to keep the acquaintance very short, I could live up to an honesty-all-the-time policy. "Any idea where Scooter and Jimmy might have gone? Another friend's maybe?"

"He might have gone to Paul's house. But sometimes he stays at the Light House."

"The Salvation Army place?"

"Yeah. It's nicer than the homeless shelters."

I knew better than to ask for Paul's address now. "Do you know Paul's last name?"

"Hunh-uh."

I sighed and wondered if this adventure was going to be a complete waste of time. "Can you take me to Paul's house?" I asked.

"I never been there."

"You've been a big help, Janet. Do you want me to drop you off at home?"

"I need to go to the grocery store."

"I could drop you off at the store. Where do you shop?"

There was a meaningful pause.

"How would I get home with all those bags?"

I thought of and rejected several answers, one of which was 'How the heck do I know how you get home from the store, we've only just met?' I glanced over at her. She was making puppy dog eyes at me. And she had helped me get a lead on Jimmy where I had had none.

"Okay. I can wait but not long, I've got lots of stuff to do today. Think you can do it in fifteen minutes?"

"Sure, no problem. I only need a few things. Milk and stuff."

The grocery store took a full hour and after that the pharmacy was another half an hour. Janet suggested lunch at Taco Bell, but I drew the line firmly and drove her back to her apartment building. When we got her groceries unloaded, Janet threw her arms around me.

"I'm so glad you're my friend, Meg."

I patted her back awkwardly. "Thank you for helping me with Jimmy, Janet. I'll call when I find him." I turned to go. "Wait, do you know Scooter's real name?"

"Scott Reuther. His mom's name is Ruth Reuther. Pretty funny, huh?"

The Plymouth was amazingly quiet after I left Janet. I headed for Washington and the Harbor Light Shelter. I had time to think.

Trust Lindstrom to tell me she loved me during a fight. Not a fight, really. She was the only one fighting. Was that her goodbye? I love you, grow up? Because I wasn't buying a car and a house? Because I didn't want to drive her new Jeep? Or because I was never relaxed with her—always jousting for recognition or power?

Neither Scott Reuther nor Jimmy Sills was a resident at Harbor

Light or at St. Patrick's, nor the New Life Evangelistic Center, nor the regular Salvation Army shelter. I left messages at each place for both Scooter and Jimmy to call me.

On the drive back to Miller, Jerry Cross called in. Mann was back at home after an uneventful day. Jerry was expecting the operative from the other agency to relieve him soon. I thanked him and told him his assignment would be the same tomorrow.

I was tired and dispirited. I'd spent the entire day finding out exactly nothing about Jimmy Sills' whereabouts. And I'd spent too much of the day looking at real poverty to even feel sorry for myself. Deprived of that well-worn comfort, I drove back to Miller Security.

Tuesday a little before noon the call came. It was Scooter. I introduced myself to him and said I was looking for Jimmy.

"Why you lookin' for Jimmy?"

"He's left his apartment—isn't coming to work. I'm worried about him."

"You ain't a friend of his."

"No, I'm not." I paused.."But the people who used to be his friends are the ones he is hiding from, I think. And I may be able to help him."

"How do I know I can trust you?"

"Do you have any information to trust me with?"

"Maybe."

I sighed. Scooter sounded like someone who needed a little drama in his life.

"Why don't you come down to my office and we'll talk?"

"Where is it?"

"On South Gravois, just this side of the River Des Peres."

"Man, I got no way down there. I don't have a car."

"Okay, where can I meet you?

We agreed on a Hardee's near him. I suspected part of the trust test would be whether or not I'd buy him lunch. He told me I would recognize him because he had on a Ram's ski cap and a Green Bay Packers' sweatshirt.

To my surprise, he'd already eaten when I arrived. His orange plastic tray was littered with crumpled napkins, flattened ketchup packets, and a large empty french fry container. My stomach rumbled. The french fry smell was strong and alluring. But business before pleasure. I endeavored to look trustworthy.

"Hi, Scooter, I'm Meg Darcy."

"How'd you know I was a friend of Jimmy's?" He looked rumpled, as if he'd been in the same clothes for a couple of days. His face was round, his eyes small and gray. He was slumped in the booth.

"Janet told me. Janet and I looked for you yesterday. Did you get my message from one of the shelters?"

"Yeah. St. Patrick's."

"How long have you known Jimmy?" I asked.

"Jimmy started coming into the Northside about three years back. He and Janet talked—you know, while they had breakfast. He comes over sometimes, watches TV with Janet and me. How'd you know Jimmy left his place?"

"His employer called me."

"Why'd he call you?"

"I don't know, exactly. He knew I'd been over to ask Jimmy some questions. Do you know where Jimmy is?"

"He was stayin' with me till I got kicked out."

"Then what happened?"

"We went to the shelter. Jimmy wasn't crazy about the idea, but he didn't have no place so he went with me. Right after we got there a couple guys got to fightin'. Not fightin', really, yelling and shoving. It scared Jimmy. He grabbed his stuff and took off like a rabbit."

"Where did he take off to?"

"I don't know, man. He wouldn't talk to me. He just left. He was really scared. Those guys weren't gonna hurt him."

"So you haven't seen him since Saturday?" The irritation showed in my voice.

Scooter reacted to it. "No, but I do know why he left his house."

I just stared at him.

"He's afraid of the cops."

"The cops in general or a specific cop?"

Scooter looked flustered. "He said the cops. He said they were going to come for him."

"Why would the cops come for Jimmy?"

"I don't know, man. All I know was he was scared of 'em. He was so scared he couldn't go home. I guess he must a done something. I mean, the cops don't come for you unless you done something, right?"

I thanked Scooter and left without any french fries or any clear idea of my next move in tracing Jimmy.

CHAPTER TWENTY

Jerry Cross called at three and said he was outside Mann's house but thought the other operative must have missed him because Mann's car was nowhere in sight. I told him to stick with it for a couple of hours. Mann would eventually show up at home.

Patrick called at four. He'd arranged to meet Carter Heitner at MokaBe's at five.Did. I want to tag along and meet him? I said I'd pick Patrick up at the bookstore in twenty minutes. When we were settled at MoKaBe's with hot chocolate, Patrick read my glum look.

"Trouble in paradise?" he asked.

"Yesterday morning she told me she loved me," I blurted.

He did a Carol Burnett reaction shot. "Well, that's a calamity." He leaned forward, crumbling the edge of his brownie instead of eating it. "Tell."

Suddenly I wanted to back off, shrug, dash to the unisex restroom. "Don't you think it's weird that she ignores me for months, then yells that she loves me in the middle of an argument?"

Patrick shook his head. "Sweetie, even I, who in a sad chapter of my life logged several hundred hours keeping up with *One Life to Live*, cannot deconstruct that question. Start over."

"She's more wrapped up in her work than ever."

He'd heard that before. "I thought you two were having great sex."

"Oh, sex," I said with a dismissive shrug.

"Yes, sex—you lucky witch." This was a reminder that his current significant other was still in Oxford, England.

"And she's spending as though Oprah's going to adopt her."

Patrick's eyebrows shot up. "Well, she did inherit a chunk of change from Viv."

"I can't keep up with that, Patrick. It was bad enough when she was just a cop with a great house in Soulard. Her folks have got plenty, too—affluent farmers in Nebraska."

"Maybe she doesn't love you for your checking account. Maybe she doesn't even notice that you aren't a scion of Anheuser-Busch or the Danforths."

"She keeps me at arm's length, Patrick. You know—like I'm good for recreational sex, but I never know what she's thinking."

He sighed. For once Patrick seemed to weigh what he'd allow himself to tell me.

But when he spoke, I realized I had heard the speech before. "Maybe she's afraid to get too close to you. She blames herself for Viv's death. If Sarah hadn't been a cop, if Sarah hadn't been Viv's ex, then Viv would be alive."

"Yeah, she's a typical cop—victims are to blame," I said. I had felt tears welling up when Patrick said maybe Lindstrom was worried about getting too close to me. Better to think about Lindstrom's shortcomings, her cop prejudices.

"I think Sarah believes that if you play by the rules, the universe ought to at least leave you alone," he said.

"Isn't that what I just said?" I set my hot chocolate down with too emphatic a thunk.

"Not quite." He pulled up a smile for me. "You know she's a total Girl Scout, on-my-honor kind of gal."

"A straight arrow," I said. Funny how easy it was to diss my beloved to my best bud.

"Well, she does like things tidy. But it worries her that that wasn't enough to keep Viv safe."

I skipped past that. Old news. "I must scare her to death. I don't color inside the lines."

He laughed and nodded. "Exactly. She's both attracted and scared by your scofflaw attitude." Then he looked guilty, as though maybe he'd said too much, maybe broken a confidence, maybe quoted her.

My mind was rushing ahead to sift through that when he sprang another question on me. "When did you first tell her that you loved her?"

I tried for a glare, but I admit it slackened into a gaping astonishment. Even for a best bud, he was pushing it.

"Well?" he prodded.

"That would be happening later," I said. I shoved my chair back and grabbed my oversized cup. "I need a refill." I started for the counter.

"After what guarantees?" he called after me.

I didn't have to answer that question because Carter Heitner saved me.

He was short and slim, blond and boyish—at least his face looked younger than his twenty-something years. Patrick introduced us. Carter was soft-spoken and well-mannered; I was immediately drawn to him because he was obviously fond of Patrick.

I did find myself wondering just how rich Carter was. He wore casual clothes with expensive labels. I knew Richard Heitner and his son Booth were the Heitner Group, but I didn't know if that meant nephew-cousin Carter was a "poor" relation or so rich the sources of his wealth didn't show at all. Patrick wasn't clear on what Carter "did" except for an extraordinary amount of volunteer work for the gay community.

After Patrick's introduction, I butted in with a question. "You know Jimmy Sills?" When he nodded I asked, "Did you know he has disappeared?"

"Disappeared?" Unless he was Oscar-worthy, he was genuinely surprised. He listened intently as I sketched in the few facts of my search for Jimmy. Maybe Carter had some ideas of where Jimmy might be?

Carter shook his head. He knew little of Jimmy's friends or interests outside the Heitner circle. He thought there was probably little there. Jimmy seemed to be under Uncle Richard's thumb most of the time. I asked him to expand on his early memories of Jimmy.

He considered, found no harm in it. Jimmy had been the son of a woman who worked for Uncle Richard and Aunt Adele. He'd been around the house as long as Carter could remember. When they were very small, he and Booth and Jimmy had played, more or less as equals. They'd spent hours together in the old brewery cave, developing elaborate variations on hide-and-seek.

For maybe five minutes, I lost him and Patrick as two local history aficionados rhapsodized over the caves of St. Louis and old-time breweries with names more obscure than Griesedieck Brothers. They ticked off Schnaider's and Uhrig's and Stumpf's before winding up with the wonderful Minnehaha. All one-time St. Louis breweries that took advantage of the natural caves under the city. Did I know Benton Park sat on a huge cave? That a cave had been used in 1861 to drill a Home Guard regiment? That the famous Coliseum where the 1916 Democratic National Convention nominated Woodrow Wilson was in a cave? Or that young white hooligans on the North Side had used the caves as their gang hangout?

Well, no.

Of course, they were giddy with the joy of foisting new facts on me, but then Carter's mouth took a downward turn. "Unfortunately, many of the caves were demolished to make way for new buildings or I-55."

We gave the caves a moment of silence. Naturally we'd all rather have the caves back for wonderful civic enterprises like growing mushrooms or housing beer gardens.

As much as I like to listen to Patrick's historical tidbits, I didn't want to waste an opportunity. I interrupted again—this time to ask if Carter and Jimmy were still close. Carter shook his head. Inevitably the class differences caught up with them. Carter and Booth had gone to private school, and Jimmy was put into special ed at the local elementary school. Carter saw Jimmy doing odd jobs when Carter showed up for the family gatherings; he and Jimmy remained on "howyadoin'" terms.

Carter explained that Jimmy had always been devoted to Uncle Richard. The boy had not had a father of any kind that Carter knew of. Then Jimmy's mother died when he was thirteen, and the Heitners just kept him. They didn't adopt him, but he lived at the house, suspended somewhere between serf and poor relation.

"Why did the Heitners take him in?" I asked.

He considered. "I think my aunt got little affection from her own sons. Jimmy was like a puppy. Later, Uncle Richard found him easy to use for little odd jobs."

"At the time of the Teresa Rushing murder, Jimmy was a suspect, wasn't he?"

Carter gave me a wary look. "He was questioned as a witness, but so was that other guy who worked at the brewery. Some neighborhood boys, too, I think." He took a sip of his coffee. "Uncle Richard was ready to hire a lawyer for Jimmy if it came to that, but it didn't."

"You ever think maybe Jimmy did it?"

He shook his head. "No, Jimmy's a gentle soul."

Like Toby Shaw, Carter had a protectiveness in his voice when he talked about Jimmy. I was thinking Carter and Jerry Cross could be brothers—slight, fair-skinned, except Carter, despite being older, was the one who had a teenager's sweet face and Jerry had a hungry hawk's eyes.

Carter excused himself. He'd suggested MoKaBe's because he had a committee meeting and his group had now gathered at the table in the back by the video games.

I held him up with a hand on his arm.

"You know, Jimmy might be hiding in that cave."

"I guess he might. He'd have had to take food down with him," Carter said. He shrugged. "He could do that, of course."

"Would you help us look?"

He considered it. "Do you think Jimmy is frightened of you?"

"I don't think he's afraid of me. I think he's afraid that he'll tell me something he's not supposed to."

Carter turned to Patrick. "You did some spelunking, didn't you?"

My boy blushed. "I've gone along on a couple of trips to the Ozarks. In the name of love, you know."

"Lust," Carter and I said together and laughed.

Carter turned to me, his face sobering. "It's not easy walking in the cave. We'll have to go through some tight spaces. You'll get your feet wet."

I gave him my best Girl Scout on-my-honor face. "I know."

He didn't look impressed, but he said, "All right. I'll take you. When?"

We made a date for the next night, and Carter wandered off to do his committee business.

I glanced at my own watch. Too late to go back to Miller and get anything accomplished. If we stayed longer at MoKaBe's, we'd need to move past hot chocolate into something chewable. Our felines needed feeding. We headed home to Arsenal.

I guess she'd had to park the Jeep down the block. When I opened my door and took the few steps down the entry hall, she was there, stretched on my couch as though she owned it. Even in cords and wool, she was long and blonde and fine. I tried not to mind that Harvey was perched on the arm behind her head.

"Hey," I said, not sure where we were.

She pulled herself up in the easy, enviable motion that looks like pouring water upward. She looked at me.

I pulled off my coat and tossed it over the wooden rocker. "How was your day?" I asked.

"I was distracted all day. First I kept thinking about wh...where we're headed. Then my brother Ben called." She used her strong, basketball player's hands to sketch a motion of resignation in the air. "I just wanted to say I'm sorry for losing my temper this morning."

Oh? My ears all but shot forward like Harve's when he hears package wrap crinkling. I tried to suppress a look of triumph.

"I've got a lot on my mind. Ben's got himself in a real jam. He's scared the bank's going to foreclose."

"He'd lose the farm?" I'm sorry; I couldn't help it. The words came out not with a genuine sympathy but a sort of mockery of melodrama. It just sounded so stupid to me—a bank foreclosure of a farm when we all knew the widows and orphans out on the streets were pinkslipped retail clerks and downsized factory workers.

"He might. He hasn't been in to talk to his banker yet this month. He may be so hip-deep in debt he can't move, can't make the investments a farmer has to make to get out from under."

I'd heard this in her voice before when she talked about Ben. She'd start out sarcastic about him and what a pain-in-the-ass little brother he was, then halfway through, family loyalty would kick in, and she'd try to offer a more neutral explanation of his latest predicament.

"I'm sorry," I said, trying to make it real.

"Anyway, farmers always whine about how broke they are, and Ben has been whining with a megaphone."

"And you think I'm whining." Not good. I didn't want her to think I was a mean-spirited jerk. Besides, as money always does, this scratched something deeper than bank accounts. Betty raised us as a single mother, and she had to scrabble and make pots of beans stretch. But I especially loved her for making sure we knew we weren't the only ones who'd ever pulled ourselves up from hard times. She'd succeeded with two of us. Like they say, two out of three. I was sad that three was Jen's father.

Lindstrom took a long time to answer. Then she kept her voice even and low.

"I see you don't approve of the house I'm buying, and I'm not sure why. But I think it's money. I spent a lot last night to celebrate, and you were counting every penny. I guess I'm questioning why. We're living in a time when the security business is growing as fast as dot-coms in the '90s. I'm wondering what your problem is."

My face flamed now. I could feel the heat surge through me like a sexual rush. "You think I'm a cheapskate."

She laughed, only a small laugh, but enough to pour kerosene on the fire.

"Damn it, Lindstrom—"

"No, Darcy—Meg, listen." She shook her head, still fighting a grin. "Not unless you've undergone a complete personality transplant from the time I first met you." She looked around her. "You don't spend money on housing. Your socks have holes. You say you don't send money to support your mother. For God's sake, where does it go?"

What was she implying?

"You think I'm doing drugs?" My own voice inched toward the upper registers of incredulousness.

She started pacing. "No. That's not it either. Why am I so bad at this?" Harvey jumped down from the couch and sauntered into the bedroom.

Lindstrom pulled a deep breath and waved her hands in a time out gesture. "Let's go back to my point. It's Ben. He's a married man with two young kids, and he's making a hash out of running his farm. Maybe I'm selfish to be buying a house just because I want it and—thanks to Viv—I can afford it. I don't want you judging me every time I buy a new sweater." She took another deep breath. "I don't think you're a cheapskate." Another short laugh. "More likely you'd give your last dollar to a panhandler you'd met on the street. God only knows what you're doing for a pension plan."

For just a flicker I understood her and sympathized. "You're not mad at me?" I've vowed more than once never to ask that wheedling question again, but it slipped out.

She gave me the look I deserved. "Exasperated."

I wanted her to define her terms but to press it seemed even more needy.

"You're mad at Ben?" I could feel the flush receding. My voice was leveling out.

A spark in her own eye flared, but she shrugged. "Much more exasperated."

"I don't want you to always pick up the check."

"Not likely."

"But we may have to eat a lot at Pho Grand."

"I love Pho Grand."

Funny. After the "L" word had been used for something so trivial—well, allowing for the fact that the Pho's number one in our tummies, if not our hearts—it seemed the wrong time to use it for us. For me.

Still, we were inching toward each other, our hands reaching out to touch, to smooth, to pat, our mouths eager to kiss. The smell of her morning soap hadn't worn off. Her skin was as smooth as talcum.

It was all going swimmingly when Patrick knocked his signal knock. When I opened the door, he ignored my mild disarray.

"Want to go 'round to the Pho to eat?" he asked. He looked past me and saw Lindstrom. "Oh, hi."

"Only if you pay," she said to him.

"Uh, sure. No problem," he said and looked puzzled when we laughed.

We chose to bundle up and walk to the restaurant. All the way there I congratulated myself. We'd survived a major fight. We'd discussed the taboo subject of money. We'd kissed and made up.

So why did I feel a knot of confusion tightening its throttling hold over my thoughts, choking the feelings that wanted to flow from my heart?

CHAPTER TWENTY-ONE

First thing Wednesday morning I marched into Walter's office. Walter and I never discussed anything personal if we could avoid it. Somehow salary seemed very personal. I steeled myself with a cup of Colleen's coffee.

I closed the door, which raised his eyebrows. He settled himself in his executive chair, his weight causing a wheeze. Mikie jumped up to his usual perch on Walter's beefy thigh.

"Somethin' wrong?" Walter asked.

I wanted to broach the topic of a raise—just soften the ground. I figured I'd sneak up on it, after reporting on my own workload.

I gave him a spare version of the Diane Mann matter as it now stood.

Walter puffed out his cheeks and shook his head. Miller Security doesn't do divorce cases because Walter can't stand their back-and-forth and unpredictability. He likes things black and white. The Diane Mann matter started as a personal favor for a wartime buddy; it was slipping over into the murky waters of a divorce case.

I didn't want to hear his standard rant on the issue. I hurried on to tell him Colleen had done some fine work for us, above and beyond the call.

He nodded and held up a hand. "That reminds me. I've been thinking about what you said. We oughta look around and see if we can find some girl to give Colleen some help." He looked up, expecting me to be pleased.

I smiled for him, though a tiny worm started a crawl through my stomach.

He smiled back, let it lapse to what remains of his boyish grin. "Thing is, Meg, what with starting this Galleria contract and all and not sure of how to budget all that yet, you an' me will have to be on a tight rein for a while till we see how that works out. So, if we hire another gal, our own paychecks may be on the short side for a spell. That a problem?"

I took it well. I forced a tight smile. "It's only money."

He liked that. Mikie did a little dance on Walter's leg as though the pooch approved, too.

I stood and made a limp excuse about getting back to work. I had to get out of there before I asked him if I could have a slug of the hooch he keeps in his bottom drawer, his one touch of Philip Marlowe.

When I closed my own office door behind me, I kicked the client chair and said, "Shit."

I sat behind my desk and traced the initials carved into its surface. I thought about calling Lindstrom and breaking off whatever it was we were having—a fling, an affair, a relationship, a commitment. I could keep it crisp: "Lindstrom, I'm poor. Sorry. Goodbye."

I glanced at my watch. It was only nine, and my life had already careened out of control for the day.

Colleen buzzed me. It was Diane on the phone, she reported. I grunted into the mouthpiece and stabbed the button for line one.

"Plans have changed. You are going to have to stop what you are doing," Diane started abruptly.

"Why?" I knew from past experience that softening my approach and fancying it up with lots of reassurances was probably a better way to handle a client. But she had lied to me repeatedly, disappeared and not trusted me to know where, and been entirely self-absorbed and high-handed the entire time I'd known her. I felt entitled to ask a blunt question.

"The problem is being taken care of in another way."

"What way? Are you going back to Doug?"

"No, but I think everything is going to work out. I won't need that leverage anymore."

If she didn't need the leverage I was providing, my guess was she had something she thought was better. "Diane, you can't just quit. We've stirred it up now. There is so much we don't know. Besides the police are investigating Teresa's death now. The truth is bound to come out."

"That doesn't matter. What matters is keeping Jessica safe, and I can do that. Listen, I appreciate what you've tried to do. You've stood up to Doug, and I know that takes guts. But all I've ever wanted is to keep Jessica with me and get away from him. Let the chips fall where they may with the police. That is someone else's problem, not mine."

This from a woman who had made it my problem. "What's happened, Diane? Have you talked to Doug?"

"I think I'd better not talk about it just now. After this is over, I promise, I'll tell you everything. Will you send a bill to my home address? I'll be back there in a few days, and I'll send you a check."

When she had hired me, she'd paid cash so Doug wouldn't find out. Why was she suddenly sure she could get what she wanted from him without fear of reprisals? And why was I so eager to make her continue the investigation? She could stop paying me, but she couldn't make me stop asking questions.

"All right, Diane, I'll total the expenses and send you a bill." I made no promises about my future behavior but kept my dark little thoughts to myself.

"Thanks, Meg. I will call you when this is all over."

I couldn't say I was looking forward to that prospect, so I just said good-bye. Being fired always pisses me off.

I dialed the number of the cell phone I'd given to Jerry Cross. It rang six times.

I was just about to disconnect when he tentatively answered. "Hello?"

"Hi, Jerry. This is Meg. Where are you?"

"We were at Crown Candy, and now we've just gotten off I-70 in downtown."

"Call me when he lands somewhere. I need to know where he is, okay?"

"Sure, no problem."

I hung up, put on my coat and told Colleen I'd be back when she saw me. She made a face. Outside I started up the Horizon. Doug Mann was definitely the wild card in the case. I figured much of what I wanted to know, he already knew. He was a cop. Surely he kept records of some kind. Perhaps I could find out more about the adoption, and maybe even the missing pages from the Rushing homicide file. I was traveling east on Loughborough when Jerry called back.

"Meg, we're downtown. Mann parked on Walnut, behind the courthouse. I couldn't find a spot fast enough so I stayed with the car."

Walnut was a block south of Market. My guess was that Mann had gone into the 1010 building to visit with the Heitners. "Okay, Jerry. Don't lose him when he leaves. And call me right away. I want to know exactly where you and your subject are at all times. Got that?"

"What's happening, Meg?"

"I'm going into his house, and I don't want him walking in on me.

So keep me posted."

I pushed the Horizon up another notch, or tried to; it responded with a hiccup and no noticeable change in power. I hoped Doug would have an extended meeting.

The Mann family home was in the Holly Hills neighborhood looking into the park. Like many of its neighbors, it was two and a half stories. This one was yellow brick with a Spanish-tile roof in dark brown. Big yew bushes crowded the front of the house. I tugged on a pair of thin latex gloves.

The side door was just a simple doorknob lock and, uncharacteristically, I had it open in a couple of minutes. I stood inside and listened for another minute. The house was quiet. I heard only a small whir from the refrigerator; the fan on the furnace was barely audible. I removed my boots so I wouldn't track snow through the house.

I looked down the basement stairs in front of me and up the three stairs to my left. I saw a corner of a cabinet. Up was the kitchen. Bottom up or top down? I didn't know how much time I'd have, so I wanted to make the most of it. I chose the basement. Unless Diane had lied, any papers Doug had must have been hidden well enough that she never found them in eight years.

The house was an old one—the walls in the basement were stone instead of poured concrete. The floor was damp, so the Manns hadn't stored a lot of junk. There was a new washer and dryer and a large, double-door refrigerator hummed quietly in the back corner. Nothing taped to the back of any of the appliances. Across the way, under the front of the house were some large plastic storage bins—out of season clothing—undoubtedly packed by Diane, so I didn't bother searching them. No workbench or wall of tools. Mann evidently didn't have time for fix-it projects. I was peering into the dark, slanted space under the stairs when my phone rang, taking a year off my life.

"What?"

"It's Jerry. We're on our way—heading south on Tucker." There was a pause in which I tried, unsuccessfully, to slow my heart beat.

"Where, where are you now? What cross street? Damn, Jerry, He's on his way home." I looked up the stairs. I would only need a minute or two to get out the door. I should calm down and wait. "Okay, I'm going to keep looking. You tell me when you cross Chippewa."

I scrambled up the stairs and raced through the kitchen—definitely Diane's territory—black granite counters, gleaming white appliances. A formal dining room with ornately carved table and chairs.

Surely not. Out into the hallway. Upstairs. I took them two at a time, holding the phone close enough to my ear to hear Jerry if he started talking again but far enough away from my mouth that he couldn't hear me panting in fear.

"Wait, Meg." I stopped on the landing to listen. "We're turning. I can't see the name of the street."

"What do you see?"

"Not much, Missouri Title, a car wash. This is Shenandoah."

I went into the first door to the right. The guest bathroom. Next door was the guest bedroom. Possible but still unlikely. The next room was obviously Jessica's room. A light pine double bed was covered in a mauve comforter. The curtains were cream with mauve flowers. Not in here. An eight-year-old's curiosity would have been too dangerous.

Across the hall, I hit pay dirt. Mann's study was a large room, maybe originally a parlor. It held a modern wooden desk, heavy and stained dark. There were interesting-looking file cabinets my fingers itched to get into.

"Hey, Jerry, what's happening?"

"He's just parking now, Meg. I've pulled over. I don't want to run up on him."

"Where'd he park?"

"I'm at Shenandoah and Salena by the car wash. He's down further on Salena."

Mann was at the old brewery. What on earth?

"He's looking for Jimmy," I thought aloud.

"Who's Jimmy?" Jerry asked.

"Never mind. Just stay in your car. Don't try to follow him on foot. And call me as soon as you see him again. I'm hanging up now. Don't let me down, Jerry."

"Okay, boss. I'll stick to him like glue."

"And call me when he moves."

"Right."

I sighed and hung up. What if Mann found Jimmy? I had no real reason to believe he'd hurt him. I decided to stick with plan A and search the house. Now to those filing cabinets.

It took me twenty-five minutes to figure out that there was nothing about Jessica's adoption there. Although there were several file folders of things pertaining to Heitner Associates, none of it looked incriminating to me. Certainly there was no reference to Booth's fathering a child. The desk drawers held office supplies and a pile of security supply catalogs. The bottom one was locked. Promising.

I whipped out my picklocks and fiddled. My hands were sweaty inside my gloves. I had the feeling I'd been in the house too long even though Jerry hadn't called back. How long would it take Mann to search the old brewery? Ten more minutes? Twenty? Damn. I felt the tiny nudge against my fingers. There it was, gently, gently. The lock shifted. I pulled open the drawer. His backup weapon and boxes of ammunition all safely locked away from his eight-year-old daughter. I picked up the old sock, heavy as hell, peeled it back to see the blue steel Smith & Wesson .357 magnum. I laid it back in the drawer. What now? I ran my hands along the underside of the desktop and down the interior of the sides. Nothing secreted there.

I scuttled out into the hallway, peered into the master suite. It was huge. A wall had been knocked out, leaving a long but graceful room with a king-sized bed and appropriate furniture at one end and three exercise machines at the other. I got down on my knees, looked under the bed—unbelievably clean. I felt the bottom of the chest of drawers as far back as my arm would reach—I'd never be able to move the massive thing on my own. Nothing under the dresser, either. I glanced in the drawers of the night stand. A *Playboy* and a tube of K-Y Jelly. Nothing under the twenty-five-inch TV. I called Jerry.

"Where are you?"

"Still here at the car wash. He hasn't been back to the car yet."

"Okay, just don't miss him, okay?"

"Sure, boss."

I had to stop, take a deep breath, finish the search. Darcy, where else?

Back to the first floor. The living room was directly under the master suite. The furniture in here looked new—plush and overstuffed chintz. The windows were draped in some kind of Martha Stewart combination. Nothing behind the TV. Finally—a sign of failure in the perfect housekeeping—I found a half-empty bag of chips stuck under the heavy couch. But no papers about an adoption.

I'd been in the house almost an hour. I'd give myself another thirty minutes, if Jerry didn't call before then. I returned to the second floor. Back in Mann's den I upended the wing chair. Something shifted. I looked carefully at the black material tacked to the bottom. Part of it was tacked and part of it was stapled. I pulled out my pocket knife and pried out two staples. Wrong side. I popped out three tacks and pulled a small cardboard box toward me, but there was not enough space to squeeze it out. I yanked out two more tacks. Okay, I had it. I put the heavy box in my lap. It was sealed solidly with packing tape so there was no way to open it undetectably. I pulled out the long blade on my pocket knife and slit the box open. Inside were two plastic bags.

The first held a big wrench, not particularly clean. I looked in the other bag and carefully pulled out a blue work shirt, man's size small. Reddish brown stains smeared the front. I sniffed it. No smell after all these years, but it looked like dried blood. Evidence of what crime? Folded into the bottom of the box was a brown envelope, unsealed.

I took a deep breath and pulled it open.

Evidence log-in sheets:
wrench with blood/hair evidence from vic T Rushing, 17
    belonged to Heitner Assoc. collected Dec. 23 D. Mann
work shirt blue, with blood/hair evidence from vic T Rushing, 17
    belonged to Jimmy Sills. collected Dec. 23 D. Mann.

I stared at the sheets as if they held the meaning of life. I tried to consider the scenarios that would make what was in front of me possible. There seemed to be only one. *This* was the dirty laundry that Jimmy had told Janet about. Mann had taken Jimmy's bloody shirt and told him to keep his mouth shut. Mann hadn't logged this evidence in—Vernon Cole had said there was no physical evidence and there were no initials on the form where it was checked into the evidence room. Mann had just written up the logs and stashed them. I carefully slid the evidence forms back into the envelope and folded that into the bottom of the box. Was it the wrench on the bottom or the shirt? No matter, Mann would know his stash had been broken into either way if he checked his hidey-hole.

I put them both back into the box, then stared at the open flaps. I didn't want to shove the open box back into the bottom of the wing chair and dump out its contents. I got some scotch tape from Mann's desk drawer and pressed a strip over the end of each flap. That ought to hold it for my purposes. I placed the box back into its hole and shoved in all five tacks, placing one over the spot where I'd removed staples so the material didn't droop. Then I pulled the wing chair flat onto the floor and sat down on it.

So it looked as though Jimmy was guilty and Mann had arranged a cover-up. But instead of destroying the evidence, surely the safest thing all around, he'd kept it. Stashed it for eight years in the room across from where Teresa Rushing's daughter slept peacefully. Why?

My first thought was not of my client. I didn't yet wonder if this was enough—accessory after the fact of murder—to satisfy her need for power over her husband. My first thought was of Teresa—that silly seventeen-year-old who was never given a chance to grow out of her adolescent romanticism. And her young daughter. All these interlocking secrets—how much would Jessica know or guess or wonder about her adoptive father's link to her biological mother?

My cell phone rang. "He's getting in his car, Meg."

"Is he alone?"

"Yes."

"Okay, thanks, Jerry. I'll be out of here in a couple of minutes. Just stick with him and log his movements."

"Did you find anything?"

Instinctively I lied. "No." Then I amended it to give him a partial truth for all he'd done for me. "Nothing about the daughter here at all. But I appreciated the chance to look."

"He's heading south on Jefferson."

"Thanks, Jerry. I've got to go, got to get out of here."

I looked around the room. Everything was as I'd found it. At the landing I shoved my feet into my boots. As promised, I was back in the Horizon in less than two minutes. I didn't pause to think again but ripped off the latex gloves, started her up, and drove quickly to Miller.

Once there I played solitaire and tried to think about what my obligations were to my ex-client. To justice. To Jessica, orphan of a crime. To Lindstrom.

I called Patrick when it was time to leave the office and told him I was on my way to meet him at home for our planned expedition that evening. I saw no reason to cancel our date with Carter.

CHAPTER TWENTY-TWO

Carter was five minutes late and apologetic. Parking was tight on Arsenal with snow piled everywhere.

He hunched over my kitchen table table and asked, "Have you found out where Jimmy is?"

I shook my head. "No luck so far, but before we leave, I wanted to ask you about something else. You said the police talked to Jimmy after Teresa Rushing's body was found."

"I think Doug Mann—the detective in charge—talked to him."

"Was it only Mann that questioned him?"

"I don't know. I wasn't there when they did it. But I'm sure Jimmy didn't kill that girl."

I kept my mouth shut. Carter hadn't seen what I'd just seen. "You said that Richard Heitner was going to hire an attorney for him but that wasn't necessary."

He nodded.

"Did they arrest Jimmy?"

"No, but I guess Uncle Richard thought they might. I remember he was talking to Gardner, his corporate attorney, about it."

"How did Booth handle all this?"

"Booth was out of town when they found the body—on a school trip. Later he didn't seem too affected by it."

"Were you surprised by that?"

Carter looked wary. "I'm not sure. We didn't talk about it, really. The family just sort of went on."

"What do you know about Booth's relationship with Teresa?"

"I don't know much. By high school, Booth and I weren't really spending social time together except for family gatherings." He paused, weighing something, then added, "I suspect he paid for her abortion."

"What makes you think that?" I asked.

"One afternoon I went over to Uncle Richard's house. I was supposed to pick up an extra punch bowl for my mother. Alberta, their maid, let me in. She went looking for the punch bowl, and I walked upstairs to say hi to Booth. He and his father were arguing in the den. I heard Uncle Richard say that Booth was dumb for believing her. Like the girl was saying Booth had gotten her pregnant because Booth's family had money. Booth didn't say much. Uncle Richard yelled that Booth had better take her to the clinic himself and make sure it got done. Uncle Richard isn't used to hearing the word no. And, unfortunately, Booth is just like him."

Carter met my eyes, shrugged.

"I went back downstairs," he continued. "I didn't really want to know any of it. I figured it was Booth's problem. I didn't even know they were talking about Teresa." Carter ducked his head. "I really didn't put it all together until Patrick told me you thought Booth might be the father of some baby. There was no other talk about pregnancy or anything that I heard."

"Did the police question you about Teresa's murder?"

Patrick looked appalled.

"Since you knew the cave so well?" I added to appease him.

Carter was grinning. He'd interpreted that interplay. "No, I hadn't hung around Booth and his friends much once high school began. I knew Booth took girlfriends there—a safe, dry place to have sex—but I didn't play that game, and I didn't want to be asked why. At the time of the murder no one questioned me."

Of course. Mann had known who was guilty.

We'd followed Carter's instructions to dress for clambering over rocks, but he pronounced our household flashlights inadequate and drove us to the K-Mart on Gravois so that Patrick and I had Mag-lites to match his own.

Traffic was thin but moved slowly. The melt had refrozen, leaving treacherous black ice in spots. We stayed quiet and let Carter drive his big SUV. When we arrived, Carter pulled past the loading dock and turned up the little side street where the houses grew shabby and parked next to the fenced yard of the abandoned corner house.

"This is where they found Teresa's body," Patrick said.

"On the lot behind," Carter said and led us around on the dark side. The chainlink fence that surrounded the lot looked as discouraging as it had when we'd been there with Lindstrom. But we hadn't checked closely. Carter walked into the shadows and opened a section with a sharp tug. "Watch your step," Carter said. "This yard is full of loose boards and chunks of concrete blocks." He used his Mag-lite to show us.

We followed him to the rear where the back steps tilted as I remembered them. The door was open to the cold and vermin, the windows paneless.

"Watch your feet and your head; this place is a trap," Carter said, as we entered the remains of the house. "Back in the old days several St. Louis caves had entrances through private property—a basement or an old coal shed."

He picked his way through the old kitchen, watching for rotten boards but knowing the way. My light caught a sink on the opposite side, but I hadn't much time for gawking. I was right behind Carter; Patrick brought up the rear.

"Pantry," Carter said as he led us through a narrow hall with shelving floor to ceiling and then down creaking steps. The handrail I reached for wasn't there; I put a hand on Carter's shoulder and felt Patrick's hand on my back as we edged down the steps.

"This place must have been empty a long time if you guys used it as kids," Patrick said.

"Off and on. There were renters in and out. We didn't always sneak in this way anyhow. We'd just go through the brewery and down through the main chambers, then back into the parts of the cave that weren't used by the brewery." The sound of Carter's voice changed as we crossed the basement. A few galvanized washtubs lived here alongside old canning jars and lots of spiders.

Carter's light found a door, its green slats peeling paint. I thought I heard a scurry as he pulled it open, the wood scraping against the concrete floor.

The basement was dark, but as soon as we entered the narrow tunnel of rock, dark changed meaning. We'd fallen down a coal hole. Our lights bounced along unevenly and lit only where we pointed them; outside that cone was a shapeless blackness, defined only when a foot or elbow or head brushed the intruding, confining, unforgiving rock.

Our movements were slow and time slower. I consciously kept my mind a blank about what I would do if we found Jimmy. Carter thought we were there to make sure Jimmy was safe, but my agenda had changed. So many people had so many different stakes in this mess. Diane Mann would want to know that her husband had covered up a murder, but wouldn't necessarily want that to be public knowledge—it would make it impossible to blackmail him. Lindstrom would want to be able to solve Teresa's murder and to have intact evidence to prosecute the killer.

And I had questions to answer. Would Jessica be safer or happier if none of this came out? What did I think was right? I needed to know what really happened before I could know the answer.

Each step was a conscious one that required attention. We listened more than we looked, and every scrape of boot against rock sounded loud. Even my breathing was loud.

We spoke little. Carter announced trail markers. "This place is honeycombed with shortcuts, but you don't want to take a wrong turn."

He told us when to stoop, when to duckwalk. My thighs had forgotten that mode. Every now and then Carter would say, "Wait here on the main trail," as he disappeared up or down a rock wall and into some shadowy niche and back again.

"What main trail?" Patrick whispered.

We soldiered on—uphill, downhill, over a small stream. We passed through two or three small chambers that had been used for extra keg storage. These had natural rock floors, maybe chiseled smoother, and old metal braces and wooden staves from broken kegs. Then we were in a huge chamber with a concrete floor and ramps for the main storage area. This room connected to the warehouse above by a ramp, and Carter told us huge, horsedrawn carts and later even trucks had been driven down this far.

Carter said the electricity still worked down here, but he didn't want to turn the lights on in case Jimmy was in the cave. Our chances of taking him by surprise were zero, but we might get close enough to talk him into coming out.

Next Carter led us through a wooden door into another chamber. This one was taller and narrower with at least part of the rock wall plastered over. Its centerpiece was a huge metal brewing vat with a spaghetti of pipes and valves and gauges streaming from it. Carter walked us around it. Behind it was an old-fashioned elevator which had thick ropes the operator used to pull up himself and whatever load he wanted to move.

Along the wall perpendicular to the elevator were three wooden-slat doors, one of which we had come through to enter this chamber. Carter led us to another, opened it and ran his light over it. Inside was an old Army cot with thin blankets, a Coleman stove and an old wooden rocking chair. On the shelves above was a jumble of rusty tools, some canned goods and three Coleman lanterns, with old-fashioned kerosene lanterns shelved behind them.

"The men who minded the vat would get some shut-eye here. Later I think the night watchmen used it," Carter said.

I stepped forward, picked up a can of sweet corn, turned it over under my Mag-lite. The expiration date was next November. I read it aloud.

"He's been here," Patrick said.

I tilted my light so I could see Carter's face in its diffused light without shining it in his eyes. I felt a twinge of guilt, but I wanted to see his face. Had he looked everywhere for Jimmy or had he taken us on a sham search, avoiding places he thought Jimmy might hole up? My own hidden motives made me paranoid and suspicious.

"I didn't see any signs of him anyplace else," he said. He shrugged. "But he could easily circle around ahead of us or get behind us."

"Or he could come and go the way we did," I said.

"Is he capable of doing all that—" Patrick paused, "strategizing?" He made a delicate search for words to capture Jimmy's mental capacities.

Carter made a noise, half-laugh, half-snort. "Oh, he's good at this. Except if something scares him, he's apt to hunker down, stay tight in one spot."

"What scares him?" I thought of the sound of little feet as we'd opened the cellar door.

"He doesn't like being yelled at," Carter said.

"Who does?" Patrick asked.

But I was thinking of Doug Mann. Hiding that evidence had protected Jimmy, but it had also given Mann absolute power over him.

The trip back to the surface felt like traveling on speed. Carter marched us up the metal stairs that ran alongside the huge metal vat and down a hallway, up another set of stairs, and down a hall that was bordered on one side by offices whose upper halves were glass windows looking out over the warehouse opposite the hall. The warehouse was now empty with only thick metal chains hanging from the ceiling, left over from some pulley system for managing the kegs. At the far end a brick wall reached from floor to ceiling, but about a fourth of that was missing from top to bottom. Around it we could see light which came from the holes in the roof and the side of the building.

Carter hit the metal bar that unlocked the door at the end of the hall, and the three of us stepped onto a loading dock in the wintry night. In the bright security lights from the corners of the building I saw our puffs of breath. The crunch of snow under my feet seemed barely audible after the noise even our careful steps had made in the caves. Patrick jumped down from the dock and offered a helping hand to both Carter and me. Neither of us was too proud to take it.

I stretched my arms above my head, glad to unkink all the muscles that had crouched through parts of the cave.

When we were back in his car, Carter said, "Maybe I'll check back another time. If he saw us tonight, he might have been reluctant to come out with all three of us there."

"There's got to be a safer place to live than a cave," Patrick said.

"If I find him, I'll offer him one," Carter said.

I said nothing.

I liked Carter. As he'd said of Jimmy, he seemed a gentle soul. I was grateful to him for all his time and trouble.

I mostly trusted him. But I wished I could have seen for myself that Jimmy wasn't in any of the byways off the main cave.

CHAPTER TWENTY-THREE

The next morning, I was at my desk working industriously at my computer when Colleen buzzed me to say that Lindstrom was on the line.

"Hi, how's it going with the Grierson case?" I asked. I hadn't told her that Diane had fired me. For once I was grateful that Lindstrom's attention was still directed toward tying up the loose ends of that old kidnapping case.

"We're almost there." She allowed herself a rueful chuckle. She knew she'd said that before. "Have you got a minute?"

"Sure."

"I talked to Colin Lanier today."

"What did he want?" I remembered Colin as a handsome yuppie— but one who'd genuinely mourned Viv.

"I initiated the contact, actually. You remember—he and Viv co-owned the apartment building? I asked him to buy me out."

"Buy you out? I thought you'd decided that the building was a good investment, that you were going to keep it."

"I was going to keep it, but Ben needs the cash. He's got to come up with the balloon payment on his mortgage by January 31."

"You're going to sell the property to pay Ben's mortgage?" I couldn't keep the disbelief and disapproval from my voice. I could not imagine doing that for my stiff-necked brother Brian.

"It's for the kids. I don't want the boys to lose their home. And I don't want my parents to have to do it. If I don't, I know he'll ask them rather than lose the farm."

I had the uncharitable thought that the senior Lindstroms could probably afford to let go of some cash, but, for once, was smart enough not to voice an opinion.

"So, is this huge wad of cash a loan or a gift?"

"Probably a gift. Maybe he'll pay it back someday, but I'm not going to plan on it."

"If he's that bad a farmer, won't he just get into trouble again?"

"It's not all his fault, Meg. All kinds of family farms are in trouble or gone. Corporations have gobbled so many up. ADM practically owns American farming now."

We were quiet for a moment. We both knew she'd dodged my question.

"It's important that he hang onto the land so the boys will have something. So they can go to college," she said.

I felt a pang as I thought of the miserably small savings account I had started a couple of years ago. It was my hedge against the unknown for my niece Jen's college. Although Brian made more money than I did, I was afraid somehow that when the time came to shell out for Jen, he'd find a way not to. She was the child he couldn't seem to get along with.

"I figured it wouldn't really bother you, Meg. Haven't you been unhappy about the financial difference between us since I inherited from Viv? That apartment building is the biggest chunk of it. Now it will be gone."

What did I feel? Resentment about the old story of the sister having to rescue the boys in the family. Grumpy that she'd made the decision without me. Surprised to find that both of us cared so much about our nieces' and nephews' futures. Relieved that money for its own sake didn't outweigh her other values.

"That's really generous, Lindstrom." I pumped as much sincerity as I could muster into my tone. I still thought Ben a bad bet.

"Ah, well—" I thought I could hear her blush. I definitely heard her clear her throat. "Look, I'll try to get away earlier tonight. Why don't I meet you for dinner?"

"Patrick and I had loose plans." I didn't want to be the kind of gal who dumps pals to make dates with honeybunches.

"May I join you?" Polite, not humble.

I sketched in the details, and we hung up.

For days now I'd worried that I couldn't earn enough to keep up with Lindstrom. It hadn't crossed my mind she'd solve the problem by giving her money away. I'd have to think more about what that meant for us. Not Lesbian paradise.

She was still bossy. And somehow, without really thinking about it, I had decided not to tell her what I'd found in Mann's house…yet. First of all, she wouldn't have approved of my breaking in. She would need a search warrant to get it. I would need to convince her and a judge that it was evidence in a murder case. The evidence I had seen in Mann's house seemed to make this an open-and-shut case against Jimmy, but it nagged at me that I couldn't quite understand why Mann would protect Jimmy and still save evidence against him. It didn't feel right. I tried not to think about having to tell Lindstrom later that I'd let myself in, found something, and kept it from her.

We said goodbye and I sank back into the computer, grateful for an excuse not to brood about the paradox that was Lindstrom and got an hour's work done before Jerry Cross barged in.

He was out of breath, as if he'd run from his post. "Meg, Mann was arguing with some guy. He was screaming at him. Sounded like he was ready to kill the guy."

"What guy?" I hit two keystrokes to save my additions to the file. I had been adding up Diane Mann's bill and struggling with myself about how much to charge her for expenses—including Jerry Cross's surveillance of Doug. I'd have to call him off now.

"I don't know," Jerry flopped into one of my scarred oak captain's chairs.

"What did he look like?"

"I didn't really see the other guy. Just the top of his head. He had brown and gray hair."

I pondered. "White guy?"

"Yeah."

"Where were they?"

"I tailed Mann out to Ladue. He drove up to this house—huge thing—the drive was really long, so at first I didn't know whether to follow him in there. But I thought what the heck. No 'no trespassing' sign. If they caught me, I could always say I was lost. I parked the car and started in. There was this row of bushes so I figured they couldn't see me from the house. I was just getting to the end of the row of bushes when this guy comes out around the side of the house—like with this big snowblower. He's gonna do the drive, and no way is he not gonna see me. So I jump around behind the bushes. Then I look across, and Mann is in this glass room. You know, all windows like. So damn, I think. I gotta get out of here, too. But I can't go around the bushes 'cause the snowblower guy has started up. So I look around and there's this big tree in the corner of the glass room. On the inside, like a banana tree or something. I figure they can't see through that, so I run across the lawn there and crouch down on the outside—at the corner of the house and the glass room.

"The snowblower guy is going down the drive so the noise is letting up a little, and I start to hear them talk. The other guy is talking a lot at first. I couldn't hear much of what he said, but then Mann said something about what belonged to him. The other guy is saying be reasonable and stuff.

"But Mann is getting really mad. I hear him yell that they weren't gonna do that to him after he'd put his career on the line to save his sorry ass. And then something about the other guy had a lot to lose, too. Then the damn snowblower was coming back up. Those things make a hell of a racket. And I'm like freezing out there. I'm practically sitting in the snow. Anyway, next thing I hear is this huge crash. I look up and this flower pot comes sailing out. Mann just chucked it right through this guy's window. It was a huge pane, too.

"Then Mann yells that he's got the stuff and both you fucking idiots are going down and I don't hear anything else. The snowblower guy goes by about three times more, and I'm getting worried about how I'm gonna get out of there.

"Finally I just decided to risk it. I walked close by the other side of the bushes until I was to the end of the driveway. I waited until the snowblower was up near the house, then I ran like hell for my car. I don't think anybody spotted me."

He looked at me expectantly—one of his angelic 'didn't I do good?' looks. It was going to break his heart that I'd gotten us fired from his first real detective job.

Ladue sounded like Richard Heitner to me. Booth lived in the city in the old family house. So Doug and Richard had had a falling out. Sounded like a big one. What could that be about? And what did it mean that Mann wasn't going to take it? It didn't sound like it could be good for my erstwhile client. I had just decided that PI ethics required me to try to get this news to Diane when Jerry interrupted my thoughts.

"So I lost Mann. He must have gone right after he broke the window. I decided to come here and tell you right away. Should I go back to his house, see if I can pick him up there?"

Briefly I considered how I'd break the bad news to Jerry that he'd have to go back to being a security guard instead of a crack detective.

He interrupted my thoughts. "Do you know who the other guy was?"

"I'm pretty sure it was Richard Heitner, Mann's employer."

Jerry grinned. "Bet he just lost his job. That guy couldn't be happy about his broken window."

I made up my mind. Diane was the most unreliable client I'd ever had. And she'd landed me in the middle of a mess. Tightened belts or no, Miller could swallow a few days of Jerry's pay.

"Okay, Jerry. You should try to pick up Mann at his house. We'll stay on him a couple more days at least. He is looking for Jimmy Sills." I sketched in a description of Jimmy. "If you see Mann with him, call me ASAP."

"Sure thing, boss." He practically skipped out of my office.

I called SASSY SALLY: Custom Fashions. I told Sally that the wool material was in. She got it right away. There. My obligation was fulfilled. If Diane called me back, I'd tell her what Jerry had heard and what I surmised about it. But for now I wouldn't tell what I'd found in her home. That was going to be my little secret.

After I hung up, I leaned back in my chair and tried to think about the problem before me. Why would Doug Mann protect Jimmy from the consequences of killing Teresa? Had it been an accident? Maybe Jimmy hadn't meant to kill Teresa. And what was in it for Doug? What would make him risk so much? Only his connection to the Heitners. Why was it that important to them to protect Jimmy?

How had it happened? Had Jimmy confessed? And how had Mann gotten away with hiding the evidence? There had to have been other officers at the scene. The uniforms would have arrived before a homicide detective. Unless the Heitners knew. Maybe Jimmy confessed to Richard before the body was found. Then Richard called Mann. But how had Mann gotten the baby? If Teresa had the baby with her when she was killed, then someone had that baby until the body was found.

The pieces just wouldn't mesh. I could think of a thousand questions but not nearly enough answers. Vernon Cole had been on the scene—I would try him again.

I decided not to give Cole the option of avoiding me by warning him that I was coming. When he answered his door, he wasn't particularly happy to see me.

"I thought Diane fired you."

"She did. But she can't make all the little pieces go back in the box neatly, can she?"

"What?"

"She can't undo what she has already done."

He shook his head and stepped back, allowing me into his house.

I headed directly for the kitchen and sat down.

"Did you know that Jessica was Teresa Rushing's baby?" I asked.

"Not then. While we were investigating, Mann told me Teresa's baby was with her friend. I didn't know Diane at the time, and it was months before Mann told anyone at the station that they'd adopted a baby. There was no reason to connect the two until Diane told me you said Teresa was Jessica's mother."

"Why was Mann willing to risk so much to protect Jimmy Sills?"

Cole shook his head. "I don't know. In one way it wasn't that much of a risk. No one was checking what he did. He had a great rep, and this was just an ordinary case. At the time I figured it was Heitner's idea. Once the connection was made between Teresa and Booth, they'd have looked bad. Looking back now, I guess Mann thought he'd protect Jessica by making sure the case wasn't made."

"Richard Heitner just handed over his granddaughter to Mann?"

"I don't know, Darcy. I never heard any of them mention the baby. It was like the baby never existed to Mann and the Heitners. I knew Teresa had a baby, but I sure never knew Booth was the father. I'm not sure I believe it now. It was like the baby never existed to them."

"Didn't you think it odd that you didn't find any physical evidence at all?"

"No, we searched that cave three times. The only things we found were that drop of blood and the baby blanket."

"Who found that blanket?"

"I did."

"And then it disappeared?"

Cole nodded. "I don't know—you connect the dots. Mann didn't want that case solved, and he managed it."

"Until now."

"Don't do it, Darcy. Whatever happened, dragging it out in the open won't help Diane or Jessica. That little girl just needs her mother, and they both need Doug Mann to let them go—the controlling bastard."

"You'd better warn Diane that it's not over yet. I've left a message for her, but she hasn't called me back. Doug has had an argument with Richard Heitner. I'll do all I can to protect Diane, but Doug Mann is coming apart at the seams."

I wasn't any happier when I left Cole's house than when I'd come. The story didn't fit together for me. Why would Jimmy have killed Teresa? I could think of no convincing motive. The story that he wanted sex and she didn't sounded dubious. Seemed to me everyone who'd advanced that motive was relying on old prejudices about the developmentally disabled. No one who knew Jimmy well had ever suggested that he was a likely rapist.

And what could have provoked Mann to protect Jimmy when the stakes were so high? Despite what Cole said, if something had gone wrong, Mann would have lost his career. Surely that was what Mann had meant when Jerry overheard him complaining about how he was treated after all he'd done for them.

Mann would have felt safer arranging this cover-up if he had known about the murder before the boys found the body. If Jimmy had confessed to Richard and Richard had called Mann to the scene—to protect Jimmy, to protect his son. Because inevitably Teresa would be linked to Booth who had fathered that child. And Teresa had brought the baby to him, not to Jimmy.

What if I substituted Booth for Jimmy? Teresa brings the baby to Booth. They argue. Booth whacks her in the head with a wrench. Booth tells Daddy. Richard summons Mann, and Mann says he'll handle it. He makes sure there is no physical evidence of Booth at the scene. Moving the body gets the corpse off Heitner property and gives Mann a couple of days to make his arrangements. He puts blood on Jimmy's shirt. Or maybe he makes Jimmy help carry the body, to frighten Jimmy, to keep him from telling. So Mann makes Jimmy take off his shirt and threatens that if he ever tells anyone about the body, the shirt is evidence that Jimmy killed Teresa. That keeps Jimmy quiet and allows the Heitners the added safety of a fallback position in case the pressure to solve Teresa's murder gets too great. Mann can prove Jimmy did it.

And Mann picks up the baby and takes her home to his wife. Jessica is his reward for protecting Booth Heitner.

CHAPTER TWENTY-FOUR

I went to get Patrick. I wanted a chance to talk things over with him before I had to spill this story to Lindstrom. While I was out, she'd called to say she was running late—surprise, surprise.

When Patrick and I got back to Miller, we had the place to ourselves. He propped his boots on the edge of my desk and listened attentively while I recited what I'd done and what I thought. Talking about the cover-up made me itchy.

Something hit the door outside three times—hard. Then came a sharp rap on the glass. We both jumped to our feet with dumbfounded looks and hurried to the front. While we weren't paying attention, dusk had become dark, and the streetlight behind the small figure initially concealed her identity. Then recognition came—my recent client, Diane Mann. I unlocked the door.

She wore wool slacks and a casual top and the open car coat was cashmere, but otherwise she in no way resembled the woman who had walked into my office and demanded that I help her find her daughter's mother. Diane's face was an unnatural white with only smeared mascara remaining as makeup and strange red blotches and gray grime around her mouth.

"Meg, you've got to help!"

Something in her voice made me hear beyond the command.

"What happened?" I asked.

"He's taken Jessica." As though that explained everything, as though it always would for Diane.

"Doug?"

She shook her head. "No. Booth Heitner."

Patrick and I exchanged a quick, befuddled glance.

"Why?" I asked.

"He's using her against Doug. You've got to help me."

Patrick had taken her elbow and was steering her toward the nubby orange couch.

"Sit," I said. "Tell me what happened." I squatted in front of her, looked into her eyes.

"We don't have time." Her voice was scratchy. I saw tears well, but she fought them off.

"I can't help you unless I know what happened," I said.

She nodded and sniffed and used the back of her wrist to wipe her nose. That unselfconscious gesture sent her credibility stock soaring—not least because I saw an ugly red welt on her wrist.

"Booth found Jessica and me at the motel where we were staying. He forced his way in, tied me up and took Jessica. He promised he'd bring her back, but he needed her to get to Doug."

Her stories always had loose ends flapping.

"What was happening with Doug? Was it because Doug and Richard fought?" I asked.

She nodded. "Doug was threatening to go to the police unless Booth and Richard helped Doug get Jessica back."

"To the police about what?"

"About Teresa's murder." She looked up at Patrick, a faint ghost of her usual manner in her glance. "Could I have a drink of water?"

My boy hurried to the kitchen.

Diane leaned toward me, lowered her voice. "Booth admitted that Doug helped him after Teresa was dead. Booth killed her, and Doug was able to make sure the investigation failed. Booth said Doug was supposed to blame Jimmy, but it was too late now."

I rocked back on my heels. "If Doug goes to the police with this story, he'll lose Jessica."

"It was all or nothing. He'd lose Jessica, but Booth would be charged with Teresa's murder. Doug figured Booth would rather help get Jessica back than go to prison."

I thought a moment.

Patrick was back, offering the glass of water. She sipped it delicately at first, then drank it half down. "Thank you," she said.

I stood up.

Her eyes widened as though I'd intimidated her. But she steadied herself, went on. "Doug was furious with the Heitners. He thought they'd betrayed him, helped me hide Jessica. He thought the only leverage he had was to threaten to expose Booth."

And Booth had decided his best leverage to get to Doug was Jessica. I mulled over the implications.

"How did you get away?" Patrick asked while I was thinking.

"Vernon Cole knew where I was hiding. He came to warn me after he talked to Meg. He's gone now to try to find Jessica."

I didn't ask her why she hadn't gone to the police. But I looked at Patrick and said, "Lindstrom."

He got it and walked back to my office to call her. I looked at Diane. "Can you drive?"

"I got here."

"Good. Drive to your Uncle Truman's and stay put till you hear from me. Give me Cole's cell phone number. If I get a lead, I'll call him. You call and tell him to do the same for me."

I offered her a hand up. "We'll find her."

The look she gave me showed how desperately she wanted to believe me.

CHAPTER TWENTY-FIVE

A cold three-quarter moon shone on the refrozen piles of snow, a noirish play of light and shadow from buildings and streetlamps. Patrick and I rode in silence. My brain buzzed. What if I was wrong? This melodrama could be enacted on any stage—in the cave or miles away in another motel room or somewhere else where I'd never find them in time, miles from where the Horizon churned through the night.

Five minutes from the Heitner Brewery I told Patrick to try Lindstrom again. He ran through the short list of numbers that might reach her. No luck. Damn woman. What was wrong with her pager?

But my thoughts snapped back: Jessica, Jessica. For the first time I'd seen Diane's face unguarded. Her urgency was contagious. If any of them wanted Jessica safe, Booth was the least likely candidate.

When we reached the brewery, I made a slow circuit, checking out the vehicles parked nearby. Along Lemp I recognized Toby Shaw's SUV in front of his house. Patrick caught my eye and nodded. Other vehicles were scattered along the curbs on Lemp and on Victor, which ran perpendicular to it. On the brewery's back side, where the loading dock ran, I saw no cars. But down James, the stubby street that ran into this area, a dented old Chevy was parked outside one of the street's shabby but still occupied houses, and, farther along, a sleek, supersized SUV. The license read Koenig, the old family name, the old Heitner lager. I pulled behind it.

I shut off the Horizon, reached under my parka for the .38. Patrick looked away. I expect him to start closing his eyes at the sight of guns. I had no time for sympathy. I got out, and he followed. I shooed him back with a wave of my hand while I kept my eyes on the SUV. It was empty. I touched the hood. Still some warmth there, despite the sharp cold of the night.

"You got your Mag-lite?" I asked.

He nodded. He looked at me, waiting for my plan. But except for the thudding repetition of Jessica's name, my mind careened from thought to thought, panic to panic, without any coherent plan.

"You think he went in that way?" Patrick asked softly, indicating by the nod of his head the old house where Teresa's body had been found on the back lot.

"Maybe. Though if he's handling an eight-year-old who's struggling—" I didn't finish. Maybe she wasn't struggling.

"Or maybe he went through the front way but plans to leave this way," Patrick said.

Even harder, to come out this back way with a struggling eight-year-old.

But suppose Booth had lied to Diane. Maybe he had no intention of returning Jessica. Or maybe, and this was no comfort, he hadn't decided. He was going to wing it, improvise.

My shudder wasn't from the cold. Patrick didn't notice. "If we pay attention to the landmarks Carter gave us, we'll be all right," he said.

I didn't answer.

"We could go in the front way or through the hole in the warehouse building on Lemp," he said.

I shook my head. If I were Booth, I'd be waiting for Doug to come in one of those ways. Booth knew the cave intimately from years of playing in it: first hide and seek, next hide and sex, then hide and death.

"To get behind Booth, we need to go this back way," I said.

I hadn't seen any sign of a vehicle that looked like Mann's.

"Try Neely," I said and dictated the number. But Neely had gone for the evening, and no one was giving out his home number to just any citizen who asked.

I thought about Jessica. We were going to have to do this. Plan or no. Booth had chosen the stage, but he was going to have a couple of extra actors.

"Okay, you lead, Tonto," I said.

"Yeah, white man. I notice who always goes first." His smile cheered me. When this was over, we'd have hot chocolate and chocolate chip cookies and whatever else chocolate we could concoct from his kitchen. If Jessica behaved, we'd let her have some, too.

I was sure Patrick had grasped more of Carter's tutorial on the cave. Still, I didn't like it that he was unarmed, though reason told me someone so gun-shy was likely to be more endangered than protected by carrying one. All these conflicting thoughts flickered through my mind as I followed his long legs down the sidewalk, around the house, and up the tilted wooden steps.

I wasn't sure how much ahead of us Booth was. Had he taken Jessica straight from the motel to the brewery? Did he stop to call Mann or did Booth bring Jessica here, planning to leave her while he called Mann? From here on we were in Booth's territory.

We had to use our Mag-lites as soon as we stepped inside the house. Despite the open doors and windows and moonlight, too many shadows obscured the floor for us to see. We picked our way over rotting boards to the pantry door and from there down the basement steps, slanted and unsteady.

When Carter had led us through, had he pulled the door back to its original position? Would Booth have noticed? I wanted every advantage and hoped that Booth thought no one had been in the cave in years.

Then we were in the narrow tunnel that led toward the brewery, making the long, claustrophobic trek with my eyes focused on Patrick's bluejeaned bottom or on my own clumsy feet. All the sensations that had crept through my senses the first time rushed back: the damp, earthy smells; the harsh, scraping rock face; our echoed breathing magnified by silence.

We kept the flashlights low, wanting their illumination for us, not Booth. I gave up trying to think about the larger picture and simply inched forward. Already my back longed to stretch upright. I thought how easily we could have crossed the few yards into the building if we were on the surface.

Just as I felt I couldn't duckwalk another minute, Patrick uncoiled in front of me and patted a big, trashcan-size rock to his left, slanting his flashlight so I could see. I remembered it, but how he had spotted it, off the immediate trail as it was, I had no idea. I leaned forward and squeezed his arm to say thanks. We moved on, passing the temptation to turn left into that spur.

Suppose Booth was hidden down that offshoot? Then he'd be behind us. But surely not. He'd want to get closer to one of the main chambers of the cave, somewhere Doug could find.

We inched on. I was sweating. We'd left behind the biting cold of the surface world. The rock I touched still felt cool, but I smelled my sweat and felt it trickle down my spine. No use lying: this was fear sweat. I tugged at Patrick's coat to get him to stop and cocked my head to listen. All our foot scuffles sounded amplified to me. If Booth were anywhere near, he'd surely hear us even if he didn't see our lights. I opened my parka to the waist, made sure I could reach my gun. I patted Patrick's arm to signal him onward.

Carter's next trail marker was impossible to miss. The loose gravel under my feet was slippery and dark from mud, and abruptly our trail tilted down the steep, short incline to the shallow creek burrowing under the rock. Patrick slid down on his bottom, regained his footing, paused in the creek bed, water trickling around his boots, and offered me help down. Damp seeped into the hems of my jeans. He pointed his light to the left, then right, and moved forward, slipping.

I saw the beam of his Mag-lite falling, maybe sensed rather than saw Patrick's desperate grab, heard the small crack against rock. The glow went out like a doused match. Only then did Patrick, who avoids casual swearing, emit a "Damn." I used my light to find his; we clicked, shook, and rattled it to no avail.

"It's okay," I said before he had to say anything.

He stuck the flashlight through his belt. "Sometimes they have a resurrection. Or I can use it for a club." He started to maneuver behind me. "You lead."

I caught his arm. "No. You're doing a great job. Here." I passed my Mag-lite to him, using my other hand to guide his to it. I didn't let go till I felt his fingers tighten around the shaft. I've often thought I'd trust Patrick with my life. Trusting him with my light source was the same— my mind created a fast-forward scroll of tragedies—an ankle turned on loose rock, a plunge down a shaft. Suppose we got separated? I swallowed, tapped his back twice to signal him to go ahead.

Our progress was slower with my riding his coat tail. My steps were more fumbling, and I kicked his heels. Then, just as we seemed to be on a flat stretch, I tripped him and we fell in a heap.

We lay there, my nose buried between his shoulder blades, both giggling so hard our stomachs jerked,. He twisted and whispered, "Hush." He doused our light. My nervous laughter died.

We lay still a moment, the immensity of the darkness swallowing us whole. Then I heard it faintly, off and on, like a bad cell phone connection. Two voices at least, one female, surely.

Delicately we untangled our limbs to lie side by side, heads near, whispering distance.

"Where?" I asked. In this dark my ears lost up and down, backward and forward. I heard but wasn't sure.

"Ahead. There should be a bend near here." He sounded confident. Was it a boy thing? Or were those afternoons spent spelunking—about which he'd complained so often—paying off for us?

We eased to our knees, then upright. "I have to use the light," he said into my right ear. I nodded and braced myself.

The light clicked on; no one shot us dead. Patrick directed the beam down, then slowly panned upward and forward. Our path widened, not a good thing. We couldn't feel our way along, using rock walls to guide us. Ahead I saw the entrance to a side spur. The closer we got to the big chamber, the more opportunities there were to get lost. The cave wasn't just two main branches but a series of capillaries or a honeycomb, some bits too small to crawl into, others a perfect niche for hiding—Jimmy or Jessica or Booth.

I tapped his shoulder twice. We moved forward slowly. I envied a dog's ability to prick its ears forward, the better to catch sound, because I couldn't hear any words above the crunch of our feet, even though we stepped with painstaking care.

But he was right. We rounded a bend which sloped down, then twisted back. How did I know that? I blinked. I saw a soft glow at the end of the slope, from around the next bend. I didn't have to signal him. Patrick snapped off the Mag-lite. We inched forward, and now in the darkness I could hear better.

Hearing but hallucinating, surely. Because what I heard was the distinctive voice of NPR's Terry Gross and a '60s rock musician she'd interviewed some months before.

Patrick stopped, no doubt as flummoxed as I was. None of Sergeant Lopez's wisdom for MPs had prepared me for Terry Gross on the enemy's side.

Nerves bubbled up into another giggle, but I twisted it into a fake throat-clearing. "Follow me," I whispered, pulling the .38 from its holster and stepping past Patrick.

He handed me the flashlight. We inched forward, and the interview became clearer; now the giggle was Gross' chuckle of appreciation at something the musician said.

When I reached the turn of the bend, I motioned Patrick down and dropped into a duckwalk to peek around the corner. Sergeant Lopez again: Don't put your head where they expect it to be.

What I saw would have stopped me if caution hadn't. Along the trail was a relatively flat shelf of rock; the ceiling above was like a sloping attic roof. The light was a Coleman lantern, sitting in the middle of a little tableau like a campfire scene. Except the bad guys had come and gone, leaving two captives tied hand and foot.

I had never before laid eyes on the little girl whose arms and legs and mouth were secured with gray duct tape. She'd had a blanket over her but lost it somehow; now she lay shivering, her eyes squeezed shut against horrors past or horrors to come. I don't have a maternal nerve, but my heart lurched. Nearby lay a more familiar form, hogtied with a combination of rope and duct-tape, his dark eyes large and calf-in-a-slaughterhouse, his thin body twitching as animals do. I heard one of the musician's songs start, then cut off, followed by more dialogue from the interview.

I wanted to rush forward and start cutting them loose. Where was Booth? For that matter I didn't relish being shot by Doug Mann either. I suspected his hand would be steady and his aim true. I pressed my fingers into Patrick's parka, holding him back, while my eyes checked an imaginary grid imposed on the scene before it. The Coleman cast shadows. I needed x-ray vision to see around the next bend.

I was sketching a plan—how I'd go first, ease around the corner, gun ready, while Patrick stayed behind to free the prisoners—when I heard the new noise. Someone else's plan was paying off.

"Jess-i-ca! Jess-i-ca! Where are you, Jessie?"

I'd know that hoarse voice anywhere, its usual imperious assumption that he'd be obeyed wavering now, undermined by a father's panic. Doug Mann was coming after his daughter.

Jessica heard him. Her eyes opened, wide and dark in the dim light. She struggled to sit up.

I glanced at Jimmy. His twitches grew more agitated; his head jerked.

Patrick was straining beside me like a dog about to snap his leash. I wanted us all out of there, and none of us dead.

I leaned into him. "I don't know where Booth is. Maybe he's up ahead waiting for Doug. Let me look around the bend, make sure it's clear. You get the little girl and go back the way we came."

I handed the Mag-lite over. He looked at me.

I nodded. "You'll need it."

"I'll take her to Toby Shaw's house. We'll call the cops."

I grabbed his wrist. "Don't come back for me. I won't know who you are in this mess and I don't want to shoot you. One more thing." I paused a second so he'd know I meant it. "Don't pull the tape off her mouth till you get her out of the cave. She will call for her daddy."

He gave me a look I understood in my own gut.

"Trust me, Patrick."

He nodded, and we started to move. When he reached the prisoners, he patted Jimmy's shoulder, then scooped up Jessica, whispering reassurances. Her sandy hair was smeared with mud; her pink dress, dainty with lace, had a dark stain in back. I stooped and hugged the rock wall and scooted around the bend.

"Jessie! Where are you, sweetie?" Mann's voice sounded farther away.

I saw nothing. But I saw. This bend led to another, and from around that corner I saw more light, this of a different quality, more evenly diffused. Maybe Doug, maybe Booth, had turned on the lights strung in the main chambers used as work areas. That would work to Booth's advantage if he waited in some dark nook for the well-lighted Mann to come searching for his daughter, traveling toward the recorded voice.

Didn't Mann realize that? Was he confident that he could always impose his will on Booth?

I moved toward the light, not wanting to poke my head around any corner where Booth might be waiting, but guessing Booth would be looking toward the sound of Mann's voice. I hesitated. I had Doug Mann in front of me and Jimmy Sills behind me. I chose Jimmy.

I hurried back to the niche where he lay, clambered up and pulled the tape off his mouth after delivering a stern warning that he must be quiet. He tried. He was sobbing from fear or relief. Terry Gross was still calmly conducting her interview; I was close enough to see the tape spooling in the black boom box. I hoped it would cover Jimmy's gurgles.

I gave him an awkward pat on the head, then shoved him over and tackled the rope. Booth had done an amateur's job combining rope and duct tape; the results baffled me. I looked around. Booth had left the tape roll and a coil of rope and a box cutter. The world's dullest box cutter I soon discovered, as I sawed away at the thick rope, swearing up to Lopez's standards. By the time I'd yanked the last strip of duct tape off, Jimmy had numerous nicks and scrapes, but he clung to me like a cub burrowing into Mama Bear's pelt.

I gentled myself away and tried for a soft but firm tone while massaging some blood back into his limbs. "Jimmy, you've got to go out the back way, out through the abandoned house. Do you know what I mean?" I tried to look commanding. His eyes were huge and moist. He nodded. Did he really understand?

"Okay, okay," I said and stood and pulled him up. He leaned against me, but I shoved him back. "Here. You take the Coleman."

He looked at it. I picked it up and clamped his cold fingers around the handle. He tried to take a step, stumbled.

"Go that way," I said, pointing, and left him while I scurried up the slope and around the bend toward the next light before I lost the Coleman's glow. Behind me Terry Gross laughed.

The fear of being shot dead without warning was a lump of ice in my stomach, but the dread of falling and becoming as helpless as an overturned turtle swirled around that ice. The trick is to think of something else, to let the brain and body merge into a survival machine. And to stay low.

A pause at the bend, then ahead to the next. Another pause. I willed myself to be all eye and ear, to filter out the tape. To note the unusual in a world unfamiliar. Nothing. No moving shadows. No blobs that transformed from boulder to body. I crept on.

"Jessie—where are you?" Doug again. I could hear the familiar edge of impatience creeping into his voice.

Nearer or farther?

Should I call out, let Booth know there'd be at least one witness, that he was caught in a squeeze play?

The shots rang out before I had the chance to wrestle with the pros and cons. One, two.

The sound was huge, reverberating. I fell flat, clasped my left hand to my ear, buried my right ear in the crook of my arm. It was too late to stop the shock of it. Counting five, I shook my head, but couldn't shake the ache out like water. I stood, moved forward, upward now. Sweat greased my palm. I used both hands to grip the .38, arms extended.

The lights went out.

The ice lump melted and sent its cold spilling through my every vein. I froze in the dark, squeezed my eyes shut. Oh shit, just shoot me and get it over with.

But I wanted my body to tell a different story when they found me afterward, the one where the brave PI presses on against all odds. I started forward, moving up. I remembered the slope from Carter's tour. Because I traveled slowly, my ears recovered and I heard a new sound just as I saw another refracted light—not electric. The sound was hard to pick up between the tape's words—the drip of water down the walls. Then I was over a little rise and saw the flickering beam of a Coleman lantern beside a stream in a large chamber that had once held huge kegs of beer: St. Louis Ale, Koenig, and their successors.

I crept down the slope, checking the shadows not lit by the lantern. Then I saw the figure bobbing in the stream like some terrible cork. His face, drained of impatience, anger, and life, tilted upward, amazed to be dead because he was the man in control. His chest resembled road kill, and the water around him was inky. The force of the water spread the ink downstream.

I'd wanted to get even with him, to see him humiliated and brought low, fantasized kicking his balls, thought of a dozen scalding ways to make him pay.

My gorge rose in my throat. I swallowed hard. Doug Mann.

The lantern called me back; it hiccuped off a half-beat, came back on. But that scant second's pause had jumped my heart. I knew I was tampering with evidence, but I picked up the lantern and gingerly turned it up. Sometimes that works, and it did then, but I wasn't counting on the fuel lasting.

I risked another look at Mann's corpse. He was, ironically, concrete proof that Diane's story was at least partially true. Which meant I was now in a chess game. Had Booth left by backtracking Doug's route? Surely he'd go back to check on his prisoners. Did he really intend to keep his promise to Diane, that he'd return Jessica to her, let them both go? Return to the old way of keeping people quiet—pay money, keep them happy?

And what about Jimmy? Would Booth risk Jimmy's telling the story? Or did he intend for there to be one more body or two? And if he killed his own daughter, he'd have to go back for Diane.

Did Booth realize there was no end to it? Or did he think he could stop with Doug?

I thought it was a safe bet that in either case he'd be heading back to check on those prisoners. Had we crossed paths without knowing it? Or was there another short cut among the many chambers of the cave?

It didn't matter. I had my own plan. I gripped the lantern and turned back the way Doug had come. I was headed toward the main offices, and every step I took became easier. The next chamber's floor was smoother, then I reached the doors that led to the area where the big tank was. Up the stairs, down the hall, repeat, turn, offices on one side, open warehouse to my left. I was now loping toward the outside door. I put down the lantern.

I opened that door cautiously, took a look outside. At each end of the loading dock bright security lights spotlighted the area. I took a deep breath, holstered my gun, and made a dash for the dock's edge. I jumped down, landing with a little skid on the snow but keeping my feet. Mann's car was parked nearby. I moved into its shadow, looked around. Nothing moving; there was nothing new.

I should have run toward Toby Shaw's house then. But I didn't. The moon stared down at me. I raced down James, dashing from shadow to shadow. The Horizon was still there, Booth's SUV, too. I hurried to the end house, cut around the corner, clinging to its rotting siding. I unholstered the snubbie. I found myself a tree and a pile of debris to hide behind and waited.

His face, peeking around the open doorway, was just a white smear in the moonlight but enough to be recognized.

"Booth!"

I didn't even get the warning out before he fired a shot.

I answered right away and better because I spent more time on the firing range. But I missed anyway. Sergeant Lopez always said, "Shoot to kill. Don't try no fancy-pantsy arty-smarty Annie Oakley shots where you shoot the gun out of his hand or just nick an arm or a leg; you'll miss every time."

But I couldn't quite do it, just kill him cold. So I aimed for his thigh. If I missed one way, he'd have one of those terrible gut shots that deliver an agonizing death. But I missed the other direction and nicked a leg after all.

I'd hit him—he yelped. But he ducked back, and so did I. His first shot had gone way wild, but then I'd startled him. He'd managed to drill Mann, so I didn't dare underestimate him. I figured I might be able to just hold him tight till the cops came. Surely the cops were coming, weren't they?

Then Booth dragged his ace out—and it was Jimmy. Well, that was bad luck.

Booth wrapped Jimmy in a tight, one-armed embrace and waved his gun at me. "We're leaving here. Toss your gun down."

"Give it up, Booth. We've got Jessica. You can't get away with it." I tried the de-escalation route.

"I'll kill him." I saw Jimmy jump, maybe one of his little involuntary spasms.

"Then you won't have a hostage," I said.

That pissed him off, and he fired off a shot my way. It took a bite of bark off my tree. I dropped back into the shadows and kept my mouth shut.

He waited. I could hear Jimmy's rattling breath.

I waited.

Booth nudged Jimmy down the steps. I heard the creaking wood, saw the lurch when Jimmy put a foot wrong. But Booth was glued to him. I couldn't see a shot. I eased back farther into the night, closer to the debris pile behind which they'd found Teresa's body. Booth's face turned my way. I imagined his eyes straining to pick me out, but not, I thought, quite managing it. I was still breathing.

They reached the ground, moved away in a crab-like sidle. I heard Booth mutter a curse as Jimmy stumbled again. But Booth wasn't letting go.

Maybe I should just stay still, let Booth slip away, pass this problem onto the police.

Maybe I'd have done that if I hadn't seen the quick movement from the shadows behind Booth, the slight figure picking up a loose board.

My throwing arm isn't as good as it once was, but I grabbed a chunk of concrete off the debris pile and lobbed it toward the house—not at Booth, off to his left, so his attention would go that way. Once again I missed the exact point I was aiming for, but it was like hitting the side of a barn, and I heard the good, solid thunk of it. Booth did, too and swiveled around firing off three shots into the splotchy shadows. And the mystery figure swung the board like a bat and connected with Booth's head hard enough that I heard that thunk, too.

I raced forward, still keeping my gun at the ready. "Jeez, did you kill him?"

Jerry Cross grinned at me. "Might've." But it seemed to me his pale face was even whiter than usual.

Jimmy had folded into a heap, his body shaking. When I put a hand on his shoulder reassuringly and said "It's okay Jimmy," I noticed I was trembling too. I walked over and kicked Booth's gun farther away from his unconscious form. I never believe in those movie villains who keep coming back like the Energizer Bunny, but I wasn't taking any chances.

I always liked the heavy-handed irony of the old Greek and Roman gods and goddesses. They poured some out now. Before Jerry and I could exchange another word, the night split with the sound of St. Louis Police Department sirens racing our way.

The sirens grew louder and louder until the white St. Louis Police Department sedan jerked to a halt a few feet from Jerry and me, catching us in the insistent glare of its headlights. Mercifully, the sirens stopped but the headlights kept us pinned and the revolving reds and blues accused us again and again.

The two grim-faced officers that came out of the cruiser had their nine millimeters pointed at us. "Get 'em up!" the white officer said; he was short and stocky. The taller, thinner officer was black and female. Both were looking equally aggrieved.

Without being asked, Jerry dropped his board, and I put my snubbie down by my feet. We both raised our hands, just until we could get things sorted out.

That took awhile.

CHAPTER TWENTY-SIX

Lindstrom arrived at the scene two minutes before the still unconscious Booth was loaded into the ambulance. She was dressed for dinner, not murder, but her face was grim. "You again," she said when our eyes met. But to everyone's astonishment, including mine, she marched straight over and gave the chief witness a tight hug. "Okay?"

"Sure," I said, a little embarrassed.

She turned around and gave the scene a quick assessment. She pointed at Jimmy. "Get him an ambulance, too, and stay with him at the hospital," she said, addressing the white male patrol cop. "Simpson, you secure the scene," she added to the black female. She looked at Jerry, then me. "He belong to you?"

I nodded.

I summarized the facts, remembering to mention Patrick and Jessica's whereabouts. Before I finished, another patrol car and a plain Crown Victoria arrived. The patrol car spilled forth two more uniformed cops while the white sedan spit out bad news—Lindstrom's nemesis, Judith Rosero, and her partner, Ray Major. Rosero was short, white, ill-tempered, homophobic, and jealous of Lindstrom's success. Major was tall, black, stiff, and loyal to his partner.

"We caught this case," Rosero informed us in a growl Harvey uses when protecting pork chop bones.

"This goes back to a cold case I'm working," Lindstrom said with calm certainty. She was relying solely on my version of events, and my throat tightened at that evidence of trust.

She inclined her head at Jerry Cross and said to the white patrolman, "Take him in and get his statement." She looked at Rosero. "He probably saved at least two lives."

"Call a lawyer," I said to Jerry. Saving lives doesn't always get you a parade.

His eyes widened and he shook his head.

"I'll call one for you," I assured him.

Lindstrom, using her greater height to advantage, walked closer to Rosero. "There was a child involved in this situation. I'm taking Darcy over on Lemp because she can reassure the little girl. I'll be responsible for keeping her separate from the other adult witness." She then sketched in the basics of what had happened in the cave for Rosero and Major.

I used my cell phone and caught Rhonda Tucker still at her office at Randall and Bond, one of St. Louis's premier law firms. I had worked with Rhonda on a previous case and trusted her judgment. It took me only a few minutes to put her in the picture. She agreed she'd meet Jerry at the Clark Street Station and stick with him until they let him go.

Rosero and Major are cops, so they have to pretend they've heard it all and seen it all. Lindstrom's recital was succinct, but with each sentence Rosero's mouth tightened. I saw the look in her eye when Lindstrom reported that Doug Mann had been shot and killed. If Rosero could figure a way to pin this mess on me, she would. I felt like peeking around Lindstrom's broad shoulders and sticking out my tongue. Rosero said she and Major would stay at the scene and give directions to the evidence techs and then meet us back at Clark Street.

Lindstrom soon had me in her Jeep and headed toward Lemp Street. Toby Shaw's house was lit up like a carnival tent; so many cars were lined up along the curb that we had to double-park.

My boy Patrick hadn't rested on his laurels with one call to the police. He'd finally gotten through to Lindstrom, then called Colleen to get Walter here. Somehow the news had traveled to Neely, Lindstrom's old partner, and he was on the scene as well. Toby's well-appointed living room lacked only the elephants for a three-ring circus. Toby had provided the coffee and hot chocolate. Jessica, clad in a too-large Cardinals t-shirt, was sitting across an ottoman from Patrick. The two, amid the chaos of many conversations, were concentrating on a game of Chinese checkers. From time to time Jessica petted Mikie, Walter's mutt. Only then did her serious face relax.

Patrick stood when Lindstrom approached. "Excuse me, Jessie, I need to talk to Detective Lindstrom," he said. Lindstrom topped her previous capacity to surprise by giving him a short, tight hug. A man I surmised was Toby Shaw's partner squatted down to take Patrick's place at the game.

We stepped away from Jessica's hearing. "She knew her Uncle Truman's phone number. She's called her mother. Diane is on the way over," Patrick said. He lowered his voice another notch. "Jessica doesn't know about her father yet."

About either of her fathers, I thought.

Lindstrom put her hand on my shoulder. "You and Patrick stay separated. I don't want some slick defense lawyer saying you conspired to throw the guilt on Heitner. Go attach yourself to Neely while I interview Patrick."

Neely and Walter were huddled together in a far corner. Walter gave me a broad wink as I approached.

"You won't stay out of it, will you?" he said in an aggrieved tone that didn't match his wink.

"You got me into this case," I said, trying to put manly joshing in my voice. But it was too soon; my nerves were raw.

Walter's were too. He excused himself so Neely could get first crack at me. I recited my story to Neely, a good practice run for retelling it to Rosero and Major. It was easier than telling Walter would have been. Except in a general humanistic way, Neely didn't care if I got my sorry self shot up. When I asked him how Jessica had gotten the t-shirt, Neely explained that Toby had provided it, but Neely admitted he'd had her remove her soiled dress so he could bag it for evidence.

We hadn't long to wait before Diane arrived, accompanied by Vernon Cole. We all watched as Jessica sprang up and raced into her mother's arms. Even those who hadn't been in the cave to see Jessica tied up swallowed hard watching this mother and child reunion.

After their initial embrace, while Jessica still had her face buried in her mother's belly, Diane gave us a fierce glare as though all of us had threatened her. Her eyes met mine with a look that said I had conspired in this tragedy visited upon her daughter.

So much for thank you.

Neely pulled away from me and drew Vernon Cole aside for a conversation that required note-taking. Lindstrom motioned Patrick forward and bent over to address a few soft words to Jessica and her mother. Jessica then sat on the sofa beside Patrick; Lindstrom led Diane out of the room for some privacy.

They weren't gone all that long. Diane's face was tight, but I saw no signs of fresh tears when she returned. Now she knew her husband was dead; she would have to tell Jessica. She marched straight to her daughter. Toby had anticipated the moment and had a blanket ready for Jessica's trip home. Vernon Cole asked Lindstrom for permission to accompany them. Lindstrom nodded agreement and told him someone would be by the house later to question Jessica.

Finally, Lindstrom motioned Patrick and me to her. "Ah, as a treat I get to take you down to Clark Street so you can talk to Rosero and Major. Sorry, I can't keep you all to myself, my darlings." She made a wry face to match her wretched attempt at a Greta Garbo accent. "This may take a few hours," she added.

It did.

A week later I stuck a cup of water in the microwave for tea. Sooner or later I was going to have to pay attention to my life: visit Betty, shop for Christmas, call Jen, clean my apartment. I told myself that I wasn't going to miss the high drama of the previous weeks anymore than I'd miss the fresh snowfalls.

Booth Heitner had recovered from Jerry's whacking. He'd been denied bail. Killing a retired cop put him on an especially despised list of offenders. Even so, Booth's attorneys had created more outrage by suing Jerry Cross for assault.

That hadn't fazed Jerry. He was strutting around the Galleria, enjoying his fifteen minutes of fame. Lucky for him, Miller Security carries insurance to protect its employees who get sued in the line of duty.

Toby Shaw joined up with Carter to find Jimmy a decent place to live and a salaried job as a janitor for GLBT Services. Carter hired a lawyer to help prepare Jimmy for the testimony he'd have to give at Booth's trial. Jimmy had heard more of the quarrel between Booth and Teresa than he'd first admitted. Lots of ugly words had been used; he'd heard Teresa's cry when she'd been hit. I already knew from Lindstrom that Jimmy was going to get immunity for his part in moving the body in exchange for providing the details about the day Booth killed Teresa Rushing.

When Doug Mann arrived in response to Richard Heitner's call for help, he made Jimmy help him move Teresa's body deeper into the cave. Mann had taken her feet and instructed Jimmy to pick up her upper body. After they moved Teresa, Mann told Jimmy to take the wrench back with the body. As a result, Mann had Teresa's blood on Jimmy's shirt and Jimmy's fingerprints on the murder weapon. Two nights later Mann had Jimmy help him move the body to the empty lot. To seal Jimmy's silence, Mann told him that Richard wanted him to keep the secret to protect Booth.

Lindstrom figured the original crime had been impulsive rather than planned. Booth had seen Teresa through his father's eyes—a money-grubbing slut using her bastard to pry money out of Heitner hands. An old-fashioned view, really.

As for finding Diane's hideaway motel, Booth had simply followed her after her second meeting with his father—the one where Richard Heitner had explained that Doug wasn't accepting their suggestion that he give Diane custody of Jessica. Diane had been keeping a sharp eye out for Doug, but she hadn't suspected the Heitners of being a danger to her. Bad decision.

Not surprisingly Diane Mann and Jessica left town about five minutes after the police released Diane from their initial questioning. But Vernon Cole followed her and persuaded her that she had no choice but to do her part at the trial.

Lindstrom reported that the cop shop was divided. Half thought I was a hero for nailing Booth within an hour of his killing Doug Mann, and the other half considered me a menace who had somehow been responsible for Mann's death.

Lindstrom, embarrassed, had explained a dozen times that she'd been in the shower when Patrick and I called for help. My intention was to hold this over her for as long as I could. But it was a mistake to assume I could keep a permanent advantage. She'd already resumed her imperious ways. Even now I was waiting, on her command, for the phone call that signaled me to come downstairs. She had a surprise.

She pulled the Cherokee to the curb at Claude. I looked up at the dark red brick. We were quickly losing the sun.

"You bought it?"

"Yes."

Inside, she'd spread the blue duvet from her bed in front of the fireplace. She'd tossed pillows on top and supplied a basket with cheese and bread and a red wine.

"You want to open the wine?" I asked. She was fussing with a plastic-wrapped bundle of firewood.

"You do it. I hope the chimney's clear." I heard the scrunch of paper, the scratch of the match. "So, what do you think, Darcy? With the mortgage for this place, I'm back to living paycheck to paycheck. You'll get to pay for your share of everything."

"Don't know, Lindstrom. I was working up to the idea of being kept." I handed her a glass of wine.

"Were you now? Somehow I don't think of you as a woman with a secret hankering for diamonds."

"A trip to Europe would have been nice. Maybe someday I'll be able to take you."

She looked into my eyes. "Does that mean you think there will be a someday?"

"What?" Oh goddess, suddenly we were in deep water, and I wasn't sure I'd decided to join the Navy. "Um, Sarah…the other day when you were talking about my not wanting to be close to you…that isn't really true."

Over the rim of her wine glass she watched me squirm. The fire crackled and leapt behind her. She reached up and touched my face. "You were saying, Meg?"

"Uh, I am glad that you love me. I mean…I was—"

"Say what you feel, Meg. Give me something more than that army tough girl you do so well."

I looked at her. She never stopped turning me to jelly. "I want to touch you."

"That I already knew." She arched a brow.

Somehow I was flunking. I moved closer to her. "No, I mean touch your heart—break through that perfect exterior and get to you."

She put up a restraining hand. "The perfection is all in your mind. You know that. You've got to do better."

What did she want from me? An admission of some kind? An accounting of how I'd shortchanged her, how I'd kept her at arm's length and whined to myself that she was all surface? A panic gushed through me; I mustn't lose her. I'd been an idiot.

"I'm sorry…I didn't mean…" I reached for her.

She arched a brow, stepped back.

My cell phone chirruped. I felt the misery on my face.

"Answer it," she said. Her voice said she had in mind the call she'd missed a week before.

I wasn't surprised when I heard the voice. "Meg, this is Diane. Look, my situation's changed. Could you not cash that check I sent just now?"

"Don't worry, Diane. I'm going to frame it." I pushed End and walked to the front door. A grimy snow pile stood near the stoop where the walk had been cleared. I tossed the phone into the snow and closed the door.

"You were saying?" she asked.

Without closing my eyes, I leapt. "I love you."

Then she reached for me and we warmed her house.